Dear Yin,
I'm so glad that we
met each other. You are
such a great vibe & a truly
Creative Soul. You and
I are destined to do
great things. I'll meet
you at the top!

Love + Light
Alicia

RETROGRADE

The Darkness

A. O. Godmasch

Hardcover: ISBN: 978-1-7353555-0-4

Paperback: ISBN: 978-1-7353555-1-1

E-Book: ISBN: 978-1-7353555-2-8

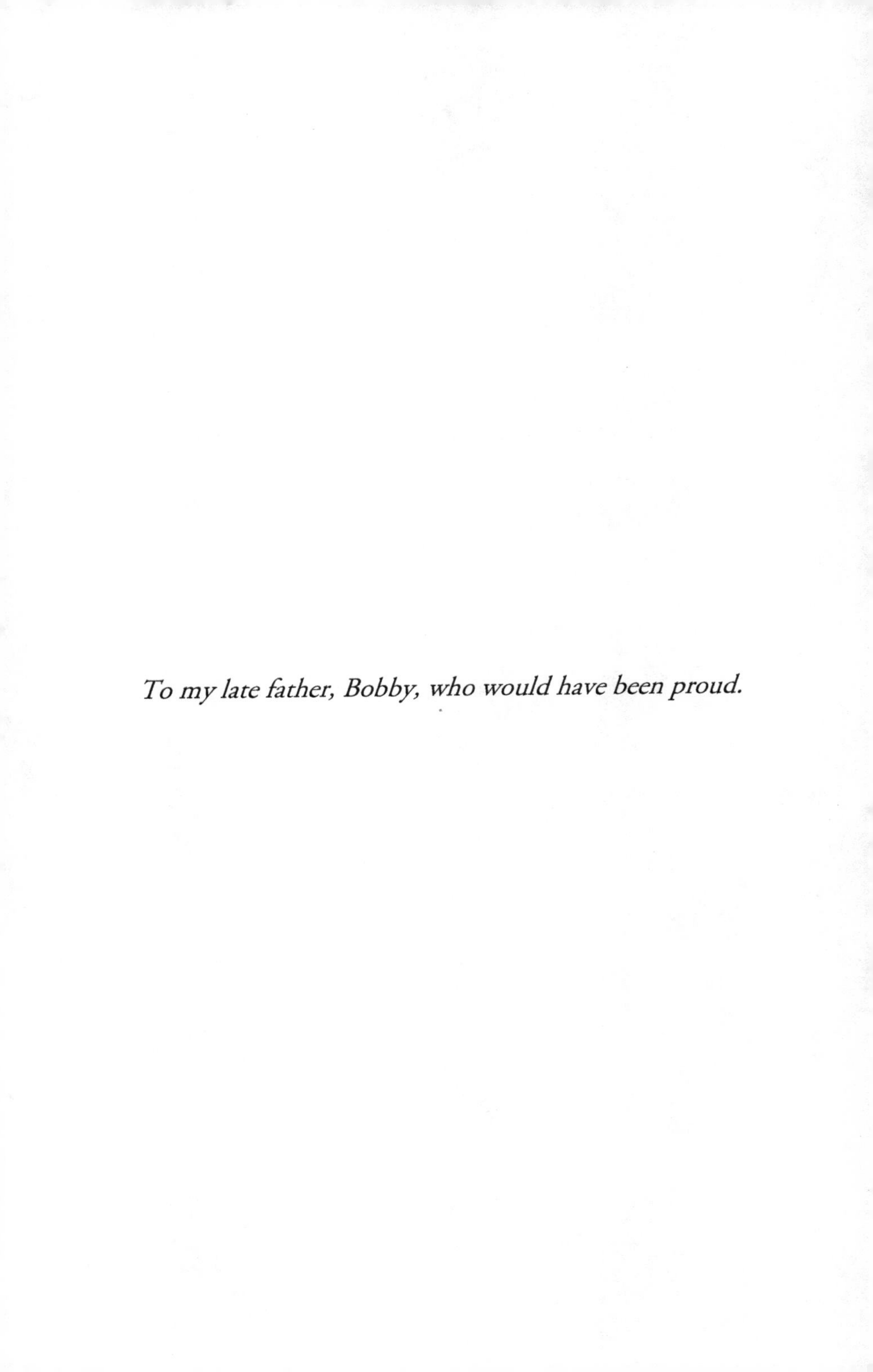

To my late father, Bobby, who would have been proud.

CHAPTER 1

Isis Pnina Mahmoud slowly opened her eyes, stirred awake from her nap by the gentle breeze dancing across her face. It felt like fresh air, but she knew it was just the ventilation from the air system that had been recently installed, only giving the illusion of fresh air. The Retrograde may have been still a while away, but her father, her *pa*—Maat Mahmoud—was not the type to take chances.

And frankly, neither was Isis.

She sat up with a groan, her muscles taut and tired from the long morning of training she had endured. It was all worth it, though, as far as she was concerned. She'd been too young the last time the Retrograde occurred, but she'd been studying it extensively ever since. This time around, whether her parents liked it or not, she was going to fight it.

Isis's eyes roamed her locked bedroom window, watching the curtains flutter with the fake breeze. She took in the glorious sky outside, which glowed in the rays of their Sun, *Ra* filling it with purple and orange hues. Despite the seemingly peaceful atmosphere outside, The Mahmoud complex had already been put on lockdown in preparation for what was to come. There were times when Isis found the whole thing to be a little excessive, given they still had a few months before the Retrograde even started. But this was a thought she kept to herself, not caring to receive her *pa's* tirade regarding how it was better to be safe than sorry. Nevertheless, Isis always found it slightly disconcerting the way upper-class citizens of Damara handled times like these. Her father had come from wealth, and he was the third in succession of the Mahmoud Family to lead the region of Cairo, so it was important for them to be secure. But Isis still thought that the preparation process was nothing more than a showy display of their means.

Deep down, though, she knew it was probably guilt making her feel the way she did. Those who were less fortunate than her family had no such safety precautions and luxuries to rely on during the Retrograde. It was an ugly truth that no one liked acknowledging. Still, it was no secret. The Retrograde always made the poor suffer most. It was the knowledge of this guilt that made Isis train so hard; there was a dire need inside of her to help fight for those who didn't stand a fighting chance on their own.

Isis stood and stretched, glancing down at what she knew her mother, her *eva*—the stunningly beautiful Rania Mahmoud—would consider the most unladylike of attires. Yet, Isis couldn't care less.

She exited her sleeping quarters, intuition guiding her down to the foyer, where she could already feel the tension in the air. Her skin prickled, hearing the hushed voices drifting down the halls. For one wild moment, she feared the Retrograde had somehow already begun while she'd been napping. She quickened her pace, running down the corridor with her shoeless feet slapping noisily on the shiny marble floors.

When she turned the corner, she found her parents, along with Khalfani Abaza, huddled together, giving their undivided attention to the broadcast on the screen before them.

Isis moved closer, her *eva* being the first to turn around and acknowledge her presence, clearly annoyed by the way she'd been running through the corridors; she had told her time and time again not to do so. Rania never missed a chance to tell Isis that with her tall frame, she was too big to run in the house, and needed to adopt a more ladylike gait. Eyeing her daughter, Rania Mahmoud pressed her lips into a grim line.

Isis tried not to squirm as her *eva's* gaze roamed over her unkempt hair and the training attire she had yet to change out of. Her training gear was rather form-fitting, and probably—according to her *eva*—not appropriate to be wearing in front of young male company.

Isis blinked back at her innocently. After all, it wasn't like she'd known ahead of time that Khalfani Abaza was there; he usually stayed in his own wing, his presence barely detectable. Most days, Isis forgot he even lived there. "What's going on?" she asked, ignoring her *eva's* stare, although neither her *pa* nor Khalfani bothered to turn around when she spoke.

"My daughter, you should know," Maat answered, his voice just as grim as Rania's expression.

Isis moved forward, positioning herself within viewing distance of the screen they were huddled around.

Yes, she knew. Because everyone knew what the approaching Copper Moons meant. Nevertheless, everyone also knew that there was something different about it this time around…

Isis wanted to say something, but words failed her as her eyes became transfixed on the screen. A cold chill ran down her spine, practically reaching to the tip of her toes. She shuddered.

She knew the images before them were captured from a neighboring planet rather than their own, but that was of little consolation. The Retrograde would come for them too, and being forced to witness the havoc it was causing on the neighboring planet simply intensified the dread of knowing their time was nearing. Furthermore, it gave them ample time to witness just how strong the Retrograde had grown since its last occurrence.

Isis nearly had to clench her teeth against the nausea she felt, watching the wayward people in the streets, no longer even looking human. They were pale shadows of their former selves, roaming about mindlessly, their eyes void of all emotion. Their mouths hung agape, dribble running down their chins like rabid dogs. No words were spoken among them, just hysterical groans and grunts. They seemed like zombies as they shuffled around, running into vacant buildings and occasionally each other—some of them tipping over and lying in the streets, scratching at the pavement until their fingernails bleed or tore off completely. The darkness around them looked so sinister, it was almost as if it had a life of its own—and that's because it did...

Dark mist swirled through the streets, infecting everyone in its path. And though there was no audible thunder or visible storm, lightning flashed across the hazy sky. The dark mist below thickened and Isis eyed it curiously, feeling that something was wrong...Something more than the obvious...

Temporarily tuning out the infected people running through the streets, Isis found herself concentrating on the strange dark mist. She wasn't sure if it was just her imagination, but for a split-second, she thought she'd seen the mist swirl into a shape that looked suspiciously humanoid, with legs and feet. More disturbingly, however, was the fact that just when the lightning had cracked through the sky, she saw a flash of red and white resembling what could only be described as eyes and teeth. The strange sights had gone across the screen so quickly, though. Isis couldn't be sure she'd actually seen them.

She glanced at her *pa*, *eva*, and Khalfani. While they all closely watched the broadcast of the devastation, none of them reacted as if they'd seen anything particularly out of the ordinary. Isis was pretty certain they would have said something if they'd seen a pair of random red eyes and sharp teeth.

Convinced her eyes must have been playing tricks on her, Isis decided to keep the strange observation to herself. Nevertheless, she still felt somewhat disturbed and had to wrap her arms around herself to suppress another shudder. Afraid to see the strange images again, she eventually tore her eyes away from the screen, taking in her *pa* and Khalfani as they continued witnessing the terror unfold.

Maat watched with his arms folded across his chest and a deep frown set on his lips. Khalfani, on the other hand, returned Isis's stare, albeit only briefly.

Thoughts of the unusual images momentarily pushed aside, Isis's eyes lingered over Khalfani a moment longer than necessary, a patter going through her chest that she couldn't quite explain. Though Khalfani lived on her family's property, he lived in a separate wing. Hence, they rarely encountered each other. Nevertheless, it was no secret that he was her *pa's* favorite soldier. In fact, Maat was so fond of the boy, Isis often suspected he thought of him as an honorary son. And perhaps, Isis thought, she couldn't exactly blame him. Khalfani was strong, handsome, virtuous, and from what she knew, a damned good fighter. When she reflected on the unusual feeling that occasionally squirmed through her when their eyes met, she sometimes wondered if it was jealousy. Even the other soldiers occasionally thought of him as Maat's protégé—an honor that Isis desperately wanted, as his daughter.

She could only hope, one day, that her *pa* would share the same pride in her, though in her heart, she had a feeling he already did. It was simply that her *eva* complicated things, seeing as she was so against Isis training for the Retrograde army in the first place. Rania wanted nothing more than to raise a prim and proper young lady, but Isis was determined to show that there was so much more to her than that. She had a warrior's spirit, and there was simply no suppressing it.

Isis looked back to the screen, her lips twisting into an involuntary snarl at the sight of a woman running down the road with a knife in her hand, stabbing herself repeatedly until she collapsed. Again, lightning flickered across the sky as the woman hit the ground, her blood seeping into the pavement.

Sometimes, Isis was certain that sort of thing was really the worst part of the Retrograde; not only was the madness it induced terrifying, but it was humiliating. Dehumanizing. And those who tried to fight against it often ended up self-destructing, just like that poor woman.

Yet, Isis grit her teeth, refusing to be discouraged. She loved her home planet of Damara too much to idly sit back and do nothing when the Retrograde arrived. And when the time came, she was determined to prove that she was just as capable of defending it as any of her *pa's* soldiers—even one as skilled as Khalfani. Just thinking about it, she squeezed her hands into fists at her sides, mentally reviewing the training she'd had thus far.

"Isis, why don't you help me prepare some tea?" Rania suddenly said, stepping away from the screen. There was a look in her eyes that also silently suggested Isis changed into something more respectable as well.

Isis bit her tongue and forced herself to take a deep breath before she accidentally said something rude. Slowly, she eyed her *eva*—with her beautifully curled hair, petite frame, and elegant dress. As a whiff of Rania's fragrant perfume reached Isis's nose, she thought about how she would never be the woman her *eva* was, even if Rania refused to accept it.

"Three months," Maat abruptly said, interrupting before Isis had a chance to respond to Rania. "We have three months before the Retrograde reaches us..."

Isis and Rania both turned back to the screen, where the devastation continued to unfold.

No one ever questioned Maat and his declarations, well aware that he often tended to be correct. Plus, with his chiseled jawline, strong build, and wise eyes, he was the type of man whose mere presence commanded respect. Furthermore, the fact that he happened to be the president of Damara's region of Cairo also meant people automatically listened when he spoke.

"Is this really what we'll be up against?" Khalfani asked in a low voice, as if he meant for Maat alone to hear. Anxiety filled his green eyes, so stunning against his olive complexion.

Maat nodded solemnly. "The Retrograde has been growing stronger and stronger every decade. We're going to be up against something no one could ever imagine in their worst nightmares. The time to amp up our preparation has already passed. I can only hope we've been doing enough..."

"Good thing we've already been training hard then," Isis said, her teeth clenched as another flash of lightning showed on the screen while dark clouds swirled around the infected people in the streets.

CHAPTER 2

"*Ella*, Isis." *Good morning.*

Retrieving a canteen of water from the refrigerator, Isis slowly turned around to face her *eva*—her mother—recognizing the faked cheerfulness in her morning greeting. Yet, after having witnessed what the Retrograde had become, Isis was in no mood for another argument, and therefore pretended not to notice the disapproving wrinkle in Rania's brow. "*Ella, Imma.*" *Good morning, Mommy.* Isis had a habit of using the term '*imma'* when she wanted to keep the peace.

Rania stood at the kitchen counter, eyeing her daughter with pursed lips. Her chest rose and fell with a deep breath—a clear indicator that she was trying her best to remain calm. She tossed her long curly hair over her shoulder and forced a smile. "So, what are your plans for today? I was hoping you could help me prepare dinner for this evening, if you aren't busy."

Isis blinked, unable to help the grimace that formed on her lips. She glanced down at herself—at the obvious training attire she wore.

Her *eva* knew precisely what her plans were…

Isis shook her head and barked an exasperated laugh.

"Isis, *please*," Rania said, cringing. Her hands clenched the kitchen counter.

Isis blinked innocently. "What, *Imma*?"

"That laugh of yours…" Rania shook her head, annoyed.

In response, Isis laughed again. Her *eva* hated her laugh, always complaining that it was too loud and boisterous. Too much like her *pa's*. Unladylike.

To Rania Mahmoud, there was no greater insult to a woman than being unladylike.

"Well, I'm sorry to break it to you, *Imma*, but I am busy today." Isis placed the canteen of water into her duffle bag, with the rest of her training equipment.

"Really? I hadn't noticed," Rania responded, frowning at the training clothes her daughter wore. She shook her head again. "Isis, honestly, no activity that causes a young lady to dress like *that* is appropriate. How do you think it makes me feel? As if I haven't raised you better than to wear clothing that fails to preserve a single ounce of your modesty. And I know the majority of the soldiers are men…Why are you so determined to give people the wrong impression?"

Isis clenched her teeth and took a deep breath, forcing herself to speak calmly. "The only impression I am trying to give is that I'm serious about my training."

"As if it isn't bad enough that you're training," Rania muttered. "And if you insist on training, surely you do it in something more...modest."

"Oh?" Isis's eyebrows shot upward. "And what would that be, *Eva*? Shall I change into a dress so that when I kick, all the gentlemen can see my knickers? Would that be better than these?" She ran her hands along her form-fitting pants and then placed her finger on her chin, posing as if deep in thought. "Yes, I can see how practical a long, flowing dress would be. When I'm out fighting, someone could step on it, and it would come ripping off of me entirely. Then I'll be standing there naked! I'm sure nudity would bring a stop to any fight in progress, eh? Maybe it'll even stop the Retrograde." Isis shrugged her shoulders. "Then again, if the dress doesn't rip when someone accidentally steps on it, it could wind up awfully unfortunate for me. I could get caught in a bad position and be killed, unable to free myself. So, which would you prefer, *Eva*? Me in this, able to fight, or me in a dress, where I'm bound to end up either naked or dead?"

Rania glared at her daughter, not at all amused. The frown lines on her typically beautiful face deepened. "Where did you get such a crass sense of humor? Between the way you dress, and the way you talk, people are going to think—"

"To think what? That I'm a loose floozy?"

Rania threw her hands into the air, exasperated. "You see what I mean? What are you doing, using language like that? What has happened to your virtue, Isis?"

Isis rolled her eyes. "If you're implying what I think you are with that question, *Eva*, you can relax. I assure you, I am still a virgin."

"You'd better be," Rania said. "But you sure will make it hard for anyone to believe that if you keep carrying on the way you do."

Isis shook her head. "What does that even mean?"

"That your actions need to match what you are."

Isis opened and closed her mouth wordlessly, so offended she couldn't even think of a reply. "I don't care what people think," she finally said. "I know who and what I am, and that's all that matters. Anyone who's dense enough to make such judgments about a woman just because of the way she speaks or dresses…" Isis's voice trailed off, and she clamped her mouth shut, afraid that if she permitted herself to keep speaking, she would end up saying something she regretted. She may not have agreed with her mother, but she knew she had to respect her.

A smug look spread across Rania's face, suggesting that she believed herself to have won the argument. "Modesty is one of the most important things for a young woman your age, Isis. And it is necessary that you preserve your modesty until you are married." She gave Isis a meaningful look, making it clear what she was insinuating. "And even then, it will be your duty to your husband to still present yourself in a ladylike fashion in front of society."

Isis turned her back to Rania, still not trusting her mouth, and in that moment, not even trusting her expression. She rolled her eyes but knew that arguing further with her *eva* was a lost cause, and ultimately, Isis felt it didn't matter anyway. Men and relationships were the farthest things from her mind, not at all on her current list of priorities. Hence, regardless of what her *eva* thought, her modesty, virtue, virginity, and everything else pertaining to the matter were not at stake anytime soon, and she didn't need to dress or act a certain way just to prove it. She knew where her focus was.

Sometime in the future, when marriage was on the horizon for her, she would know when the time was right. Until then, it wasn't a concern.

"*Sahha, Imma.*" *Goodbye, Mommy.* Isis then hoisted her bag onto her shoulder and made her exit, running carelessly down the corridor, anxious to leave the house.

"Stop running like that!" Rania yelled after her, grimacing. "You sound like a colt."

* * *

Isis fought to control her labored breathing, not wanting the others to see how winded she was. Heading over to the break area to grab her water canteen, she flinched at the stitch that had formed in her side. The breathlessness and pain were worth it, though; with every ache in her muscles and each labored breath she took, she reminded herself that it came at the cost of being prepared to fight the Retrograde, which was all that mattered.

Digging through her duffle bag, Isis retrieved her water canteen and quickly twisted off the cap. The cool liquid felt like heaven going down her throat. After drinking enough to feel refreshed, she lowered the bottle and took several deep breaths, willing her heart rate to slow back to normal. She breathed in deeply through her nose and exhaled through her mouth, eyeing the soldiers still practicing around her.

Off to the left, there was quite a bit of laughing and chatting. She glanced over, seeing a shock of brown hair flying through the air as Jacey Burnell bounced around. She was one of few female soldiers in Damara's army, and upon first meeting her, Isis had tried to strike up a friendship, presuming a sense of comradery amongst the fellow female soldiers. She quickly learned, however, that Jacey didn't share the same sentiments.

Jacey primarily interacted with a limited number of soldiers, most of whom happened to be male. They were like a clique, always showing up to and leaving practice together, and usually sticking together throughout the duration of practice, just as they were currently doing.

Isis took another sip of water as she watched Jacey dodge a swing from Farhad Spinks—a soldier whose attitude was as tough and burly as his appearance. Standing off to the side, watching and cheering them along, were Hydrus Rode—a quiet and observant soldier, and Garth Sturla—a fair-looking guy with a well-groomed beard and prominent look about himself.

After Jacey dodged a few more of Farhad's heavy swings, he ducked out of the fight and let Hydrus take his place. Isis watched, intrigued. She'd seen Hydrus fight a couple times before and had marveled at his nimble style. As he went to take his place fighting Jacey, he stretched his long arms and positioned himself firmly in front of her. She stood, her fists at the ready with a smug smirk plastered on her face. Without warning, she took a swing. Hydrus, however, bent his spine backwards to dodge the punch, immediately snapped back upright, and then kicked out his leg, tripping Jacey. Garth laughed as she tipped over and fell, and Farhad let out a low whistle.

"Gotta do better than that!" a loud voice called from across the room. Isis let her gaze travel in the direction of the voice, where she spotted Mirko Ele—a handsome, muscle-bound soldier with a squared jaw, brown hair, and gray eyes, who was currently lifting weights while closely watching Jacey fight her friends. Every time Isis saw Mirko, he seemed to have a couple of dumbbells in his hands.

"Oh, shut up, Mirko!" Jacey retorted.

"Just saying—what good of a fighter are you if you're so easily tripped up?" Mirko taunted.

So intrigued in watching their practice and listening to the exchange, Isis gave a start at hearing movement behind her. She spun around, surprised to find Khalfani standing on the opposite side of the table, also taking a water break. "Stop instigating!"

Mirko shrugged his shoulders innocently and laughed. "Not instigating. Just motivating!"

Khalfani chuckled and shook his head. Taking another sip of his water, his eyes met Isis's and they simply held each other's stare for a moment.

Isis nodded curtly in greeting, and Khalfani returned the nod before averting his gaze, a slightly flushed tint suddenly spreading across his face.

Isis eyed him, not understanding what a guy like Khalfani could possibly be embarrassed about; he'd been doing amazing with his training—something Isis had become even more aware of today. The two of them had been training near each other, and she had gotten a closer look at Khalfani's technique and skill than she'd ever gotten before.

Again, she couldn't help feeling slightly jealous. She had noted, begrudgingly, that nearly the whole training area hadn't been able to take their eyes off him, though, she suspected, at least in terms of the handful of women present, Khalfani's good looks were partially to blame for the attention. Even in her periphery, Isis was aware of Lia Falzon—with her bright red hair—glancing their way, probably at Khalfani.

Realizing she had probably been staring at Khalfani for a bit too long herself, Isis finally averted her gaze, catching glimpses of the others still training, silently sizing them up as she did so. Some of the others were good, she had to admit, but most of them paled in comparison to what she'd seen from Khalfani. Sensing him still standing there, Isis decided that another attempt at camaraderie couldn't hurt. She turned back around, wanting to tell Khalfani that he'd been doing a good job, only to notice that he was already looking at her—or parts of her, rather.

His eyes had been roaming her body. When they made it back to her face, and he realized she'd caught him in the act, the flush over his cheeks deepened.

Isis smirked and suppressed a laugh. On some level, she knew her mother's gripes about her training attire weren't without warrant. The other female soldiers either wore looser fitting attire or simply didn't have the same kind of curves filling out their attire the way Isis did. For the most part, though, Isis usually didn't care and typically paid no attention to men and where their gazes traveled.

But with Khalfani, for some reason, it was a little harder to ignore.

Isis presumed it was because she knew how disciplined and gentlemanly Khalfani typically was. Hence, rather than feeling annoyed or offended, she merely felt amused and a bit flattered, if she was being honest.

Besides, it was hard to feel offended when he looked so ashamed of himself. The great Khalfani Abaza was human, after all, it seemed.

"What?" Isis said, boldly looking at him and trying not to laugh.

He practically jumped at the sound of her voice. "Huh?" he said.

"What are you looking at?" she challenged, her head tilted sideways.

Khalfani stammered, opening and closing his mouth but failing to say anything coherent. "I…I…Umm, what? Nothing…" he eventually said. "I just…" He swallowed. "Uhm, you're doing really well. With the training, I mean. And I'm not just saying that because you're a girl…" Yet, the instant the words left his mouth, he cringed. "Okay, that sounded really pompous. I'm sorry. I didn't mean it that way. I just meant, you're good, Isis. *Really* good." He awkwardly rubbed the back of his head. "I wouldn't want to fight you myself, that's for sure. You'd give me a run for my money. Your parents would be so proud, if they weren't so worried."

Isis blinked, stunned. Coming from Khalfani, the magnitude of the compliment was not lost on her. Granted, the 'because you're a girl' comment had initially rubbed her the wrong way, but she still understood the sentiment behind it. It was the double-standard of society at play—something she resented deeply, for she knew it was so much easier for her male contemporaries to train without the same kind of judgment she received.

"Well, you're pretty damned good yourself," Isis said. "I've seen how hard you train and how disciplined you are. It's impressive."

Khalfani shrugged his shoulders. "Yeah. Well, fighting the Retrograde gives me a purpose. Gives me something with meaning to do, you know? So I might as well put my all into it. I've got plenty of time since I've sworn off women until marriage..." His voice trailed off, and the flush returned to his face. He averted her gaze.

Understanding he'd accidentally said more than he meant to, Isis turned away as she smirked to spare his feelings. While she'd found his confession adorable, she figured he probably wouldn't appreciate her saying so.

She cleared her throat, looking for a way to diffuse the tension. But when she spoke, words she hadn't anticipated came out. "It's fine. I'm a virgin too."

Her statement lingered in the air, and she couldn't resist watching Khalfani's reaction, primarily because her mother's tirade came back to mind, making her wonder if there was any truth to people doubting her purity based on the way she presented herself.

Khalfani stared back at her, but she couldn't quite place his expression. "I think it's a little different for men," he said after a moment's hesitation. "Maybe. I don't know." He shrugged. "Stereotypes, I guess. But uhm...it's fine. It's important to me to wait for marriage. Besides, I was advised to do so by a man I have great respect for."

"Oh, yeah?" Isis said. "Who?"

Khalfani smirked. "Your *poje*. He once told me that it's worth the wait when you find the right person, and I believe him."

Isis nodded. "Yeah. Well, I guess the old fart is pretty wise. I've learned to believe him most of the time too." She winked.

At this, Khalfani laughed, and Isis smiled in return. She found that she rather enjoyed the sound of his laugh, and consequently wondered if he would mind the sound of hers. Or would he find it too boisterous, like her *eva* did?

"Well, I'd say there are no doubts about it," Khalfani continued. "Your *poje* is a very wise man. As a matter of fact, both of your parents are wise and only want what's best for you—your mother included. That's something to be valued."

The smile slipped from Isis's face, getting replaced with mild irritation. She knew Khalfani meant no harm, but a part of her couldn't help feeling slightly lectured. She slowly took another sip from her canteen, though her thirst had already been quenched. "Enough about my folks," she said. "What about yours?" She met his gaze, genuinely curious as to why Khalfani seemed to idolize her parents so much. Surely, he had parents of his own to be concerned with.

Khalfani turned away from her and finished the rest of his water. It took him a moment to speak, and Isis had a distinct feeling that he was stalling.

"Parents are parents," he finally said. "We all have them." He shrugged his shoulders again. "Well, it's been nice talking to you, Isis. Now, if you'll excuse me, I have some more training to do." He nodded toward the door where a dark-skinned soldier stood, looking in their direction with his arms folded nonchalantly across his strong chest. Isis stared at him for a moment, scanning her memory for his name as her eyes roamed his smooth dark skin. She'd seen him hanging around Khalfani frequently during practices.

"Tekem and I usually make time to do some training and strategizing in the other room. You know, with less...distraction," Khalfani explained. As if right on cue, Jacey's laughter drifted towards them as she goofed around with her friends.

Isis nodded, looking towards the soldier at the door again, Tekem Iswe. She remembered him now, with his dark brown skin, striking hazel eyes, and squared shoulders. He was widely considered one of the smartest in Cairo's army. If memory served her correctly, she thought she had even seen him a few times around her home, likely there to visit Khalfani in his wing of the Mahmoud complex. Catching Isis staring at him, he politely nodded his head in greeting. She nodded back.

Her eyes then snapped back to Khalfani as he began walking away. "See you around, Isis. *Sahha.*" *Goodbye.*

"Okay, yeah. *Sahha,*" Isis said, watching him disappear with Tekem. Still looking at the doorway after they'd gone, she wondered what Khalfani was hiding pertaining to his parents. Her thoughts were soon interrupted, though.

"Hey, Isis. *Kif int?*" *How are you?*

Isis turned around, surprised to see Aurora Imamu heading her way. Instantly recognizable by her long dark braids and intricate tattoos, Aurora was among the oldest soldiers and one of the best. Even though Isis was the daughter of the greatly respected Maat Mahmoud, Isis was stunned that someone like Aurora would acknowledge her directly.

"H-Hi," Isis stammered. "I'm well, and you?"

Aurora stopped about a foot away from her and smiled. "I'm fine. *Ose.*" *Thank you.* "I was watching you train earlier. Just had to come over to pay you my compliments. You're doing an amazing job."

"*Ose,*" Isis said, bowing in appreciation. She stood in awkward silence for a moment, still unable to wrap her mind around the fact that Aurora Imamu was standing in front of her, complimenting her, no less. As she struggled to figure out what to say next, her eyes roamed Aurora's beautiful tattoos; they consisted of white swirl designs that framed her eyes and cheekbones, breathtaking against the tone of her dark brown skin, and standing out with her rich purple attire.

Feeling awkward for staring at her too long, Isis lowered her eyes to Aurora's neck, where a gorgeous amulet necklace rested.

Noticing Isis's stare, Aurora touched the necklace. "Do you like it? It's my little connection to the *Hallah*." *The Universe.*

"Load of hogwash, it is," a man nearby said, interrupting before Isis had a chance to respond. Isis turned her gaze over to the soldier who had spoken.

Aurora rolled her eyes. "If I'd wanted your opinion, Parr, I would have asked for it," she retorted.

The soldier called Parr rolled his eyes as well. Glancing in his direction, Isis saw that Jacey, Farhad, Hydrus, and Garth stood nearby him, snickering. Whether they were snickering at Aurora or Parr, though, Isis couldn't tell.

She cleared her throat and turned back to Aurora. "Well, I think it's beautiful."

Aurora smiled. "You know, when I was a child, my mother told me to always wear it, and I've done exactly that. In exchange for wearing this necklace, the gods will one day grant me a wish, although I know that wish will cost me my life." She paused thoughtfully for a moment and then shrugged her shoulders. "I say it is a fair exchange, though, especially considering the gifts this amulet gives me. It regularly gives me visions, and those visions tend to come true."

"Wow…" Isis said, astounded. Yet, in her periphery, she could see the skeptical soldier—Parr—shaking his head. It appeared that he was about to make another retort, but Farhad nudged him in the ribs with his elbow, effectively stopping whatever it was that Parr had wanted to say. Parr pursed his lips, agitated, but refrained from arguing.

Listening to Aurora, Isis could understand why others might not believe her. Isis, on the other hand, had grown up with a *pa* who had his own mysterious ways of predicting the future. Thus, the idea of Aurora's necklace possessing mystical powers didn't seem too far-fetched to her. Just looking at it, Isis had already been able to tell there was something special about it. She met Aurora's eyes and smiled. "I believe you. That's an incredible gift to have. I don't blame you for never taking it off."

Aurora smiled amicably and pat Isis on the shoulder. "Well," she said, "enough of that. If it's all right, I have some moves I want to show you." She leaned in closer to Isis, lowering her voice. "From what I've seen of your training, I think you're actually skilled enough to pull them off."

CHAPTER 3

The day of training had been long and tiring, but rewarding—particularly with the one-on-one sessions Isis had been fortunate enough to have with Aurora. Afterwards, she'd done a few more group training sessions, in which Aurora had introduced her to some more soldiers she'd only seen before in passing, and then Khalfani and Tekem had returned to watch a bit before they all called it quits for the day.

Nevertheless, by the time Isis made it back home, her muscles screamed in agony. She headed straight for the shower, letting the warm water massage the soreness in her limbs and wash away the sweat from her body. Then, she headed straight to bed, falling asleep the instant her head hit the pillow and feeling soothed by the artificial breezes coming through the ventilation system near the windows.

Isis woke the next morning, rejuvenated, and ready to face the new day. Still lying in bed, she stretched extravagantly and then spent a moment simply listening to the sounds of the house. It took a bit of time for her to realize that the morning wasn't as quiet as normal. Though her bedroom was on the second floor, the opened vents due to the newly installed ventilation system permitted noise to drift through the Mahmoud dwelling more easily.

Judging from all the voices Isis heard, they clearly had company.

Her curiosity mounting, she quickly got out of bed and dressed. When she made it down to the main floor, she headed for the kitchen, under the assumption that some sort of breakfast gathering was taking place.

"*Ella, Imma,*" Isis said, greeting her mother good morning, yet confused as to why she was seated alone in the kitchen.

Clutching a cup of hot tea, Rania turned toward her daughter and blinked, a flash of relief crossing her expression. Knowing her mother so well, Isis knew Rania's look of pleasant surprise had to do with the fact that she was not dressed in her form-fitting practice gear.

Rania smiled. *"Ella, iva." Good morning, baby.* "Would you like to join me for a cup of tea?" she asked, already preparing a cup for her daughter before receiving an answer.

However, Isis hardly heard her mother; her attention was captured by the voices coming from the foyer. "What's going on? Is *Pa* having some kind of meeting?"

"Yes. Don't worry about it. It's nothing of your concern," Rania said, handing the cup to Isis.

Hearing the forced nonchalance in Rania's voice, though, left Isis convinced that whatever was going on definitely should be her concern. Abruptly turning away from her *eva* and ignoring her protests, Isis hurriedly made her way to the foyer.

She stopped in the entryway, momentarily stunned to see the crowd. Rows of chairs had been lined before a podium, where her *poje* stood, addressing the crowd of soldiers before him. Maat's eyes briefly landed on Isis, and he nodded slightly in greeting.

Instantly, Isis was aware the gathering was about the Retrograde. Why else would her mother have been trying to draw her attention away from it?

As Isis stood there, still stunned for a moment, perhaps sensing her stare—or having noticed Maat nod at her—some of the soldiers began to glance back at her. Jacey and Farhad shot smug looks in her direction. Parr looked her up and down before turning back to face forward. Aurora caught her gaze and nodded politely, and a soldier named Kaiden Taha flashed her a tentative smile. Behind them, Tekem nodded in acknowledgement, and beside him sat Khalfani, listening attentively to Maat. A few rows away from them sat several of the other soldiers she'd recently met.

Seeing them all there, Isis couldn't help but feel a brief but strong flicker of annoyance. Why hadn't anyone told her about the meeting? Did none of them really think to even mention it at the previous day's training?

Or was it simply that as the daughter of Maat Mahmoud, they had all assumed she would have already known about it?

Or was it something a little more unflattering than that?

Isis grimaced, knowing that deep down, many of them believed her to be training simply for sport, out of boredom. Not many genuinely believed the daughter of President Maat Mahmoud would actually participate in fighting the Retrograde. Behind her back, she knew the majority of them probably thought of her as a spoiled and pampered princess, just playing pretend. Even as she'd been leaving practice the day before, she'd overheard Easton Losco—a pretty, yet gossipy girl-next-door type—quietly insinuating as much to Kaiden.

Isis grit her teeth. How she couldn't wait to prove them wrong…

Deciding not to dwell on her annoyance any longer, Isis simply scanned the premises for an available seat. With her cup of tea still in hand, she realized the seat on the other side of

Khalfani was vacant and quickly made her way over. "*Ella*," she said, settling down next to him and taking a sip of her tea. She then leaned forward and nodded hello to Tekem on the other side of him.

"*Ella*." Khalfani offered her a polite smile before refocusing back on Maat Mahmoud.

Taking another sip of her tea, Isis leaned back and tuned in to her *poje's* words as well, knowing she had a lot of catching up to do, since they were all apparently fine with leaving her out of the loop.

"I'm afraid none of this is an exaggeration," Maat was saying, looking out grimly at his captivated audience. "The Retrograde has always been known to worsen with each decade. Many of you are too young to remember much about previous Retrogrades. However, for those of us who can remember and compare past attacks—or who've heard stories from elders regarding the Retrogrades of the past—it is common knowledge how the conditions gradually grow worse. This Retrograde, however, I can say with certainty, is panning out to be the worst we could have ever imagined." Maat paused, taking a handkerchief out of his breast pocket and patting his forehead with it. "It's so bad, in fact, none of us may be exempt from exposure to it this time around. So extra precautions will be necessary.

"Now, more than likely, based on the Retrograde's typical travel pattern over the last thirty years, it will reach either Zahara or Illyian first. As you know, Illyian is our neighboring region, which is composed primarily of woodlands. It has no existing army. Zahara's army is a third of our size and far too remote to even consider protecting Illyian, so it is up to us. Our army is the most powerful in all of Damara, so we must do our part. We will still have a little bit of time before it reaches us here in Cairo. That, however, doesn't mean conditions won't be just as harsh when it finally reaches us. We might be last to get hit, but we will undoubtedly get hit just as hard." He paused again for a moment before continuing.

"Just last night, I received some devastating news about our neighboring planet of Ximxija. The entire planet has been overrun by changelings, and they're killing themselves and each other off to the point of extinction. This is the end of Ximxija as we know it."

At the mentioning of Ximxija, Isis shifted in her seat, remembering the images of the Retrograde attack she'd watched with her *pa* and Khalfani. She glanced sideways at Khalfani. Noting the way his brow furrowed, she suspected that he, too, was remembering those disturbing images of the changelings—the planet's inhabitants who had been rendered into something less than human due to the Retrograde's infection.

Khalfani folded his arms tightly across his chest, and Isis was pretty sure she'd seen him shudder.

"For those of you who still don't know exactly how the Retrograde works," Maat resumed, "here's a quick crash course. The typical pattern is as follows. You'll know the Retrograde is about to strike because the day before, the sky turns dark, and daylight never arrives. Typically, residents seek to evacuate concentrated cities long before it reaches this point. Because of the denseness of city populations, we find that the Retrograde's effects are the most severe in those areas. Those who can't leave will barricade themselves in their homes, trying to block out as much of the outside world as possible. Some people will even go as far as to surround their homes with impenetrable armor..." Maat gave a brief and ironic smirk, for his own home was surrounded with such armor, albeit, much stronger than what the typical Cairo citizen could afford.

"As to be expected, though, it is the working class and the poor who are left the least prepared and able to protect themselves. They can't leave, and they can't secure their homes, so they just wait for the inevitable and hope to survive.

"In the passing hours, a dark and hazy fog fills the streets, and slowly, it invades the systems of anyone breathing it in. That's when the symptoms begin to manifest. The first symptom is irritability and confusion. You'll find an increase of lawlessness all around, in every way imaginable. This is because the fog has a way of making people lose their sense of self-control. And without self-control, more and more people will give in to their darkest urges.

"The following day marks the first true day of the Retrograde, which is when the chaos really begins. By this point, the fog turns into complete Darkness, which is an entity in itself. Some of those who've been exposed to the previous day's fog will begin to spontaneously combust with what is called the Blue Fire. The infected get engulfed by the fire from the inside out until they disintegrate into a pile of ashes—a process known as deliquesce. In contrast, others melt—literally dissolving into water before evaporating and becoming a part of the Darkness in the air. Why some combust, and others dissolve, no one knows; it's just a part of the Retrograde's mystery. In either case, the pain felt by the victims is incomprehensible.

"And then there are those who just disappear altogether. Vanish without a trace. As for those left behind, anger and violence consume their minds. This even happens with the animals at times. Normally docile creatures turn into rabid, vicious beasts, willing to attack anyone and anything that cross their paths. And all of this is just *Day 1...*"

"Leum," someone in the crowd said, uttering an explicative. Isis scanned the tops of heads, trying to figure out who had spoken. Instead, however, her gaze stopped on a soldier she recalled being named Amam Keita. Even with all the others surrounding him, his bulging figure stood out. He was a huge man who made Isis feel a little uneasy from time to time. He, too, was a good fighter, but there was something particularly unnerving about him. Even now, as he listened to Maat, there was an expression on his face that seemed mildly inappropriate. Everyone was riveted by Maat's speech, but not in the same way Amam appeared to be. If Isis didn't know any better, she'd say he looked excited about the descriptions of the Retrograde...

Suppressing a shudder of her own, Isis forced herself to look away from Amam.

"On Day 2, the pandemonium increases," Maat said. "This is usually the stage when the army tries to intervene, killing off anyone showing signs of being consumed with the disease. But the Retrograde's effects are usually so fast and far-reaching, it's impossible to exterminate everyone truly affected by it. Sometimes even people barricaded in their homes begin to display symptoms—the Retrograde still managing to reach them through the tiniest cracks and crevices. In consequence, they often develop the same violence and rage as those outside, even if it takes a little longer to reach them. The only people documented to be unaffected by the Retrograde are nursing mothers, strangely enough. Something about the changes in their hormonal chemistry during that time period makes them immune to the Retrograde's effects. But you can imagine their terror, trying to keep themselves and their babies safe while everyone around them is turning into changelings…Lots of families are ripped apart by the Retrograde.

"By Day 3, virtually everyone still remaining has changed over into what can only be called the walking dead, and there is no cure for their condition. As for the few who manage to survive, they're trapped, listening to the sounds of the changelings outside, scraping at their houses until their fingernails fall off. Even still, some of those who've survived can feel the evil slowly consuming them and are left to commit suicide to prevent becoming changelings themselves. The third day is the darkest and most vile of the Retrograde.

"That, my friends, are what we are up against." Maat wiped his forehead with the handkerchief again, a stunned silence following his words. For a long moment afterwards, the entire room was quiet enough to hear a pin drop. Slowly, yet, frightened murmurs filled the room.

Isis sat, gripping her cup of tea that had now grown cold. Listening to her *poje*, she couldn't help thinking about all the precautions he'd already been taking, months in advance. It all seemed useless in light of what he had just described. Yet, deep down, Isis couldn't bring herself to believe that all hope was lost in fighting this Retrograde. If that were really the case, none of them would be training so hard.

She narrowed her eyes, watching her father carefully as he continued standing at the podium, a deep crease forming between his eyebrows.

Maat was an intelligent, intuitive, and sometimes seemingly all-knowing man, but if there was one thing Isis knew about her *poje*, it was that he had a knack for saying precisely what needed to be said in order to bring about the best results. Hence, the more she reflected on his speech, the more she grew convinced that Maat's method was to instill as much fear as possible about the upcoming Retrograde to make sure that everyone took it seriously. He wanted to see to it that Damara's army was completely prepared and would be motivated to acquire the necessary skills and plans to defeat this Retrograde, no matter how bad it was.

The tension that had been slowly building up throughout Isis's body eased up, and she leaned back in her seat. She turned her head sideways, seeing how distressed Khalfani still looked.

Isis smirked. As skilled as Khalfani was, she was certain that he had little to worry about; the Retrograde wasn't going to know what hit it when it encountered Khalfani Abaza.

Without thinking, she reached out and touched his knee. He jumped, startled by her touch. Not meaning to alarm him, she gave his knee a reassuring squeeze, a bit slow to realize how the gesture made him blush. From the corners of his eyes, he looked at her with raised eyebrows.

She removed her hand from his knee. "Don't worry," she said confidently. "We'll be ready."

Khalfani scratched his chin and looked ahead again, trying to focus on Maat now that he had resumed speaking. Nevertheless, his face remained flushed, and Isis couldn't deny something about it made her want to grin despite the circumstances around them. She also recognized how recklessly flirtatious her gesture of touching Khalfani's knee had been, yet she couldn't find it in herself to regret it, especially as she noticed how he kept glancing at her even though he was trying desperately to keep his focus on her father.

"Are you afraid?" Isis whispered, watching Khalfani out the corner of her eye.

He blinked. "Afraid of what?"

"The Retrograde."

"Oh…"

Isis raised an eyebrow. "What did you think I was talking about?"

"Uhm...I don't know. But yeah...I mean—you know what we saw. The Retrograde is nothing to play with this time around. Not that it ever was, but you know what I mean."

Isis nudged him with her elbow. "Do you really think you'll have anything to worry about? The Retrograde probably won't be able to do anything to you. Your looks will stop it in its tracks. You know, just like it does every female in the room when you're training."

On the other side of Khalfani, Tekem snickered. A muscle clenched in Khalfani's jaw as he shot Tekem a look. He then glanced at Isis, clearly unable to believe she had the nerve to flirt with him while in the middle of such an important meeting.

Yet, Isis didn't care; her only thoughts were on easing the tension permeating the room. Purposefully this time, she pat Khalfani's knee again.

Maat spoke for a little while longer, and then the meeting was adjourned.

Isis remained seated for a while, merely watching as everyone stood, their chairs scraping against the floor, and their voices hushed as they discussed amongst themselves what they'd just heard.

"Hey," Tekem said to Khalfani, "let's try to meet up with Mirko later to discuss tactics." He grinned. "And uhm...from what I've heard, Easton and Orsel plan to sit in if you're going to be there." He winked and laughed before walking off, leaving Khalfani glaring after him.

Isis sat there, her mind working over who Easton and Orsel were. Suddenly, a doe-eyed blonde and a petite girl with beautiful almond shaped eyes came to mind, respectively. She pursed her lips together, glancing the premises to see if they'd been there but got distracted by the sound of Khalfani clearing his throat. Still staring after Tekem, who was now chatting with Lia, Khalfani slowly stood.

"Hey," she said, also standing. Though her voice was soft, it was still enough to stop Khalfani in his tracks. He looked at her, his expression almost as riveted as it had been while listening to Maat. "I just want you to know," she resumed, "all of this was meant as motivation, so don't feel discouraged. Just use it as ammo to train harder so that we can put an end to this Retrograde, no matter how big and bad it's supposed. I know my *pa*. That was his intentions with that little speech he just gave."

Khalfani thoughtfully weighed her words and then nodded his head. "Yeah, I can see that."

Isis nodded back at him curtly, watching as the others began to file out of the room, on their way to training. "So, uhm…how about you wait for me while I get changed? Then we can head out to training together. That is where you're going, right? To meet up with Tekem, and uhm…Easton and Orsel, was it?"

Again, Khalfani nodded slowly, the corners of his lips twitching as if holding in a smile. He rubbed the back of his head. "Yeah. Sure. All right. I can wait for you."

"Okay. It'll just be a second." Isis looked around briefly, thankful to see her father preoccupied talking with several soldiers and, consequently, paying her no attention. Taking advantage of her *poje's* distraction, she sprinted out of the foyer, hoping to avoid running into her *eva* as well.

Right as she turned the corner, however, she almost slammed right into Kaiden Taha.

"Oh!" she cried out in surprise.

Kaiden's arms shot outwards, clutching Isis by the shoulders. "I'm sorry! Are you all right?" he said.

Isis stepped back and nodded. "Yeah…What are you doing?"

Kaiden smiled sheepishly. "Nothing. I…just needed the restroom…" He cleared his throat and nervously folded his arms. "Umm, nice place. I think this is the first time I've been inside the Mahmoud complex."

"Oh…" Isis said and then shrugged her shoulders. "It's all right, I guess." She was just about to excuse herself, but noted the expression on Kaiden's face and suspected there was something else he wanted to say. "Are you okay?"

He nodded his head too vigorously. "Yeah, yeah…Sorry. I guess I just wanted to let you know that you've been doing a good job. I've been watching you…I mean, not in a creepy way." He laughed awkwardly. "Seeing you at practice, I mean…"

"Oh," Isis said, her mind darting back to what she'd heard Easton saying about her to Kaiden. She narrowed her eyes at Kaiden, wondering if he was being sarcastic. But suddenly, she noticed the way he looked at her, and realized that sarcasm was likely the furthest thing from his mind.

"Are you coming to practice today?" he asked, looking at her hopefully.

Isis nodded. "Yeah. I was just about to change into my training gear. And as a matter of fact, Khalfani is waiting on me. So, I really should get going. It was nice talking to you, though…And I'll see you around practice too, I presume?"

Kaiden's eyes went wide. "Oh. Umm, yeah. Yeah. I'll see you around then. Sorry…" And with that, he cleared his throat and darted off.

Isis continued on her way to her room, thinking of Kaiden. He was handsome in his own way, and in terms of Cairo's army, he almost ranked as highly as Khalfani. But that was the thing—he wasn't Khalfani…

* * *

Isis had heard cat-calls before, but the training grounds was the last place she expected to hear them. "What in the world?" she muttered as she entered the building with Khalfani trailing behind her. She glanced back at him, only to find the familiar flush spreading across his cheeks.

"All right, Khalfani," a voice called out. Isis recognized it to be Tekem's. He stood several yards away, grinning in their direction. Several other soldiers stood around him. "I knew you were brave, but I didn't know you were *that* brave. You actually left Mahmoud's house *with* his daughter? Wow…" Tekem gave a mocking clap, and several of the soldiers around him cat-called again.

Isis blinked, simultaneously stunned and amused. A surprised bubble of laughter burst from her throat.

Meanwhile, Khalfani flipped off Tekem, though it was clearly in a good-natured fashion.

"Hmm," Isis said, playfully raising an eyebrow. "So, you're hanging out with me to be rebellious, huh?"

"*Duro,* Isis," Khalfani said. *Stop it, Isis.* Yet, Khalfani smirked nonetheless.

"What's wrong? Do I make you uncomfortable?" she teased. "Is it still all right if I train with you? I mean, I wouldn't want you to feel awkward around your friends..."

"Of course, you can train with me," Khalfani scoffed as they walked farther into the building. "It pays off to train against a formidable opponent." He turned around and yelled over his shoulder towards the soldiers still chortling at them. "Unlike some other lousy soldiers that I know!"

Isis laughed and then placed her index finger on her chin in mock contemplation. "So, is it me that you find formidable, or is it my training outfit that you keep looking at?"

Khalfani stopped dead in his tracks, his mouth dropping open.

Isis unashamedly laughed her full and boisterous laugh. "Relax, I'm just teasing."

"You are unbelievable," Khalfani muttered, recomposing himself.

Isis winked. "You have no idea," she said as they turned the corner, entering their favorite training spot.

While everything was all in good fun to Isis, she couldn't help noting how flustered Khalfani seemed to be despite trying to keep on a brave face. "Hey," she said, "in all seriousness, I really don't mean to make you uncomfortable. You know that, right? We both know who my *pa* is. If something about training with me seems…inappropriate to you somehow…you can let me know. I won't be offended. I know you have a respectable reputation to protect—"

"And don't you as well?" Khalfani interrupted.

"Yes, I suppose so." Isis shrugged. "But what I mean is, if you don't want people talking or getting the wrong idea about us, I can back off. I don't mean to start any trouble."

Khalfani turned to look Isis directly in the eyes. "Isis, I don't care what people think."

She stared back at him, not entirely sure she believed him, fully aware of how virtuous and conservative he was.

"And more importantly," he continued, "neither will anyone else once the Retrograde gets here. So, our training together isn't a problem for me, and I hope it isn't for you."

Isis smiled. "Well, I guess we're in agreement then."

* * *

Keeping up with Khalfani was a challenge, but Isis was up for it and proud of herself for succeeding.

"Good work," he said, grinning as they stopped for a break. He tossed her a bottle of water, which she easily caught.

"Thanks," she said, grinning back at him and coming to stand at his side.

The two of them sat, drinking their water in companionable silence, the only noise around them being the clinking sounds coming from Aiari Adisa across the room as he made some kind of weapon out of a strip of metal.

Isis shifted in her seat a bit, turning to look out the window beside them. As she stared at the grassy green field outside, decorated with colorful pnina flowers, her mind began to wander.

She'd known Khalfani for a while; he'd been living in a wing of the Mahmoud complex ever since he was a child. Yet, in all these years, she had never felt this close to him. Granted, she supposed she never quite had reason to before. Despite living on the grounds of her family's complex, he had primarily kept to himself, making it easy for them to live their separate lives. But now, with the Retrograde approaching, their paths crossed so much more frequently. In consequence, Isis couldn't help the mounting curiosity she'd started to feel towards him. It was almost as if something, somewhere, was drawing them closer together.

She thought back to their previous conversation, recalling the way he had become distant at the mention of his parents. For the first time, it struck her as weird that he had grown up away from them, especially from such a young age.

She could recall when her *pa* had called her and her *eva* to the living room for a family meeting all those years ago, informing them that they had a new housemate. He had then brought a young Khalfani into the room, and Isis had been astonished to see that he was just barely older than her. Maat had explained that the boy needed a place to stay, and planned to grow up as a part of Cairo's army—something Isis had found strange back then, considering how young Khalfani was.

From that point on, Khalfani had frequented the house for breakfast, lunch, and dinner. But he typically disappeared, retreating to himself in the hours in-between. As the years went on and Khalfani became more capable of taking care of himself, the meals he shared with the Mahmoud family became less frequent until stopping altogether. From that point on, they hardly saw him anymore—at least that was the case for Isis.

Her curiosity growing by the second, Isis hoped that after spending so much time together as of late, he might be willing to open up to her more…

"What is it?" he abruptly asked, catching her off guard.

"Huh?"

Khalfani tilted his head sideways. "Well, you keep staring at me, so it seems like there might be something on your mind."

Isis shrugged her shoulders and looked out the window at the pnina flowers again. "Maybe…"

"Isis, playing coy?" Khalfani chuckled. "Who would have thought that possible?"

She laughed. Then, noting that Khalfani was in a more playful mood than usual, she decided to take her chances. "So, what's your family like? I know you're close with my *pa*, but what's your own *poje* like?" As soon as the question left her mouth, though, she regretted it, seeing the way Khalfani's posture tensed. "I'm sorry," Isis said, confused but still curious. "Is it hard for you to talk about?"

He sighed and shrugged his shoulders. "Well, it's just that…my *poje* is a control-freak, to say the least. And let's just say his favorite thing to try controlling was me. He wanted me to be like him, but I've never found that option very appealing." He paused, a thoughtful look coming across his face. "My *poje*, he's the type of man who craves admiration. He *needs* to be respected. But it's my belief that in order to get respect, you should be a respectable person…" His voice trailed off, and it became evident that he didn't intend to speak any further on the subject, at least for now.

And that was all right with Isis; she simply appreciated that he had opened up to her, even if just a little. She reached out and touched his shoulder, meaning it as a comforting gesture. "Thank you."

He looked sideways at her. "For what?"

"For sharing that with me. I can tell it's hard for you to open up to people, so I really do appreciate it."

Khalfani fell silent, now turning his gaze to the window to look out at the flower-covered field.

Sensing that he was feeling awkward and didn't quite know what to say, Isis looked out the window again as well. "Beautiful, aren't they? The pnina flowers." She let her gaze roam over the flowers for a moment longer. They resembled tiger lilies, except they were colored deep blue, purple, and fuchia—the colors bleeding together as they reached the flowers' buds—something about them always reminded Isis of an ocean tide on a sandy beach. "Did you know my middle name is Pnina, after the flowers?"

Khalfani looked at her, his expression somewhat appraising. He then nodded his head. "Pnina," he said, as if testing the name on his tongue. "Suits you. You're just as colorful and vibrant."

Isis pressed her lips together, holding back a grin. "Well," she said, "shall we resume?" She gestured to the training area, where Tekem, Lia, Aurora, and a young blonde soldier had just entered.

Khalfani finished the last of his water. "Yeah, I suppose so," he said, and then smirked, "Ninna."

Isis paused for a second, evaluating the new nickname he had just used for her. Smiling silently in approval, she followed him back onto the floor.

"Hello, there," Aurora said, making her way over to them. Trailing behind her was the young blonde soldier. Isis had seen her numerous times before; she was quite easy to remember, with her hair as golden as the Ra and her eyes as blue as the sky. Each time Isis saw her, she felt the girl looked far too sweet and innocent to be a soldier.

"Hi," Isis said in greeting, while Khalfani nodded at them.

"Doing a good job, as usual, the both of you," Aurora said, smiling. "I want to formally introduce you to someone." She turned around and put her hand on the girl's shoulder, gently nudging her forward so that she was in better view. "This is Apple."

"Hi, Apple," Isis said, glad to finally have a name to put to the face.

Khalfani nodded hello and gave the girl a brief wave, a sense of familiarity between them, considering he and Aurora were already old friends.

Apple smiled broadly, looking both friendly and shy at the same time. "Hi," she said, focusing primarily on Isis. "You're amazing, by the way. Sometimes I get distracted just watching the two of you train."

Aurora laughed. "As you can see, Apple plans to follow in your footsteps."

Isis smiled at Aurora. "Well, we're just following yours. So, if she's following us, at least you know she's going in the right direction," she joked, though she inwardly wondered whether Apple truly had it in her. There was such a doting tone to Aurora's voice, not to mention in the way she looked at Apple, that made it evident the girl was like a daughter to her. It was no secret that parents sometimes exaggerated their children's capabilities, which was one of the reasons Isis was so determined to prove herself on her own merit, not wanting people to think she was just being given a pass as Maat Mahmoud's daughter.

Isis exchanged glances with Khalfani, wondering if he, too, got a sense that Aurora's fondness of the girl was what drove Apple, rather than actual skill and desire to be a soldier.

* * *

Tired from another long day of training, Isis entered her house, making it past all the security doors and gates that had been installed in preparation for the upcoming Retrograde.

"Isis, is that you?" Rania's voice called out.

Isis sighed. "*Ano, Imma,*" she answered reluctantly. *Yes, Mommy.*

Moments later, Rania appeared. As usual, her eyes roamed Isis's training attire with disapproval. Nevertheless, she forced a smile onto her face, though it didn't reach her eyes. "How was your day?"

"Productive."

"Isis—"

Isis pinched the bridge of her nose, already agitated. "*Imma*, can we please not do this now?" she said, already knowing from the tone of Rania's voice that she wanted to have another one of her serious talks.

Rania pressed her lips into a tight line. "I just don't understand you sometimes. Or more accurately, I don't understand why you refuse to understand me…"

"*Imma*, I understand you perfectly."

"Really? Because it most certainly doesn't feel like it. From my point-of-view, it looks like you think my only purpose is to make you miserable and complain about everything you do."

Isis clenched her teeth to keep from agreeing on the accuracy of Rania's statement.

"That's not the case, Isis." Rania sighed. She gestured to the table in the dining room. *"De'ku je." Come to me.* "Sit down."

Seeing no way out of this, Isis headed to the table and took a seat, already deciding the only way she could quickly make it through this was if she sat quietly and just let her mother rant uninterrupted.

It'll be over soon, she thought, praying for her own patience.

"Isis, I can see it in your eyes all the time that you think I'm always being judgmental of you for no reason."

"That's not exactly true. You're judgmental for a reason, and that reason is that I'm not like you," Isis said, already breaking her own rule. As she uttered the words, she thought of Khalfani, recalling the brief words he'd spoken about his father. Was this what their relationship was like? If so, Isis could relate more than Khalfani realized.

Rania shook her head. "You have to know how much I care about you, and how much respect I have for you as my daughter, Isis. You're my *iva.*" *My baby.* "We may not see eye-to-eye, but I only want what's best for you. You may not think I have any clue as to what that is, but as your *eva,* I beg to differ. I know a whole lifestyle that you can't even fathom—and I'm thankful for that, because it's a lifestyle I was determined to make sure you never have to deal with.

"Isis, I didn't come from wealth—you know that, right? My family..." Her voice trailed off for an instant, and she sighed, casting her gaze downward to the floor as if recalling painful memories. "When the Retrograde hit, they had no way to defend themselves. I'm old enough to remember how it was sometimes. And honestly, it's only by the grace of the gods that I'm still here, to begin with. The grace of the gods, and your father…"

Isis sat quietly, reflecting on her mother's words. She didn't really need her elaboration to understand what she was implying, which was that marrying Maat Mahmoud had improved her quality of life. And no doubt, it was the reason she wanted Isis to be a 'proper lady'—so that she could ultimately marry well.

The tension in Rania's mouth while she'd been speaking relaxed, and a soft smile spread across her face. Suddenly, she looked so peaceful—in such contrast to how she had looked just moments before.

Isis tilted her head to the side, eyeing her mother. "What are you thinking about?"

Rania blinked, suddenly snapping back to the present. "Oh, the wedding, I suppose. As a little girl, I never imagined having an extravagant wedding. Not where I came from. Everyone I knew had used the poor man's method."

Isis furrowed her brow. She'd heard of the 'poor man's wedding' before, but never exactly knew what it entailed.

Truthfully, she had never really given it much thought, since weddings and marriage typically weren't on her mind. Hence, all she really knew was that the lower-class had a much simpler and humbler way of getting married than the rich, who celebrated their nuptials with fancy gatherings that they occasionally invited working-class people to, as if they were charity cases winning a prize.

"Do you know the poor man's method?" Rania asked, correctly identifying the confusion on her daughter's face.

"Well, not really…"

Rania held out her arm. "You know the chip that is embedded under everyone's skin?" She rubbed her hand across her forearm, where her own chip resided to mark her marriage to Maat.

Isis nodded, having seen a number of weddings before. "Yeah. Where you touch arms during wedding ceremonies."

Rania nodded. "Right. You don't need an extravagant ceremony to activate it. The poor simply touch arms and recite their wedding vows. That's really all it takes. Once this is done, the chip activation automatically causes an announcement to go off throughout your home region, informing residents of the two people who have joined together in matrimony."

"Huh," Isis said. "I always thought the chip could only be activated by a wedding officiant or something."

Rania smiled and shook her head. "No, not at all. The poor can't afford such luxuries." A faraway look fell over her face, and she stared off into the distance for a while. Then she abruptly shook her head again, as if shaking away whatever thoughts had temporarily run off with her. "Anyway," she resumed, "you have to understand, Isis, that everything I've done has been with the hopes that when I brought an *iva* into this world, he or she would have it better off than I did as a kid. My goal, as a woman, was to make sure my child had all the safety and protection that my family could never provide for me. I wanted to make sure my child didn't have to rely on fate and chance to survive. So, can you just imagine for a second what it feels like for me to see you, my only *iva,* willingly—voluntarily—going out and inserting yourself into this…this chaos?" She waved her hand at Isis, gesturing to her training outfit. "Honey, I want you *safe*. I want you to meet a good man and end up happily married with a family of your own to grow old with. Not out there, putting your life on the line unnecessarily. We have soldiers for that, and your pa and I have provided you with a lifestyle so that you *wouldn't* have to be one of them." A look of fear suddenly came over Rania's face. "*Iva*, you don't know what it's like to see a loved one get taken over by the Retrograde and turn into a changeling. You don't know what it's like to see someone you know personally—someone you care about—turn into something you can't understand."

Seeing the terror that had so abruptly seized her *eva's* expression, Isis suppressed a shudder. Again, images of the changelings she had witnessed in the live stream of their neighboring planet came to mind. No, she hadn't ever seen anything like that directly. It suddenly struck her just how terrifying it probably was to experience such a thing.

She swallowed, imagining her *eva*, *poje*, Khalfani, Aurora, Apple, Tekem, or any of the other soldiers she'd come to know, suddenly forming expressionless faces, grunting, drooling, and clawing at buildings. Or worse, falling victim to the rage the Retrograde induced, making them viciously lash out at others, if not seizing weapons to do damage to themselves…

She clenched her jaw. As horrifying as the thought was, it only made her more determined to make sure the Retrograde didn't come after the people she cared about. She halfway considered that maybe she was being a *gozo*, an idiot—but the more she feared the Retrograde, the more she wanted to fight it.

Rania had been sitting silently, watching the varying emotions go across Isis's face. In return, Isis stared back at her, rather surprised to hear all of this from her *eva*. She felt somewhat guilty, having always dismissed her *eva* as being shallow. But now, it occurred to her that there was far more to Rania than what met the eye—and that there was quite a bit of logic and rationality to the way she presented and conducted herself.

"Thank you for sharing that with me, *Imma*," Isis said, truly meaning it. She appreciated having this new view of her mother. Nevertheless, she also wanted her mother to have a solid understanding of where she stood in regards to all of this.

"Thank you for finally listening," Rania said, reaching out to tenderly rub her hand down the side of Isis's face. "You're *harika*, Isis." *Beautiful.* "You're smart. You're intelligent. You deserve the best that life has to offer."

Isis cleared her throat. "I appreciate you feeling that way, I really do. But *Imma*, I want you to know where I'm coming from too. Don't get me wrong; I appreciate being born into all of this." She waved her hand around at her lavish surroundings. "I know it's a blessing that others would kill for. But still, in good conscience, I can't always take pride in it, knowing others don't have it so easily, all for no fault of their own." She leaned forward and held her mother's gaze. "And that's especially true now, knowing that you were once in that category. You've been able to make it out of that lifestyle, but those are still your people—and I can tell by the way you speak, you still feel that way about them too. So, do you realize what that means? That means they are *my* people too. They need people to fight for them. *I* want to fight for them. Besides, you've heard what Pa said. This Retrograde is different from past ones. Even the wealthy are going to have to put more effort into staying safe this time around. So, when you think of it that way, isn't it best that I'm prepared for it?"

Rania remained silent for a long time—so long in fact, Isis thought she wasn't going to get a response.

With a sigh, Isis stood, believing that she had tried her *eva's* patience too much this time. Yet, just as she turned and started walking away, Rania sighed. "I see your point, Isis," she said. "Just please, my daughter, *schvak se.*" *Be careful.*

Isis halted, staring at the back of Rania's head, for she hadn't turned around when she spoke. "I will, *Imma.* I promise."

CHAPTER 4

It was nighttime, and the house ordinarily would have been quiet, but a young Khalfani had stirred awake after hearing water running. Listening to the water, he rolled over in bed, the movement triggering a pressure low in his belly, letting him know his bladder was full and in need of relief.

With a yawn, he sat up and groggily rubbed his eyes. He then slowly swung his legs out from under the covers, letting his bare feet hit the cold floor. Crossing his room, he exited out into the hallway, where he heard muttering voices drifting through the otherwise quiet house.

Walking down the hall, Khalfani wondered why his parents were awake at this hour. He bit his bottom lip uncertainly, hoping they hadn't had another argument.

At the end of the hall, he saw light shining through the space at the bottom of the closed bathroom door. He stopped outside the door and pressed his ear against it. "Eva? Pa?" he said tentatively.

But he received no response.

He stood a moment longer, the pressure in his bladder intensifying. Standing on tiptoe and squeezing his legs together, Khalfani knocked again. But although he heard his father's voice, he still receives no response.

Pa was a strict man. Regardless, even if he was occupying the bathroom, Khalfani had a feeling he would be in greater trouble if he had an accident on himself rather than letting it be known that he needed the toilet. Thus, setting aside his trepidation, he creaked the door open and peeked inside.

He blinked, his eyes temporarily watering from the bright bathroom light after waking in the dark. When his vision adjusted, he was able to take in the scene in front of him.

There, kneeling at the bathtub and not even noticing the door opening, was Khalfani's father, Kek.

And inside the tub was Khalfani's beautiful mother, Tije.

Kek had a sponge in his hand, gently rubbing his wife's back with it as she leaned over the tub, her head resting in his lap with her eyes closed.

Khalfani meant to ask if he could use the washroom—to let them know that it was an emergency and he needed to go really badly. But his words caught in his throat as he breathed in the aroma coming from the steaming bathwater.

Khalfani crinkled his nose. The scent wasn't the usual perfume and bath salts he was accustomed to smelling in the aftermath of his mother's baths. This was something different, and he couldn't place his finger on what it was or why it disturbed him so.

Still not noticing his presence, Kek spoke in soft, soothing tones to his wife—or at least that's how it sounded at first. Khalfani, however, soon realized that even though his father was trying to sound comforting, there was a strained edge to his voice that hinted at distress. Listening more carefully, Khalfani realized his father was apologizing for something.

He gritted his teeth in dismay, assuming that the two of them likely had been fighting after all. Granted, he knew it shouldn't surprise him, given how cruel his father could be, especially towards his mother…

Khalfani shifted his gaze to his mother again, an uncomfortable swoop going through his stomach.

Something was wrong; he could feel it.

Upon first glance, he thought his eva had merely looked relaxed, enjoying her strange-smelling bath. But the more Khalfani stared at her, the more he realized she looked a bit too relaxed…

Drugged, more accurately.

Every now and then, she opened her eyes but didn't seem to actually see anything. Furthermore, she only seemed capable of keeping her eyes open for a few seconds at a time before her eyelids started drooping again and inevitably shut.

As for her body, it looked far too limp, hanging over the tub while Kek continued running the sponge down her back.

When her lips began moving, Khalfani realized she was saying something, though it was almost inaudible.

"I loved you..." she slurred to Kek. "I really did..."

"Shh, darling," Kek said.

There was no doubt about it this time; Khalfani was positive. His father sounded bothered by something.

But Tije continued. "All I ever wanted was for you to change..." When she said her last word, it sounded as if she had also used the last of her breath. Her eyelids fluttered shut, and Kek's hand went limp, the sponge he'd been using to rub her back hitting the floor with a wet plop. He audibly sniffed, and then proceeded to stare at his wife for several long seconds.

Watching from the cracked door, Khalfani felt as if his own heart had stopped when his pa proceeded to bodily lift Tije's limp body from the bathtub.

Apparently, she actually had said her last words and used the last of her breath...

Khalfani blinked, still staring but unable to believe his eyes.

It couldn't be…

His eva couldn't be dead…

Kek lowered his head, his shoulders slumping. "What have I done?" he muttered in a whisper, cradling Tije in his arms. Despite their long years of marriage, he looked at her as if he had never quite seen her before. "This is all your fault, Tije. I couldn't let you leave me, you know that…" He shook her for an instant, as if trying to revive her. But it was useless. The damage was already irreparably done.

Unable to resist anymore, Khalfani pushed the door open, finally drawing his pa's attention. His breathing came harshly out of his body, shaky and difficult. "Poje, what did you do?" he asked, forcing the words out around the lump in his throat. Though his eyes had already filled with tears, he was able to make out the unusual tint of the bathwater, confirming what he had suspected all along—something was wrong with it, hence the smell. He swallowed, staring at his pa in disbelief. "You k-killed her…"

Finally, Kek looked up at his son. It was the first time Khalfani had ever seen tears in his pa's eyes. His stomach squirmed uncomfortably, and he felt like he was going to be sick.

"What are you doing in here?" Kek said, the harshness of his voice in stark contrast to the anguish on his face. "Get out of here! Go!"

"You killed her..." Khalfani repeated, the tears now running down his face, hot and fast. And in the midst of his sadness, he felt pure rage. Hatred. All for the man he was unfortunate enough to call his poje. His father.

His legs wobbled, but he backed away from the door, running away...

Wanting to run away forever, as far as he could...

"No...no...How could you? How could..." Khalfani said breathlessly. With a jolt, he sat upright in bed, finding himself covered in cold sweat and tangled in the sheets.

"Shh..." a voice drifted towards him through the darkness.

Still confused and disoriented from the dream, Khalfani jumped, his heartrate skyrocketing even more.

"Hey, it's all right. You were just having a nightmare..."

Khalfani blinked, rubbing his eyes before finally recalling where he was— in the guest quarters of the Mahmoud complex. And the voice he heard...

"Isis?" he whispered, still out of breath and jittery from the dream. Before he could fully process it, a gentle hand was on his back, rubbing soothing circles on his sweat-dampened nightshirt.

"Are you all right?" she murmured.

It was still dark, so he could barely make out her face, but the tone of her voice made her concern evident. He opened his mouth to answer but realized he didn't know what to say.

"It's all right," she said, seemingly sensing his difficultly speaking.

Khalfani took a deep breath, trying to calm himself. Sleep had been difficult for him ever since his childhood. Far too many nights, he revisited that horrible day, haunted by what his *pa* had done to his beloved *eva*. However, the nightmares had been plaguing him a bit more than usual lately. So much, in fact, that after training that evening, he had literally feared being alone, with nothing to distract him from ruminating over such a horrible memory.

Isis, whom he'd been training with again, proved herself to be too intuitive for her own good—or perhaps for his own good. Somehow, she had sensed something wrong and had subsequently tried cheering him up by inviting him over for dinner after training.

Eager for an excuse to avoid being alone, Khalfani graciously accepted the invitation, pleased to find the Mahmoud family welcoming and accommodating when he showed up to their private living quarters rather than his own wing of the complex. After dinner, Maat Mahmoud took him for a walk around the grounds, discussing training tactics and the

Retrograde in general. Before they knew it, the hour had grown late, and the Ra was setting. Proving to be just as intuitive as his daughter, Maat offered Khalfani the guest quarters in his family's wing, perhaps sensing the young man didn't want to feel so isolated that night.

Now, he sat in bed, cold sweat still running down his face while Isis's comforting voice echoed in his ear. "I'm s-sorry," he stuttered. "Did I wake you?"

"No," she said quietly. "I was going to get a drink of water and just happened to hear you… Are you okay?"

Khalfani hesitated. For a moment, he felt like he wanted to tell her no—that he was not all right. That his father was a murderer who kept haunting his dreams.

The only person he had ever confided in about his father was Tekem. The two of them had met during childhood, after Khalfani had run away in the wake of his mother's death. Walking round with a chip on his shoulder and hatred in his heart, Tekem had been one of few people who could ever get through to Khalfani, likely because Khalfani had always admired Tekem for his prowess in combat sports. Noticing his interest, Tekem began teaching Khalfani not only martial arts, but meditative techniques as well to help with his mood swings. Not before long, the two of them became best friends.

Appreciating what Tekem had done for him, Khalfani eventually told him the reason behind his anger…

To this very day, Tekem was the only one who knew the truth, and out of loyalty to Khalfani, he had never told another soul.

Yet, in that moment, Khalfani seriously felt like Isis was someone else he could safely confide in. But instead, Khalfani caught himself and refrained. He took a deep breath, concentrating on the flow of air going in and out of his lungs, as Tekem had taught him to do long ago.

Feeling the way Isis continued to stare at him, Khalfani forced himself to nod. "Yeah, I'm okay," he said. "Just tired."

"Easy then, try to sleep now, handsome." Gently, Isis pushed his shoulder until he was lying down again. And though he wanted to resist, he let her. It was in that moment that he realized Isis nearly had an effect on him just as soothing as meditation…

With her hand still on his shoulder, it was only a matter of seconds before he drifted off into the most peaceful sleep he'd had in ages.

All the while, Isis sat on the edge of the bed, watching him.

When she'd heard his distressed voice drifting from the guest quarters, her legs automatically carried her over to him. The bedroom door had been slightly cracked open, and for a moment, Isis had been terrified someone had somehow broken in. Her mind had momentarily started to race, wondering if she needed to sound the alarm. But instead, she ended up cautiously pushing the door open and stepping inside, checking things out for herself against her better judgment. Once inside, she breathed a sigh of relief to see that it was just Khalfani. However, her heart gave a pang when she noticed the way he was kicking and thrashing in his sleep, and she had wanted nothing more than to comfort him.

It had been a curious sight to see someone as strong and brave as Khalfani, looking so vulnerable and frightened in his slumber. Isis couldn't fathom what horrors his dreams brought to reduce him to such a state.

Now that he had drifted back to sleep, however, he was still a curious sight—so peaceful and youthful-looking, the intensity and seriousness that usually accompanied his face, absent.

Losing track of time, Isis wasn't sure how long she sat there, watching him sleep, but eventually, her senses returned to her, and she realized the last thing she wanted was for either of her parents to wake and find her there. She understood that they'd invited Khalfani to stay in their wing of the complex that night, but that by no means was an open invitation for her to visit him. So quietly, she leaned over, gently kissed his forehead, and left the room to get her water and return to her own bedroom.

What Isis didn't know, however, was that it wasn't her parents she needed to worry about seeing her with Khalfani…

Although miles away, it was another parent who watched them. The very same parent who had inspired Khalfani's nightmare in the first place…

Kek Abaza himself.

With his hands in his lap, twirling his thumbs with a snarl on his face, he sat before his Sharir—a device he'd spent many long hours across many years perfecting. The hard work had paid off, though. For now, his Sharir worked perfectly, easily permitting him access to moments he had no business being privy to, letting him spy on any location of his choice.

It was astonishing what he had been able to do with technology, and he absolutely loved it.

Watching his one and only son take refuge in the Mahmoud compound was enough to set Kek's blood boiling, partially because he knew all too well how easy it was to fall for the Mahmouds. After all, Maat had once been a source of respite for Kek during his troubled youth…

And as for Maat's daughter—she was just like him. Kek could so easily see what was budding between Khalfani and Maat's young female offspring. She was beautiful like her mother, but had the same fiery spirit as her father. With a girl like her, Kek knew his son didn't stand a chance.

The closest Kek had come to being in love was what he had experienced with Khalfani's mother. Yet, Kek was strong. His son, on the other hand, had his mother's heart, which meant love would become a liability for him.

Kek hated admitting it, but in his eyes, the boy was weak. And nothing infuriated him more than the thought of having produced weak offspring. Then, adding insult to the injury, the boy had run away before Kek had gotten the opportunity to toughen him up in the absence of his eva's coddling.

He scowled, watching the image of his son sleeping like a baby while Isis kissed his forehead…

* * *

"*Ella*, sleepy-head," Maat greeted from the kitchen table when Isis entered. He, Rania, and Khalfani were already seated, having worked halfway through breakfast already. "Must have been a tough day of training yesterday for you to sleep in so late. Although you probably needed to rest, so we didn't want to wake you."

Isis blinked groggily. She'd had a hard time returning to sleep after her impromptu visit to Khalfani in the middle of the night. By the time she'd made it back to her room, she had lied awake for quite some time, wondering what had been giving Khalfani nightmares. She had been taken aback by how the sight of him in distress, even if just due to a dream, had bothered her so.

Feeling her parents' eyes on her, she forced a smile. "*Ella*," she greeted. "Yeah, training has been pretty tough, hasn't it?" She turned her gaze to Khalfani.

He did not look back at her, though. Instead, he clutched his glass of orange juice and merely nodded. "Yeah. But that's to be expected, considering what's coming," he finally answered, still not making eye-contact with Isis.

Rania cleared her throat, and Isis paused, hoping her *eva* wasn't going to be so bold as to give her another lecture in front of company. She watched cautiously as Rania stood and forced a smile. Abruptly, Isis's fear shifted. *Evas* were intuitive, and she found herself praying hers hadn't somehow figured out that she'd stopped in the guest quarters that night.

"Take a seat, honey. Let me fix you a plate," Rania said.

Isis breathed a sigh of relief, and then covered her mouth and disguised it as a cough. "Thanks, *Imma*." She then rounded the table and pulled out the chair beside Khalfani, only for him to abruptly stand.

"Thank you so much for your hospitality," he said, bowing his head at Maat and then at Rania, "but I really should be going now."

"Are you sure?" Rania said. "Do you want anything more to eat? There's plenty left. It's been nice having you over for meals again. Feels like it's been so long…"

"No, no, I'm stuffed." He smiled and pat his stomach. "You've fed me quite enough between yesterday evening and this morning, and I greatly appreciate it. Thank you so much."

"Anytime," Maat said, reaching out to clutch Khalfani's hand in a handshake. Nevertheless, there was a slight gleam in Maat's eyes, indicating that he perhaps sensed something was wrong, but kept his suspicions to himself, for Khalfani's sake.

Again, Khalfani avoided her gaze. "See you later, Ni…Isis," he said, catching himself before using the nickname he'd given her. He then quickly headed for the kitchen doorway.

"Wait," Isis said, still standing and clutching the back of the chair before her.

Khalfani came to a reluctant halt.

"Let me walk you to the door," she offered. She followed after him, and they silently made their way to the front of the house. When they reached the door, Khalfani kept his back towards Isis.

Pushing aside her reservations, she grabbed his shoulder, making him turn around. "Is everything okay?" she asked.

He nodded, though his eyes flicked in every direction but hers.

"Khalfani, look at me," she said, her voice full of authority.

He clenched his jaw, but finally, for the first time that morning, their eyes met.

"What's going on?" Isis asked, her voice low.

Khalfani blinked and shook his head. "Nothing," he answered. Although his voice was steady, his expression betrayed him as he hovered on the spot.

As Isis held his stare, she got the distinct feeling that he was holding himself back, inwardly fighting himself about something. She took a step closer to him, noting the way his chest rose and fell with the deep breaths he took. So close, she could practically feel the nervousness radiating from him. Tentatively, she touched his shoulder again, feeling his muscles tense. He raised his arms for a second and then dropped them, as if torn between wanting to hug her and wanting to flee.

Thus, Isis took matters into her own hands and gave him a quick hug of her own.

"I...I should go," he stammered as Isis's body briefly pressed against his. He took a step back.

"All right," Isis said, and reached behind him to open the door.

Khalfani exited the house, and while Isis wasn't entirely sure, she thought she heard him mutter, 'Thank you, Ninna' on the way out.

* * *

"What's on your mind?" Rania asked, sitting perched on the edge of the bed in the master bedroom of the Mahmoud complex. She watched her husband idly pacing the room with his brow furrowed.

"Hmm?" he said.

A knowing smile curved Rania's lips. "You're pacing, *ti biyeh.*" *My love.* "I know something is troubling you."

He sighed. "It's obvious, isn't it? This upcoming Retrograde…" He shook his head and sighed again. "The more I think about it, the more it feels like it's going to be impossible to get through. I've never seen anything like this before. At the very least, it's going to cause more damage than any other before it. I just hope I'm preparing correctly." He swallowed and came to a halt. "I'm scared, *ti biyeh.*"

Rania stood and approached her husband, raising her arms to rub his tensed shoulders. She then wrapped him into a hug, which he gratefully returned. "If anyone can figure out how to defeat this thing, it's you," she said. "There's still time. Just do your best, which is always enough. I trust you. Our city trusts you…"

Maat squeezed his wife closer and kissed her forehead. "Thank you. Now, your turn. What's on your mind? I can tell something's bothering you too."

Rania pulled back and looked down to the floor, shaking her head. "That daughter of ours…"

"Oh, that lovely feisty creature we brought into this world?" Maat chuckled. "Yes, she is something, isn't she? Now, what is it about her worrying you this time?"

"Well, don't you think she's spending too much time training?" Rania asked, folding her arms defensively across her chest. "I talked to her the other day a bit. You know, she truly intends on being on the frontlines, fighting this thing." She shook her head again. "The girl is just so headstrong. When she has her mind set, no one can talk reason into her. Not even us! It worries me."

"She'll be fine," Maat assured. "The thing about Isis is that you just have to let her be."

"Easier said than done."

"I know. But look at it this way, *ti biyeh*—there's no stopping what lies ahead. With that in mind, I don't necessarily think it's a bad thing for our daughter to be as prepared as possible."

Rania huffed, looking at her husband sideways. "I swear, she is definitely your daughter."

"Well, that's reassuring," Maat said with a hearty chuckle.

Rania smirked and slapped his arm. "Oh, stop it. You know what I mean. She's just like you. When I was talking to her, trying to get her to reconsider participating in this fight, she essentially said to me exactly what you just said now."

"That's my girl." Maat laughed.

"Ugghh," Rania sighed. "She even laughs like you!"

Maat grinned. "That just means she's a strong girl. Just let her be."

Rania pursed her lips, looking as if she wanted to say something else, but refraining. "Well, I think I'm going to go for a walk to clear my head," she finally said.

Maat grabbed her hand and kissed it. "All right. Be safe."

"I will," Rania said, and then exited their bedroom.

After watching his wife leave, Maat Mahmoud stepped onto the balcony outside their bedroom. While it once used to be open, it was now encased with thick, clear glass. Fake breezes blew through the ventilation system, though, creating the illusion of being out in the open.

Maat took a deep breath as he looked over the land stretching out beyond, thinking about everything and nothing in particular.

And then his eyes glazed over, filling themselves with a vision…

As if witnessing a dream playing out right before him, he saw a young Khalfani, back when the young man he knew now had first come to him as a child.

"What is it that you need, son?" Maat asked, stooping down to eye-level with the boy.

"Please, sir, I want to enlist in the army. I'm all alone sir. Please. I won't be any trouble."

Maat stared, seeing the haunted look in the boy's big green eyes, and intuitively knowing there had to be a drastic reason for someone so young to make such a request. And while Maat knew the boy was obviously too young, he also knew that for some reason, he couldn't turn him away. He cleared his throat, just about to answer him when something else abruptly caught his attention.

Maat froze for an instant, certain he saw a cloudy dark figure lurking just behind Khalfani. He peered over the boy's head, but saw nothing…

"Sir?" Khalfani said, trying to recapture Maat's attention.

"Ahh, yes…" Maat said, still casting furtive glances around, so certain he'd seen the shadow of something—or someone. Shaking his head and deciding his eyes were playing tricks on him, he leaned back down to Khalfani's eye-level and cleared his throat again. "So, you want to join the army, eh? You must consider yourself pretty tough…"

Young Khalfani nodded curtly. "I'm as tough as I need to be, sir. And with the right training, I can get tougher."

Maat studied the boy's face, the determination he saw there reminding him so much of his own childhood friend. He held out his hand in a welcoming gesture. "Come with me, son. Let's talk."

Yet, just as he was about to lead Khalfani away, he saw the shadowy figure again in his periphery, lurking some distance between where the boy stood. He realized with some consternation it wasn't exactly a shadow, but rather a cloud of smoke that had solidified into a somewhat humanoid shape. Or at least he thought that was the case. He couldn't be sure though, for whenever he tried to focus on it, it miraculously disappeared.

"Is there something wrong, sir?" the boy asked.

"No, son," Maat said, not wanting to frighten the boy. He placed a protective hand on the child's shoulder, steering him away.

As they started walking, however, their surroundings began to suddenly darken.

Maat looked up toward the sky, seeing that it had abruptly turned black, as if covered by ink. There was a flash of lightning, and then, unsure whether his ears had started playing tricks on him as well, he heard a horrific, screeching inhumane laugh drifting through the air…

Maat blinked, the eerie and inhumane laughter snapping him out of his vision and back to reality. He stood perfectly still for a moment, trying to make sense of what he'd just seen with his mind's eye.

Disturbed, he turned back around, returning to the bedroom, where he resumed pacing.

Although he couldn't quite comprehend the vision just yet, he was fairly certain it had something to do with the upcoming Retrograde. Parts of the vision he'd recognized, for Khalfani had indeed come to him as a young child offering military services, as well as looking for safety and shelter.

The shadowy, misty figure, however—if it had really been there—was harder to interpret. Try as he might, Maat couldn't make any sense of that part of the vision. Nevertheless, whatever the case might be, he knew it all had to be related to the fact that the Retrograde was constantly getting closer; every bone in his body could feel it approaching, threateningly looming ahead like a hurricane.

If only he knew what specifically was going to happen once it actually hit.

Only the gods know, he found himself thinking. *I just hope they'd clue me in better…*

CHAPTER 5

"Good morning, Isis," Kaiden said, waving as he passed by.

"Morning," she replied politely. She then took a deep breath and stretched, readying herself for another day of training. The hour was early, but that didn't seem to slow anyone down, for each passing day brought them closer to the Retrograde's inevitable arrival.

Isis bent down, touching her toes to stretch her legs, and overall enjoying the pleasantness of the day. The Ra was shining, yet there was just enough breeze in the air to keep it from being too warm. With the lovely conditions, the majority of the soldiers had decided to practice outside, enjoying the fresh air while they still could.

Relishing the breeze on her face, it took Isis a moment to realize there was quite a bit of muttering around her. While she had paid no attention at first, as the muttering and snickering grew louder, she couldn't help noticing a considerable amount of it was aimed in her direction. She looked around, her eyes settling on Parr, Jacey, Farhad, Garth, and Hyrdus, huddled together, looking her way.

When they noticed her watching them, they averted their gazes. But Isis's skin continued to prickle, knowing they were talking about her for some reason. She grimaced, irritated. The longer she trained and practiced with the soldiers, the more the hostility she felt from some of them began to frustrate her.

They were all on the same team. Why couldn't they all just get along?

Wanting the group to know that she was onto them, she flat-out refused to look away. She honed her gaze on them, even turning her body in their direction as she continued her stretches. She found it childish of them to laugh at her behind her back; if they had something to say to her, she wanted them to know that she was more than willing to hear it.

Perhaps noticing the intensity of her stare—or just no longer able to ignore it—Parr finally looked her way again. Seeing how she held his stare, he smirked, and shortly thereafter, began sauntering her way.

Isis instantly noticed the haughtiness in his gait and the mischievous gleam in his eyes. He walked with his head tilted to the side, a sly smirk on his face that foretold of trouble. Recalling the way he'd rolled his eyes at Aurora's amulet necklace, it occurred to Isis that clearly, Parr was the kind of guy who struggled in the department of having respect for others.

"*Ella*," Isis said, keeping her voice steady although her suspicions were high.

Parr nodded at her. "*Ella*, Miss Mahmoud," he greeted with a small bow that looked far more condescending than respectful. "How's it going?"

"Fine, thank you. And yourself?"

He nodded. "I'm splendid." Looking into her eyes, he folded his arms across his chest. "So, you've been doing pretty good so far, from what I've heard from those who've been watching you train. Even the great Aurora seems impressed." He let out a low whistle and then grinned. "That's really saying something, isn't it?"

Isis noted the way he uttered Aurora's name, almost as if it was a swear. Something stirred inside of her, making her dislike him even more. She already hadn't felt very fondly of him during their previous encounter; now, her dislike felt even more justified.

Parr narrowed his eyes at her. "But what I want to know," he continued, "is how much skill can the daughter of the president *really* have? For instance, can you shoot an arrow? I mean, with the prim and proper upbringing you've had, do you even know how to hold anything that's not a golden spoon?"

Isis's ears burned from the insult. It wasn't until then that she noticed Farhad, Jacey, Garth and Hydrus had made their way over, as if eager to watch a battle.

They weren't the only ones, however. As the seconds ticked by, more spectators gathered around, watching in grave silence. Even Mirko, who'd been busy doing push-ups, paused his workout session to watch their exchange. From what Isis could tell, only Aiari kept his distance, too busy making wooden weapons.

"Grixti," a voice called out sternly. Isis turned to see Khalfani quickly approaching, an agitated scowl on his face. "Lay off her."

Isis blinked, surprised to see Khalfani coming to her defense. The last time she'd seen him, he'd been determined to blow her off.

Parr turned to look at Khalfani. He stretched out his arms and shrugged his shoulders in mock innocence. "What? No harm meant. I was just asking a question."

Khalfani opened his mouth to make a retort, but Isis interrupted.

"It's fine. I've got this," she said. The two of them exchanged glances, but Khalfani remained silent, holding in whatever it was he'd wanted to say.

Holding in a smirk over the fact that Khalfani had been prepared to argue on her behalf, Isis turned back to the smug soldier scowling at her. "So, Grixti, is it?"

He nodded and bowed at her again. "That's right, ma'am. Parr Grixti, to be exact."

"Right," Isis said. "Well, how about we hold a little contest, Parr?" As she spoke, she saw Aurora approaching from the corner of her eye, coming to stand beside Khalfani to watch the exchange that now had drawn everyone's riveted attention.

She also saw that once again, Khalfani looked doubtful and seemed to want to interject. But Aurora placed a hand on his shoulder, stopping him.

"Let her go," Aurora whispered to him.

Khalfani folded his arms and clamped his jaws, literally straining from the physical effort it took him to not intervene. It wasn't exactly that he didn't think Isis could stand up for herself. Rather, he simply didn't like anyone challenging her, to begin with. Something about it irked him down to his very core.

He stared at her, taking in her fierce expression and the fact that she honestly didn't seem anywhere near as bothered as he felt. His eyes roamed downward, taking in her confident stance—her shoulders squared, and her feet spread apart. The curves of her body, so visible through her tight training gear that left very little to the imagination. She was so strong, yet so supple and feminine. So beautiful…

His breath hitching in his throat, Khalfani forced his eyes away from her, embarrassed by the way his thoughts veered so inappropriately off course. Nevertheless, those inappropriate thoughts only managed to get replaced by reflections on the way she had comforted him out of his nightmare, not to mention how well he had slept afterwards, which was so rare for him.

And then there was the fact that he had been mildly disappointed to wake up and discover she was no longer there. That, of course, was followed by immediate guilt from having the thought in the first place, knowing how inappropriate it was of him, especially while in her parents' house, no less.

He was a better person than that. He had morals and standards to abide by, and at a time like this, he couldn't let anything—or anyone—distract him in that way.

Refocusing on the issue at hand, Khalfani watched as Isis retrieved a bow and arrow, maneuvering it with skill that sent the crowd around her whispering once again. Hearing the whispers, however, only increased her resolve; if there was one thing she hated, it was being underestimated.

Her hands moving expertly and her arm tensing as she prepared to launch the first arrow, Isis focused on the target ahead—the tree with the bullseye on it that had been used throughout the army's practice sessions. Double checking that she had picked up practice arrows rather than the poison-filled exploding ones they'd be using during the war, she envisioned herself hitting the bullseye and then took her stance. When she released the arrow, she'd landed a nearly perfect shot that immediately stopped all the whispers around her.

Feeling more prideful than ever, Isis fired off two more arrows in quick succession, both of them landing more perfectly than its predecessor.

Satisfied, she cleared her throat. "Guess I'm good at holding more than golden spoons." She turned to Parr Graxti and smiled. "Your turn," she said, pleased to see the shock on his face.

He quickly rearranged his features and haughtily snatched up a bow and arrow of his own. Snarling at Isis, he tried his best to look unimpressed. Focusing on the target, he fired his first arrow and missed completely. The arrow didn't even manage to stick into the tree bark.

A few snickers sounded around him, and he grit his teeth, furious. He cleared his throat and looked at Isis, who was visibly holding back a grin. "Big deal. Everyone knows about beginner's luck."

"Well, put your money where your mouth is," a voice retorted. Isis glanced through the crowd, realizing it was Amam

Keita who had spoken. Once again, there was a strangely excited gleam in his eyes.

"Shut up," Parr spat and then turned back to Isis. "Anyway, don't flatter yourself too much, sweetheart."

Amam, however, looked at Isis and winked—a sight she found simultaneously unnerving and comforting.

Meanwhile, Khalfani clenched his fists at his sides, unnerved that anyone would dare to speak to the daughter of Maat Mahmoud in such a matter. But deep down, everyone knew Isis was being treated this way because of exactly that—she was Maat Mahmoud's daughter, and consequently, people didn't take her training efforts seriously.

Again, Khalfani felt compelled to speak up for her, but Aurora placed her hand on his shoulder and squeezed it. He looked sideways at her, seeing her gently shake her head in objection. And he understood—the only way for this to truly end was to allow Isis to prove herself on her own. While not many of the soldiers would openly admit it, plenty of them had been waiting for this kind of moment to see what Isis was truly capable of.

Turning his attention back to Isis, Khalfani saw that despite how rattled he felt watching the scene play out, she looked completely nonplussed.

She stood, nonchalantly picking at her fingernails. "Yeah, yeah," she said in sarcastic tones. "Quit talking and prove me wrong, big shot. You've still got two more tries. We're all waiting."

Parr had just been about to fire his second shot when he lowered his bow and rounded on Isis. "Watch your mouth, you spoiled brat!" he yelled. And with that, he tossed his bow and arrow to the ground. "You know what? Maybe you've forgotten, but your *poje* and his house armor aren't here to protect you right now!"

A quick hush went across the area, only broken by shocked muttering.

Khalfani felt his own heart leap to his throat, and had it not been for Aurora's steadying hand still planted firmly on his shoulder, he would have charged forward.

All the while, Isis kept her cool. She simply gestured toward the bow and arrow that Parr had tossed aside. "Come on, man. Get to it. Let's get this over with. Less talking, more shooting."

"Get that smug smile off your face!" he shouted, storming over to her. "You think you're better than the rest of us, don't you? Just admit it! Forget the damn arrows! Let's see what you're *really* made of, princess." He sneered. "Who knows? Maybe if I like what I see, I'll make you my queen..."

Suddenly, the mood shifted among the riveted audience.

"Cut it out, Parr," Kaiden suddenly said, stepping forward with a disapproving glower plastered on his face.

"Yeah, calm down. Don't turn this into something it's not," Mirko said, his brow furrowed. "You agreed to a contest, so stick to the contest. Shoot your shot."

Parr sneered at Kaiden and Mirko. "She's talking like she wants more than a contest. She wants a battle. So, I'll give her a battle, the proper way..."

Khalfani hovered on the spot, still struggling not to intervene while Aurora kept a firm grip on his shoulder. All the while, Kaiden was just moments away from wanting to pounce on Parr himself.

For the first time since the whole fiasco started, Isis suddenly felt a twinge of panic go through her. She took a step back. Noting the deranged gleam in Parr's eyes, she wondered if she had ultimately pushed things a little too far, egging him on a little too much...

She swallowed, having not anticipated things escalating so quickly.

Easily noticing Isis's shift in demeanor, Parr's taunt sent fire running through Khalfani's veins.

Maybe if I like what I see, I'll make you my queen... Those words echoing through his mind, Khalfani balled his fists so tightly he feared he might accidentally shatter his own knuckles. Unable to idly stand by any longer, he shook Aurora's hand off his shoulder and charged toward Isis, ready to insert himself in the middle of the showdown. Although Khalfani had a feeling Isis could fight her own battles, he felt an overwhelming urge to seize Parr's throat so tightly that he could never again even joke of making Isis his queen.

Yet, everything happened much too quickly for him to even get a chance to insert himself into the tussle.

His heart stuttered at the sight of Parr lunging for Isis, forcefully grabbing her. But Isis responded with a quick maneuver, twisting her body out of his grasp with incredible speed and taking ahold of his arm. Her teeth gritted, she yanked his arm upwards, downward, forward, and then backwards—sending loud cracking sounds through the air as she did so.

Gasps filled the air, but they could hardly be heard over Parr's screaming. He dropped to the ground in pure agony, his arm dangling beside him, bent in four different angles, and broken in four different spots.

Panting, Isis stepped back, resting her hands on her knees and realizing what she'd just done. She trembled. She hadn't exactly meant to hurt him so badly, but she'd done it strictly in self-defense. Although Isis was strong and fairly tall, standing at slightly over 5'7", she knew that had she hesitated too long, Parr Grixti could have overpowered her. He was bigger than her, standing over six feet tall and carrying more weight on his frame. Being the warrior that she was at heart, Isis knew the importance of not losing the upper-hand in a fight, especially when dealing with a bigger opponent. Hence, she'd acted reflexively.

"I…I had t-to…" she stuttered, glancing at the bystanders around her. But to her surprise, no one was questioning her. While Farhad and Jacey had rushed forward to help her assailant, carrying him to the medical station, the others merely stared at her with newfound respect in their eyes. Mirko even clapped a few times before walking away, some of the others trailing behind him.

Khalfani, on the other hand, stood rooted on the spot. Beside him, Aurora nudged his arm, a barely concealed smirk on her face.

Meanwhile, Isis continued taking deep breaths, calming herself down from the rush of adrenaline coursing through her body. On shaky legs, she moved forward until she ended up in front of Khalfani, standing eye-to-eye. She swallowed. "I-I had to," she uttered again, feeling that for some reason, it was important for her to relay this to him directly. She needed him to understand.

He nodded. "I know, Ninna. You were just defending yourself. You had to."

Isis exhaled, somewhat startled by how relieving it felt to know that Khalfani understood. The last thing she would have wanted was for him to think of her as rash and out-of-control.

Perhaps having too much adrenaline still running through her system—or maybe it was a reaction to hearing him call her 'Ninna' again—Isis brought her hand to the side of his face. Then, before she knew it, she pressed her lips to his.

For a few glorious seconds, a stunned Khalfani moved his lips against hers, returning her kiss as her hand slowly trailed downwards from his face to his chest. His heart pounding beneath her touch, he was hypnotized by the sensation and wanted nothing more than for it to continue…

No, he thought, his senses returning to him. Abruptly, he stepped back, breaking the kiss and distancing himself from her. In his periphery, he saw Kaiden staring.

Isis's hand, which had still been on his chest, dropped. A look went across her face too quickly for Khalfani to interpret. He stared at her, wondering if she was offended. But before he could think any further on it, the blood in his veins practically froze as he glimpsed Maat Mahmoud stepping onto the premises.

There had been excited chatter all about, but it stopped instantly as people began to notice Maat's arrival.

As a hush fell upon the area, so did the unspoken speculation regarding whether Maat had secretly witnessed what just transpired between Isis and Parr Grixti—or between Isis and Khalfani, for that matter.

Khalfani's body tensed from head to toe at the mere thought, sweat forming along his forehead as the crowd regathered to find out the reason for Maat's visit. It was unusual for him to come to the training grounds. For a moment, Khalfani felt compelled to run inside the training building, anxious to be free from Maat's sometimes-all-too-knowing gaze. But that, he knew, would only make him look guiltier. So instead, he put on a brave face and headed towards Maat, right along with everyone else. He came to a stop, standing beside Tekem, who shot him a look with raised eyebrows.

Maat glanced around and nodded at the crowd that had formed before him. The soldiers present knew that Maat had a keen eye and had undoubtedly noticed that all of them were not present. Yet, nobody wanted to be the one to explain that some of them were busy tending to Parr in their training facility's medical center—and they could only hope he would not ask.

"Good morning, everyone," Maat began, much to all of their relief. "I'm sorry to interrupt your practice like this, but it was imperative that I get here to inform you all that it is almost here…" He paused for a grave moment before resuming. "It pains me to say it, but the Retrograde will be arriving within seven days' time. And after careful studying, it seems that the first part of it will come straight for our city. I wish I could tell you more, but all I can really tell you is to be prepared. Things will happen much more quickly than I originally anticipated, and I have no idea why… The one thing I've been correct about all along, nonetheless, is that this Retrograde will definitely be stronger than any we've ever seen before. May the gods help us all…"

CHAPTER 6

A teenaged Kek Abaza stood beside his best friend, Maat Mahmoud, lounging outside the school gates one late afternoon after classes had ended. Kek easily recognized the look on Maat's face—the faraway gaze with glazed-over eyes, his slack jaw, and his unblinking stare…

He was having another one of his visions. Allegedly.

When they'd first become friends, Kek had initially found Maat's ability to have visions rather fascinating, but it didn't take long before it simply became a nuisance. Eventually, Kek found himself wondering whether Maat's visions were even real, for there were definitely times where he felt they might have been nothing more than Maat's way of garnering attention and making himself special.

In fact, as his thoughts were interrupted by the drifting whispers and giggles from a group of bypassing girls, Kek thought that perhaps now happened to be one of those times where Maat was doing precisely that—slyly drawing attention to himself.

Kek narrowed his eyes at the girls. Just as he'd expected, they were staring at Maat, practically fawning over the broodingly handsome yet aloof expression that formed on his face whenever he was having one of his so-called 'visions.'

Kek suppressed the urge to roll his eyes. For as long as he'd known Maat, he wasn't sure he would ever get over the annoyance he felt regarding the attention his friend regularly received from their female peers. And while Kek sometimes thought Maat cunningly drew attention onto himself, it was hard to know for sure, because in the same breath, Maat so frequently seemed oblivious to it all. With a guy like Maat, it was hard to tell if he only pretended to be unaware of his good looks, or if he really didn't notice the way girls obsessed over him.

Kek chewed his bottom lip in frustration, thinking about how Maat was truly nothing more than a freak of nature, yet everyone thought he was so special, especially because his last name was Mahmoud. In comparison, Kek did not have a unique last name. Half of the population of Illyian had the last name "Abaza," but he was handsome in his own right, and he had a gift much more valuable than fickle fortune-telling; he had intelligence.

Unlike Maat Mahmoud, Kek would use his brains to get him through life. Unfortunately for him, though, his intelligence and mannerisms tended to intimidate most.

Granted, he didn't always think of this as a bad thing, especially under the right circumstances.

"Hello, Maat!" one of the braver girls yelled out, enthusiastically waving in his direction and inspiring a few other girls to shyly follow suit.

Knowing his friend hardly heard a thing, Kek cleared his throat and gave Maat a nudge with his elbow.

Maat blinked, noticing the girls for the first time now that his vision had ended. He nodded at them and returned the wave, which made them all fall into another fit of giggles.

Unable to stop himself, Kek audibly huffed and failed to prevent his eye-roll this time around.

Now, it was Maat who nudged Kek, giving him a nonchalant smirk in the process. Kek eyed his friend, knowing Maat had likely seen a hint of his jealousy and was attempting to snap him out of it.

"See anything interesting?" Kek asked, referring to the vision and trying to keep the bitterness out his voice. He only asked out of habit, and wasn't sure why he even bothered doing so anymore. Maat typically kept his visions to himself, or only gave vague descriptions—all the more reason Kek found himself doubting his friend at times.

Maat shook his head. "Nah, don't worry about it. I guarantee it was nothing more entertaining than those girls checking us out, right?" He laughed.

Kek pressed his lips together, refraining from pointing out the obvious—the girls were looking at Maat, *not him. But one day, that would change—Kek would see sure to it. Because his time was coming. He had plans...*

Plans that would permit him to get his way. To get whatever he wanted, including the beautiful wife of his dreams...

What young Kek didn't know was that in his future, he wouldn't be quite so lucky, after all. He would get a beautiful wife all right—a gentle soul that he would be desperate to capture and keep in his possession. But like a delicate butterfly confined to a jar, his captivity would do nothing but kill her, both in body and spirit...

* * *

Standing at the balcony outside of their bedroom once again, Maat and Rania looked out at the land around them. In the distance, they could see the wealthy residents and neighbors of their area, following their lead in trying to prepare for the upcoming Retrograde. Houses were surrounded with workers, boarding the homes in metal and glass meant to keep the Retrograde-polluted air at bay, while ventilation systems similar to the one that had already be installed in the Mahmoud complex were put into place.

Rania placed her head on her husband's shoulder. "Looks like everyone is trying to live by your example, *ti biyeh.*"

Maat sighed. "Yes, it seems so..."

Rania furrowed her brow. "Why does it sound like that troubles you?"

"Because I watch with a heavy heart as they do so."

Rania tilted her head to get a better view of her husband. "Why? Is it because of Elias's advice about relocating underground? I thought you believed it to be a good idea."

Maat nodded, thinking about Elias Onai—an official who severed as his advisor of sorts. "I trust Elias's advice. But still, it makes me feel guilty to watch all of this." He waved his hand, gesturing towards those down below, desperate to ensure the protection of their families by paying top-dollar for the system they'd watched the Mahmoud family use. "How are these people going to feel if they find out we're having underground hideouts created to retreat to, and that all this house armor we installed was ultimately decided not good enough? If I were in their shoes, I'd feel like I'd been deceived. They'll think we've spent the whole time giving them a false sense of security. I don't want them to think that way."

"Maat, you've been very upfront about how bad this Retrograde is going to get. No one can dare say you haven't been honest. Besides, you're the president of Cairo. People will understand that extra measures have to be taken to ensure your safety. It's just the nature of your job. You're under more pressure than anyone, and you have greater responsibilities. It has to be expected that you stay safe in order to guide the rest of us through these troubled times. You still have so much work to do, and so much on your shoulders. They should understand."

"The key word you just said—*should*. I know they *should* understand, but what if they don't?"

"You can't worry yourself about that, sweetheart. Besides, the house armor will keep them protected, whether they end up doubting it or not. That's the important thing."

Maat pursed his lips and stared off into the distance for a moment. "Well, that might be true—or at least, I hope it is. But there is indeed something we both still need to be worried about..."

"Oh?" Rania said, raising her eyebrows.

Maat looked sideways at his wife. "How do we tell Isis that we're relocating underground and won't be coming back up until after this is all over and it's safe again?"

Rania lifted her head from Maat's shoulder and pinched the bridge of her nose as if suddenly experiencing a headache. "Somehow, that feels harder than everything else we're dealing with, doesn't it?"

Maat chuckled.

Rania lowered her hand, letting her arms drop to her sides. "Well, it's just about time for our inoculation. We might as well tell her then, don't you think?"

"I suppose so," Maat agreed, having a pretty good idea of how that would go. He kissed Rania's cheek. "Let me go find her then. Meet you in the dining room."

"All right, dear."

With that, Maat went to fetch Isis, and Rania headed to the first floor. Shortly thereafter, the doorbell rang, the medical technicians having arrived with their inoculation equipment.

"Good afternoon, Mrs. Mahmoud," they greeted, bowing and curtseying to her.

She smiled. "Good afternoon. Thank you for coming. Please, follow me." She led them to the dining room, where Maat and Isis were waiting.

Isis stood at the table, eyeing her mother and the guests following behind her. "It's time for the inoculations already?"

Rania nodded. "Yes, *iva.*" *Yes, baby.* "Go ahead, sit down."

Maat, Rania, and Isis all sat around the table, watching quietly as the technicians prepared their equipment and gave them the spiel about how the inoculation was meant to help curve the effects of the Retrograde, should they be exposed to it.

As the president of Cairo, Maat was the first to receive his.

Isis and Rania watched as his sleeve was raised, and his skin cleaned in preparation. The smell of antiseptic filled the air. Meanwhile, another technician prepared a syringe, filling it with bright liquid and then tying a tourniquet around Maat's arm. "Make a fist for me, sir," the technician instructed.

A vein bulged in Maat's arm, and Isis watched the needle penetrate it. "So, how many people will be receiving this inoculation?" she asked. Although she felt pretty certain she already knew the answer, she couldn't stop herself from asking anyhow.

Rania tensed at the question, pressing her lips together and straightening in her chair.

One of the technicians glanced at Isis. "There should be enough of the serum to cover the majority of your community," she answered.

Now, it was Isis who pressed her lips together in a tight line. *The majority of your community.* The phrasing wasn't lost to her, and she could picture quite well which portions of the community the inoculation supply would just happen to run short in…

The unfairness of it all drove her crazy. Soldiers automatically received the inoculation due to the fact that they were putting their lives on the line to fight the Retrograde. Isis herself fell into this category. As for the rest who would be receiving the inoculation, they were the ones wealthy enough to afford it. Ironically, they also happened to be the ones who could afford to get their houses boarded up and put on lockdown to minimize their exposure to the Retrograde, in the first place. Hence, they were essentially taking the inoculation unnecessarily, when there were plenty of others who would be better served in receiving it.

Like those who couldn't afford the expensive house armor, for starters.

But no. The working class and the poor—in other words, those most at risk who desperately needed more protective measures at their disposal—were the very ones who wouldn't receive any extra help. It was all just a part of a vicious cycle that made the most vulnerable citizens of Damara the least capable of protecting themselves.

Isis sighed as the technician who'd just finished with her mother's inoculation approached her, raising her sleeve and sterilizing her arm.

"It's all right, dear," Rania said comfortingly.

Isis balled her fist. "No, it's not," she muttered, flinching slightly as the cold antiseptic was rubbed against her skin. She shook her head, gritting her teeth and bracing herself for the sting of the needle. "It's not fair, and you all know it. There are people who need this far more than we do."

"Isis," Rania said, her tone reprimanding and instantly relaying that this was not the time for such a discussion. Yet, taking in the distress on Isis's face, Rania sighed, her own expression softening. "I know, honey. I know..."

"Okay, you're all finished up here," the technician said, removing the tourniquet from Isis's arm.

Isis rolled her sleeve back down, her arm still slightly sore from the prick of the needle. Her thoughts still running away with her, she watched as the technicians began to pack away their supplies.

"Oh, my apologies," Maat interrupted, eyeing the technicians. "Please, don't pack away too thoroughly yet. We have someone else who should be arriving soon to receive an inoculation as well. I almost forgot..."

Rania turned to Maat, questioningly.

"I told Khalfani to meet over here to receive his dose," he clarified.

"Oh," Rania said, nodding.

Maat cleared his throat and then looked across the table toward Isis. “Until then,” he continued, “there’s something your *eva* and I need to tell you…”

Isis stared at her parents, wide-eyed, and already not liking the tone of her *pa’s* voice. It also didn’t help that a line of anxiety had formed on her *eva’s* forehead, and she was worriedly chewing her bottom lip.

Isis gripped the edge of the table, bracing herself. “What is it?”

“Well,” Maat began, “I don’t want to beat around the bush. Isis, we’ll be packing up and leaving soon, going to our underground hideout to wait out the Retrograde. Everything’s being set up as I speak. We have one built under this house, and others hidden as well, such as at the outskirts of the city. So, I’ll be keeping track of everything from underground until the Retrograde passes and it’s safe for us to come back up again.”

Isis blinked. “But you’ve boarded up the house and installed the protected ventilation system already. Why do all of that if the plan is to go underground?”

Maat nodded. “Because upon further study, it’s been decided that the safest place this time around is underground, so that’s where we’ll be. It’s just an extra precaution, but it’s one that I’ve been advised to take, simply due to how unpredictable this Retrograde could be...Better safe than sorry."

Isis swallowed. "I see," she said in a strained voice. She took a deep breath and exhaled. "All right, then. I guess you have to do what you've got to do."

Maat stared at his daughter, baffled by her nonchalant attitude and knowing there was something more to it than what met the eye.

Rania leaned forward, equally stunned by their daughter taking the news so lightly. "You do understand what we're saying, don't you? We'll be relocating soon...And we *can't* come back up here until the coast is clear."

Isis nodded. "Okay. You both stay safe then. But you do realize I won't be going with you, right?"

Rania closed her eyes, her patience instantly vanishing although she'd known there had to be a catch to Isis's reaction.

Maat, on the other hand, just sat perfectly still.

The room fell silent, with the exception of the technicians tinkering about, preparing to excuse themselves to another room so as not to intrude on such a personal family discussion.

"Isis," Rania said, trying carefully to keep her voice leveled, "when we say that we're relocating, that includes *you*. No exceptions."

Isis rubbed her temples, exasperated. "*Eva,* honestly, do you think I've spent all this time training for nothing? I wish you would just stop fooling yourself already! I'm fighting this battle! Haven't we had this discussion already?"

"Isis!" Rania yelled. "*Duro*!" *Stop!*

"Wait a second, *ti biyeh*," Maat interrupted, halting the ensuing argument. He fixed Rania with a sincere gaze and reached out to take her hand, which had been balled into a fist. "You know as well as I do that we've raised a young woman who has never been afraid to do what she feels is right. This Retrograde isn't going to change that."

Rania blinked, staring back at her husband, stunned. Her voice quaked when she spoke. "What are you implying, Maat?" she said slowly. Fearfully.

He squeezed Rania's hand. "There are a lot of eyes on our family, and you know I take that seriously," he prefaced. "The one thing I don't want people to ever say about the Mahmouds is that we are hypocrites. It already pains me to have to move underground. I cannot fathom allowing my daughter to train, and then saying she can't fight."

"But Maat…"

"Rania, you make the mistake of failing to realize that Isis isn't our little girl anymore. She's an adult, and we have to trust her to make her own decisions. It's not easy for me to say this, believe me, but if she wants to fight, then she can fight. We can't force her to go underground with us. That's why I haven't been saying anything about her training. Granted, I did think maybe there was the slightest chance that once it really sank in what she'd be dealing with as a soldier, she might have a change of heart. Get cold feet. Agree to go underground with us...." He shook his head. "But I should have known better. Besides, from what I've heard, she's been doing a phenomenal job with her training." He paused to look at Isis. "Cairo's army is going to need her, and we should be proud. I *am* proud."

Rania sniffed, moisture building in her eyes that she rapidly tried to blink away. She pulled her hand away from Maat's. Her mouth moved wordlessly for a moment, too devastated to speak. "*Bann.*" *Ridiculous.* Stubbornly, she folded her arms across her chest. "Is it so wrong that I just don't want anything to happen to my daughter? But I see I no longer have a say in the matter, so *ach ma.*" *Forget it.*

"*Imma,* I'm doing this for you," Isis said quietly, her anger unexpectedly replaced with sincerity. She may have occasionally found her *eva's* attitude annoying at times, but she understood there was nothing but love behind it. "I'm going to be all right. I swear. I just know that I won't be able to live with myself if I don't fight."

To this, Rania just remained quiet, accepting this was an argument she could never win.

Maat cleared his throat. "Before you leave, Isis, we will at least make sure you are aware of the underground hideouts' locations. You know, just in case..."

Isis pursed her lips but stiffly nodded her head nonetheless. "Fair enough," she said.

A silence then stretched across the room until approaching footsteps broke it. The three Mahmoud family members glanced toward the doorway, where Khalfani appeared.

"Good afternoon. My apologies for running a little late. *Jekk.*" *Sorry.* He then came to a halt, suddenly sensing the tension permeating the room. Standing awkwardly on the spot, he looked from Maat, to Rania, and lastly at Isis, though he kept his gaze at her very brief to keep his face from warming.

Maat stood, his eyes glued to Khalfani. "I'm glad you're here," he said.

Khalfani bowed his head, though with a slightly confused expression. "Thank you, sir." He then stood back up to his full height as Maat came to stand in front of him.

Maat brought his hand to Khalfani's shoulder, while Rania and Isis remained sitting, quietly watching the two of them.

"Son," Maat said sternly, "I have a request of you."

Khalfani blinked. "Yes. Anything, sir."

"My daughter, who's been training right alongside you for quite some time now, is determined to show how committed she is to the cause. And I couldn't be prouder of her." He glanced back at Isis for a moment, as did Khalfani. "I tell you this," Maat continued, "because she will be fighting alongside you as well, once the Retrograde hits. And it would bring me great peace of mind if I knew you were looking out for her. I know she's become one of the best trainees—just as I know you are as well. I want you to keep an eye on her, please. I want you to take care of her." He glanced back at Isis again. "I want you to take care of each other."

Khalfani stood even straighter, honored by Maat Mahmoud's request. "You have my word, sir," he said, stretching out his hand to shake on the deal.

Maat looked down at Khalfani's outstretched hand for a moment. And then, instead of taking it, he wrapped his arms around Khalfani, pulling him into a hug as intimate as one that a father would give his own son. "I expect you to take care of yourself too," Maat said. "Just as I expect the two of you to make it back in one piece."

"Yes, sir," Khalfani replied.

The two men finished their embrace, with Rania and Isis still watching in silence.

Isis turned to her *eva*, seeing that there were still tears glistening in her eyes and that her bottom lip quivered. "I love you, *Imma*," Isis said. "I'll take care of myself out there, I promise. But I truly hope you understand that I have to fight this thing. I have to help…"

Blinking and permitting a couple of her tears to fall, Rania finally turned her head to look at her daughter.

Isis leaned forward, hugging her mother, and glad to feel Rania return the hug with vigor. When they released, Isis stood and approached her father, hugging him as well. After releasing him, she turned toward Khalfani, who looked back at her, finally appearing unafraid to return her stare.

"You better go ahead and get your inoculation," Isis said.

He nodded. "Yeah. Because it looks like we have a war to win."

And with that, the two of them exited the room, with Maat and Rania standing side-by-side, watching after them.

CHAPTER 7

In the neighboring city of Illyian, things were already blackening. The warm blues and purple tones of the sky, the white puffs of clouds, and the bright glow of the Ra gradually vanished, replaced with a deep, ominous darkening, like ink spilling over the atmosphere.

The Retrograde was arriving.

The spreading Darkness first made its presence known in the woods—the leaves of the lush treetops being the first to get deprived of Ra's light. The Darkness, the very essence of evil, was an entity in and of itself. It trailed the Retrograde, feeding off of its carnage. Destruction and chaos were like its breath of life, and it feasted off of negativity, fear, and despair. With the Retrograde miraculously gaining so much strength on the planet of Damara, it was only natural that the Darkness would follow it, attracted to the source of the Retrograde's momentum.

Soon, the branches of the trees got lost in the Darkness, and so did everything else. The grass stiffened in the absence of light, losing its lush green hue, though eventually, nobody's eyes would be able to tell anyhow.

The creatures populating the land sensed the Darkness on the way. They scurried across the forest floors, instinct causing them to seek shelter and safety from an enemy they couldn't fully comprehend. They tried to gather food, but the vegetation was already succumbing to it, drying and shriveling everything in its wake.

The Darkness spread, its tentacles eager to reach every inch of the land below. But there was one significant area it touched rather quickly—a pyramid that had mysteriously sprang into existence without explanation, holding plenty of secrets inside. It stood about three feet tall and was as black as night.

Had anyone been around to see this pyramid, they would have seen what seemed to be something similar to ancient hieroglyphics glowing in red and gold hues, covering the outer walls. It was quite clear that they had been painted by someone or something so long ago, with insight into what was to come long after they'd taken their last breaths.

The walls inside depicted the image of a three-headed bear, surrounded by Darkness, much like what was overtaking society. The surrounding space on the walls featured squiggles representing insects and other animals around the bear, hurriedly distancing themselves, sensing that danger was near.

Subsequent drawings showed significant changes to the beast—the middle one of its three heads raised to the sky, mouth open in a silent scream that could practically be heard from just looking at it. More interestingly, however, were the other heads on each side of it. One had morphed into a lion, and the other into a wolf. The three heads sat, perched upon one enormous body with claws that burst with red light. The heads of the beast snarled, sharp elongated teeth visible, protruding downward and looking eager to do damage.

Their eyes, which were made of small gemstones each with a symbol in the middle of them, glowed just as brightly as the light coming from its claws, a sinister, fiery red.

As if brought to life by the images on the walls, the Darkness spread out of the pyramid, oozing onto the streets of Damara, seeking victims to begin its reign of terror.

It traveled through the woods, its misty form thickening into a more distinct shape, sprouting legs and walking with a gait that was almost human. Its hue so dark it appeared blue, the Darkness drifted along, an unsuspecting victim unknowingly in its path.

A farmer, on the search for medicinal roots to store in his modest dwelling in preparation for the Retrograde, leaned over, looking through shrubbery and oblivious to the mysterious blue mist honing in on him.

By the time he felt a coldness seep over his skin, it was already too late.

The farmer straightened up and spun around, noticing deep blue swirls circling him. And then his eyes landed on the monstrous figure the Darkness had taken on—the three-headed beast illustrated on the walls of the pyramid.

The hairs on the back of his neck standing on end, the terrified farmer opened his mouth to scream, yet the scream never had a chance of sounding through the woods. Instead, the Darkness charged and clutched the farmer with its jaws, leaving him sputtering for air. Then, in one swift motion, the Darkness pushed forward and shoved itself through the farmer's throat.

Falling to the ground, the farmer's body quaked violently from head to toe. Foaming at the mouth, his saliva tinted blueish-black, every muscle in his body twitched painfully. The Darkness filled his head, and the poor man thought his skull would explode from the pressure of it. Blood ran freely from his eyes, nose, and mouth. Again, he wanted to scream but was incapable of making sound. Slowly, his body went into shock. He couldn't breathe, and his heart began stuttering to a standstill…

Another powerful convulsion sent him leaping into the air before crashing down to the ground again, face-first, his nose shattering with a sickening crunch.

As he lied motionless, face-down on the ground, the Darkness sent blood, bone, and flesh splattering into the air as it exited through the man's back, leaving a gaping hole between his shoulder-blades that showed the blood-stained ground beneath him.

Satisfied with the damage it had done, the Darkness resumed its slightly humanoid form and continued on its way through the woods in search of its next target—a particular man whose essence beckoned to it. Perhaps it sensed the power already within this man. Or maybe it was the hard and angry state of his heart that called to the Retrograde's Darkness. Whatever the case, the man—Kek Abaza—sat in his laboratory, bent over a machine without initially noticing the presence lurking behind him, ready to strike.

Kek had been busy spying on his enemies, testing his new gadgets to strengthen the effects of the Retrograde and plotting his next moves, when a cold chill ran through his body, feeling as if someone had clutched his shoulder and drenched him with ice-water. A quiver ran from the top of his spine to the tip of his toes, freezing him instantly.

He blinked, trying to make sense of what he was feeling. But his brain hardly had time to process the slithering he abruptly felt covering his skin.

Finally, he turned around, coming face-to-face with the Darkness.

His eyes widened, seeing the deep blue indistinct figure standing before him, so dark and ominous in the presence of the pristine white laboratory around him. Before he could move, scream, or do anything at all, the Darkness seized Kek's arms.

Kek struggled, wanting to fight, but already sensing immediately that the mysterious entity was way too strong for him to fend off. The Darkness spread over him, covering his body like tar. It latched onto him, squeezing him so tightly, Kek thought it would squash him to death. He wanted to cry out, but the Darkness had attached itself onto his torso so tightly that his lungs couldn't even expand to breathe, let alone scream.

Kek gaped, getting the terrifying sensation that the Darkness was not only wrapping itself around him like an anaconda does its prey, but it was also somehow going inside of him…

After a while, he couldn't tell if the Darkness was going to squish his body to smithereens or make him explode from the inside out.

He stumbled backwards, his back crashing into the nearest wall as he continued to gasp for breath he couldn't catch. An ache spread across his jaw as he silently howled in pain, only vaguely aware of the way his teeth had started elongating. In a matter of seconds, they fell over his lips like vampire fangs.

At last, feeling as if the Darkness was releasing some of its hold on him, a horrified Kek raised his head to the ceiling and finally let out a scream, the force of it threatening to rip his throat in half. His vision temporarily went red—and so did his eyes, the irises taking on a fiery red hue similar to that of the beast depicted in the hieroglyphs in a pyramid far away…

Just as quickly as the painful attack began, it started to subside. Kek breathed deeply, each breath now filling him with strength instead of unrelenting pain.

He glanced down at his body, noticing it felt familiar and foreign to him at the same time. He touched his arms, his face, his mouth, his chest—each touch making his fingertips tingle like electricity was running through him.

Glancing around his lab, Kek noticed the ominous figure that had attacked him was no longer there. Only dark swirls remained, floating around him in a circle.

Kek, a man with immense intelligence and scientific knowledge, halfway suspected he was in the middle of a mental breakdown, experiencing powerful hallucinations for reasons he did not know. Yet, also for reasons he did not know, he couldn't bring himself to care.

A jubilance was running through him, making him feel stronger and more powerful than he'd ever felt in his entire life. His evil spirits soared, and it dawned on him that the creature previously attacking him had instead decided to join him, literally. He could feel its power lurking beneath his skin, the two of them having become one.

Reveling in it all, he tilted his head back, his red eyes deranged with ecstasy. And he laughed loud and hearty, the sound of it inhumane as it bounced off the walls of his laboratory.

CHAPTER 8

Though Khalfani was asleep, his brow was creased in distress, and his breathing was far too quick to be comfortably at rest. He rolled from side to side, nearly falling off the small cot he lied on.

He shrieked, his eyes shooting open. Cold sweat ran down his forehead.

Another nightmare.

Clutching the sheets tangled around him, he took several deep breaths, trying to return his racing heart to its normal speed. With a sigh, he slowly rolled onto his back, expecting to see the ceiling above him, but seeing a face instead.

The unexpected presence of someone standing over him should have startled him, but this particular face had the exact opposite effect. A sense of peace and calm drifted through his body as she looked down at him, her nearness calming.

Isis lowered herself, kissing Khalfani gently on the forehead and running her hand through his hair before moving down to his lips, her mouth soft and soothing on his.

The muscles in Khalfani's body relaxed further, though his heart began to pound again for a different reason. Still disoriented from his abrupt awakening, Khalfani's senses were slow to return to him, and in that moment, all he could feel was Isis's soft kiss. Thoroughly lost in the sensation, he reflexively returned the kiss, allowing it to chase away his worries.

Encouraged by his reaction, Isis lowered her body until she lied on top of him.

Upon feeling their bodies touching, Khalfani broke the kiss, hastily sliding from under Isis to the point where he nearly fell off his cot.

An awkward silence passed between them.

With the Retrograde lurking so closely on the horizon, both Khalfani and Isis had taken their promise to Maat seriously. In preparation for the upcoming war, all of the soldiers had officially moved to the training headquarters—a building large enough to accommodate them all. With the building having different sections, Khalfani and Isis had moved into the same area, agreeing to sleep in the same room, albeit in separate beds, so that they could stay near each other in case of an emergency.

While Khalfani had initially taken comfort in being with Isis, it now occurred to him that it might be a problem if they started getting *too* close…

"What's wrong?" Isis asked, perched on the side of Khalfani's bed.

"Is this a game to you?" he retorted.

Through the darkness, he could see Isis narrow her eyes at him in confusion. Nevertheless, when she spoke, her voice remained calm. "What do you mean?"

Khalfani sighed and then shook his head. "*This*." Unable to slide any farther over without landing on the floor, he gave Isis a gentle push, desperately needing more distance between them. He fixed her with a stern stare, willing her to understand. "You know I'm saving myself, Isis."

She blinked, pausing a beat before responding. "Yes. And I'm saving myself too, you know…"

Khalfani huffed. "Well, you've got a funny way of showing it."

Isis tilted her head to the side and pursed her lips together, an offended tone entering her voice. "What's that supposed to mean?"

"It's just…" Khalfani sighed. "You keep doing this to me. It's not right. Temptation is the last thing I need right now. Isn't everything complicated enough already?"

"Yes, things are complicated," Isis said, shifting on the edge of Khalfani's bed to get a better look at him through the darkness. "But as for temptation, it's not just temptation if..."

"If what?" he pressed.

Isis glanced away, her face warming against her will. "How do you know I'm not the one for you, Khal? How do you know that we..." She swallowed. "What if things are meant to happen between us? What if we're meant to be together?"

Khalfani fell silent, stunned by her questions and not knowing how to respond, especially considering that he'd been ignoring his feelings towards her for quite a while already. Though he'd known Isis since he was a child, these feelings had crept up on him unexpectedly, and he'd been struggling to control them ever since they made themselves known.

He thought back to Parr threatening her that day during training, right before she broke his arm and her father showed up to warn them of the Retrograde's nearness.

He knew why it was so unsettling for him to see her get threatened in even the slightest way... He'd simply been in denial because he knew now was not the time to be developing those kinds of feelings for anyone. Yet, he'd been powerless to stop them. Now, sitting so close to her, paranoia seized him at the realization that she had possibly picked up on them.

If she had so easily picked up on them, how obvious was it to everyone else? The thought was worrying, to say the least.

"What's on your mind?" Isis asked, breaking the silence.

"Nothing," Khalfani replied too quickly.

Isis rolled her eyes, although it was too dark for Khalfani to see the gesture.

Dammit, I'm in love with you. The thought drifted through Khalfani's head, the truth of it hitting him like a ton of bricks. It may have been too dark for him to clearly make out all of Isis's features, but he could still feel the knowing stare she gave him. *How did this happen?* he wondered.

She repositioned herself more comfortably on his bed, hugging her knees to her chest. Her gaze suddenly grew far away. "We don't know what's going to happen over the next few days," she said in a hushed tone. "Going into this, I think there's a need for us to all be honest with ourselves about knowing there's a chance we might not make it out. I think we all know that, even if no one wants to say it out loud."

Khalfani silently nodded. He watched Isis, noting how still and quiet she had become. "What are you thinking?"

It took her several seconds to answer. She squeezed her arms around her knees tighter. "I'm thinking that I really want to kiss you again, if you'd let me…"

A swoop went through Khalfani's stomach. His mouth opened, uttering words he couldn't seem to prevent. "I want that too, Ninna, but I want it to mean something…"

Isis stared at him. "It does mean something—at least to me, it does." She chanced moving closer to him again, touching his hand while carefully observing his reaction. When he didn't shy away, she brought her face close to his. Their lips touched, tentatively at first, but then the kiss deepened, Isis letting go of her inhibitions and elated to feel Khalfani doing the same. It was like a force pulled them together, and neither of them had the ability to control it. So, the kiss continued, each of them willingly caving in to their urges.

* * *

A bundle of nerves, Khalfani listened to the sound of his footsteps as they echoed through the corridor while he made his way to the training headquarters' auditorium. It was a technique he had learned from Tekem some time ago—simply listening to the sounds of his own steps and temporarily clearing everything else from his mind.

Stopping before the auditorium's door, Khalfani took a deep breath before entering. Once inside, he had successfully driven his nerves away.

He glanced around the space, which was still empty at the moment. Though he had never quite thought about it before, he imagined the walls of the auditorium likely had some incredible stories to tell. He wished he could hear them, in case they could offer any advice on what was to come.

Making his way to the front of the auditorium, Khalfani paced, continuing to listen to his footsteps and mentally prepare himself for what he and his fellow soldiers would be facing later in the day.

The past few days had been trying enough, but Khalfani knew they were nothing in comparison to what awaited him and his fellow soldiers in a few hours. It had been during the early hours of the morning that Maat had tasked Khalfani with addressing Cairo's army to relay the next steps they were to take in preparation to fight the Retrograde. Notices had then been sent out to the rest of the soldiers, informing them that they were to attend Khalfani's address by mid-morning.

Khalfani glanced upwards as he heard the auditorium's door creak open.

In walked Tekem. "Figured you'd be here early," he said, quietly closing the door behind him.

Khalfani nodded. "It only seemed right."

Tekem's brow furrowed, hearing the graveness in his best friend's voice and immediately knowing that something dire was on the horizon. "Everything all right?"

Khalfani sighed. "This is it…"

"I know…" Tekem replied after a small pause. He then took a seat. "The others are on their way soon," he informed. "Anything I can do in the meantime?"

Khalfani smiled appreciatively. "Oh, trust me, we'll be discussing that soon enough."

Tekem nodded. "Got it." And then, understanding that his friend needed his last-minute concentration, Tekem sat in silence as they waited for the others.

The next time the door opened, Mirko strolled in with an easy grin on his face. "Wooo!" he said, clapping his large hands together, the sound echoing noisily through the auditorium. "Almost showtime, huh?" he said, winking at Khalfani before making his way over to sit beside Tekem, where the two of them clasped hands in greeting.

Khalfani chuckled. It was just like Mirko to be excited about a battle meeting—the guy was always ready to get pumped up for a good fight. It was something he shared in common with Amam, albeit in a less sinister way. Nevertheless, Khalfani had to admit the enthusiasm of guys like Mirko and Amam was motivational; every army needed loyal cheerleaders, so to speak.

Tekem and Mirko began chatting, and the auditorium door opened again shortly thereafter. This time, Kaiden appeared, pausing in the doorway to glance over his shoulder. A smile spreading across his face, he held the door open. Seconds later, Isis walked through.

"Thanks," she said.

"No problem," Kaiden replied, staring after her as she made her way in.

Khalfani paused from his pacing, his eyes honing in on Kaiden and Isis. A tingle of irritation went through him but quickly vanished when Isis looked his way and smiled. It was astounding, the effect she had on him. He returned the smile and gave her a wave as she made her way toward the front of the auditorium, wanting to sit up front.

Kaiden hovered on the spot for a moment, his gaze following Isis as if contemplating sitting next to her.

Khalfani gave a mock cough, redirecting Kaiden's attention. With one look at Khalfani, Kaiden seemed to abruptly change his mind, and sought a seat behind Tekem and Mirko instead.

Isis suppressed a grin, trying her best to appear oblivious to what had just happened.

The door to the auditorium opened again, and not before long, the remaining soldiers began arriving in groups until the auditorium filled with their chatter as they waited to hear what Khalfani had to say.

Once everyone was situated, Khalfani made his way to the podium. "Hello, everyone," he said, and then paused, noticing the door opening one last time. He glanced around at the soldiers, trying to see who was missing. But then, it became obvious.

Parr Grixti hobbled into the auditorium, looking lopsided with his bandaged right arm.

Isis squirmed uncomfortably in her seat at the sight of him, feeling everyone's gaze flicker to her immediately after looking at him.

After she'd broken his arm, the guilt set in pretty harshly for Isis, realizing Cairo's army would be down by one soldier. As dangerous as this Retrograde was predicted to be, she knew the army needed every soldier at its disposal. To her and everyone else's astonishment, though, Parr insisted that he was still going to fight. Thus, he'd continued showing up to practice, working through his pain, and constantly doing pushups with his one good arm, trying to build up as much strength in it as possible.

Once Parr was seated, Khalfani cleared his throat, his gaze briefly flickering to Isis just like everyone else's. Not wanting to make her uncomfortable, he quickly looked away. "All right,

I'm going to keep this short and sweet," he said, beginning his address. "So, after much consideration, it's been decided that we need to head to the center of the city. Regretfully, I have to inform you that I've received word that the Retrograde is predicted to strike by four p.m. this afternoon."

The severity of the news swept through the crowd, triggering an onslaught of anxious whispering. Off to the left of him, Khalfani heard a chair squeak. He turned his head briefly, seeing Amam leaning forward, his chair creaking under his immense weight, and his eyes glued to Khalfani, eager to hear more.

Khalfani held up a hand, silencing everyone. "I know it's disturbing, but this is the moment we've been training for all along. Our city is depending on us, and we will not let it down. That being said, we don't have much time to act, so the time to act is officially now. Please, pack your things and be ready to leave at the top of the hour. We have a city to fight for, and a war to win."

At Khalfani's last words, Mirko stood and began clapping. "You heard the man, let's go!" he said. And with that, the crowd was dismissed, the soldiers filing out of the auditorium. Khalfani watched them retreating—Jacey, Farhad, Garth, and Hydrus, huddling together and whispering as they made their exit. Lia, standing by the doorway, eyeing Tekem as he drew nearer. Aiari, walking briskly to the door with some kind of hand-made metal object in his hand that he stared at with furrowed eyebrows.

It dawned on Khalfani that half of them looked ready, and the other half looked anxious. He couldn't blame either response anyway, for his own was somewhere in the middle.

With a sigh, Khalfani realized Isis was still seated. She kept her gaze glued to him as she waited for the crowd to continue thinning out, wanting a chance to talk to Khalfani in private. However, she realized that perhaps she wasn't the only one; Aurora had stayed behind as well, with Apple right beside her.

Not wanting to stare, but unable to keep herself from watching in her periphery, Isis watched Aurora pull Apple aside, the two of them isolating themselves in the corner of the room. Though they were out of earshot, Isis could tell that they were in the midst of a heated discussion, judging from the stern look on Aurora's face.

What Isis—nor Khalfani, for that matter—knew, was that Aurora was attempting to convince Apple to sit out on the battle.

"*Iva,* I've thought long and hard on this," Aurora prefaced, staring Apple in her big blue eyes, "but I don't think you should be fighting in this battle."

Apple stared back at her; her eyes widening in confusion. "Then what have I been training for, if not to fight?"

Aurora sighed. "I want you to know how to protect yourself, but I also want you to stay safe. Things are going to get ugly out there, and…" She shook her head. "I just don't want you involved."

"If that's the case, I don't want you involved either," Apple countered.

Aurora smiled sadly. She gently stroked the side of Apple's face. "I understand that, my *iva.* But you know, I have no choice but to fight in this battle. It's not optional for me, but it is for you. You don't have to do this now. But maybe next time around—"

"No," Apple said, cutting her off. "You have to understand it's not optional for me either. Wherever you go, I go, *Imma.*"

"Please, *iva…*" Aurora begged.

"No. I'm going," Apple declared.

Aurora looked up at the ceiling for a moment, exasperated but knowing there wasn't much more she could say.

In response, Apple leaned her head on Aurora's shoulder. "We're a team. You know that," she said.

Slowly, Aurora nodded her head. "Yes, *iva.* I know." And with that, she wrapped her arm around Apple.

When the two of them separated, the auditorium was practically empty, save for Isis and Khalfani, who'd been too far away to catch the conversation but could intuitively understand the gist of it.

Aurora first looked toward Khalfani, who still stood near the podium at the front of the auditorium.

Still seated, Isis watched Aurora approach Khalfani, appearing to exchange words of encouragement with him. When their exchange was over, Aurora turned around and locked eyes with Isis. "I know that your father must be proud, Isis," she said.

Isis smiled. "*Ose.*" *Thank you.*

Aurora nodded. "Well, I guess we had better go ahead and get packed up. See you both in a bit." She headed back towards Apple, who'd been patiently waiting by the door.

The auditorium now empty, Khalfani left the podium and moved toward Isis. "You know, that's a big compliment coming from Aurora."

"Believe me, I know." Isis tilted her head. "You're pretty close with her, aren't you?"

Khalfani nodded. "Yeah, I've known her for years. She's one of the strongest—possibly *the* strongest—woman I know." He paused for an instant. "She does have one weakness, though."

"Apple?" Isis guessed.

Khalfani nodded again. "Do you know how she ended up with her?"

Isis shook her head. While she knew Apple wasn't Aurora's biological daughter, she had never given much thought to how or why the two of them had become so close.

Khalfani's stuffed his hands into his pockets, recalling the story. "Apple came from a poor family. Her parents loved her dearly, but they just couldn't afford to take care of her. As you know, there was a time when Aurora was the only female soldier in Cairo's army, so she had to live in her own residence, separate from the other soldiers. One day, she said she was in the kitchen, eating an apple when someone knocked on her door. When she went to answer it, there was a woman with a baby wrapped in a blanket on her doorstep."

Isis's mind's eye conjured images of a younger Aurora—still just as beautiful, strong, and graceful as she was now, but minus the streak of silver in her hair. She imagined this younger Aurora, baffled by the stranger and the baby at her door.

"Aurora didn't quite know how or why she had been singled out. She decided that perhaps the woman had somehow been watching her from afar, admiring her strength as the only female soldier. It can only be assumed that the woman must have come to the conclusion that with Aurora being both a woman and a soldier, she was perfect for not only protecting the baby but nurturing her as well. So, she begged Aurora to take the baby.

"Aurora refused at first, convinced there was no way she could care for a child with the lifestyle she led. She had worked too hard to become the first woman in Cairo's army, and the last thing she wanted was to give it up to become a mother to someone else's child. But when the woman unwrapped the child from the blanket and Aurora looked into the baby's eyes, she said it was love at first sight and knew her life would never be the same from that point on. The woman put the baby in Aurora's arms and ran away before Aurora could respond." Khalfani paused for a moment and then laughed. "Aurora said she still had the apple she was eating in her hand. The baby kept pointing to the apple and cooing…"

Isis smirked. "Is that how she got her name?"

Khalfani nodded. "Yeah. Although technically, her name really is Apollonia. But yes, it was inspired by her fascination with the apple." He laughed, and Isis chuckled. After another brief pause, Khalfani continued. "After that, Aurora went to your *pa* for advice."

Isis now envisioned a younger version of her father, getting approached by a young and distraught Aurora with an infant Apple in her arms, at a loss for what to do.

"Like the respectable man he is," Khalfani continued, "he told her to keep the child and offered to assign her a trustworthy nurse to help take care of it."

Yes, Isis knew her father's advice would have been something along those lines, even before Khalfani had said so. Maat Mahmoud was a man who cherished family above all else. And due to the visions he was prone to having, Isis wouldn't have been surprised if her *pa* had already foreseen Aurora's role in Apple's life.

"Of course, as the years passed, Aurora came to consider Apple as her own. She's tried to raise the girl to be a strong soldier like herself, but she worries Apple's too kindhearted to be a soldier. She worries about her safety." Khalfani shrugged. "Some people just aren't cut out for this kind of lifestyle, you know? But this kind of lifestyle is all Aurora knows, so how else could she have possibly raised Apple?"

Isis nodded, understanding the dilemma. Aurora could only pass down to Apple what she knew. Yet, it was painfully obvious to anyone who saw the girl that Apple didn't truly have the heart of a fighter. And while looks could often be deceiving, Isis had a feeling that in Apple's case, the girl was exactly who she appeared to be—a young and gentle soul not meant for this harsh lifestyle, even if she was raised by one of Cairo's most skilled warriors.

Still, Isis sincerely hoped Apple would wind up proving their doubts wrong. "Well, all Aurora can do is trust in herself and the way she raised Apple. We just have to believe that everything happens for a reason..."

Khalfani nodded in agreement. "Well, I guess we should get going," he said after a brief pause.

With that, the two of them left the auditorium. As they walked, Isis looked out the windows lining the walls, seeing that outside, the sky had already started to darken. And while the morning hours were usually accompanied by chirping birds, there was nothing outside but a still and eerie silence.

As they turned a corner, a flash of lightning illuminated the sky, although there was no thunder.

The Retrograde was gearing up for a fight, just like they were.

CHAPTER 9

To say Kek Abaza loved his laboratory was an understatement. Being the epicenter of his most impressive creativity, it was one of his favorite places in the world. However, with the newfound power of the Darkness running through his veins, even the walls of his beloved lab suddenly felt too confining.

The world outside beckoned him.

He found himself roaming the woods, experiencing the outdoors as he never had before. The sky had darkened, making visibility a challenge for most, but not for Kek. He was Darkness now; the ground and the air around him felt alive, yet subservient, as if the environment itself had agreed to be obedient to him.

He felt invincible.

Yet, that still wasn't enough. There was a thirst and hunger inside of him, eager to feel more. He wanted life—life that he could take and squeeze in his hands to feed the beast lurking inside of him.

A man of impressive size, Kek managed to move through the trees like a predator seeking prey, soundlessly with all his senses heightened.

Not before long, he caught an enticing scent in the air. He held his face upwards, getting a whiff of something that excited the creature within him. His ears prickled, determining the direction…

And there, he spotted one of the local townspeople.

Kek recognized the old man, having seen him before in passing. Taking an enormous risk, the old man was out gathering a last-minute supply of berries before the Retrograde was in full effect, undoubtedly trying to collect enough to stock up on before barricading himself inside as well as he could. Apparently, the man had drifted onto the edges of Kek's property, assuming that he wouldn't mind him picking the wild berries that flourished so freely there.

The monster inside of Kek dancing, he stalked toward the old man, careful to remain concealed in the shadows and letting the dark swirls of mist around him create additional coverage to keep him sufficiently hidden.

Nevertheless, the old man halted, sensing something wrong. His eyes widened, attempting to see better as he glanced around, but it was useless; his vision had started deteriorating with age years ago, and not even fear could improve it.

Regardless, his gut still easily sensed danger. He began gathering the berries more hastily, his old and wizened hands moving as quickly as they could.

An overwhelming sense of danger enshrouding the old man, he grabbed his last berry and picked up his bag, ready to sprint out of the woods as fast as his frail legs would carry him.

But instead, he slammed right into his stalker.

He backed away, dropping the bag of berries he had so painstakingly gathered in hopes to keep himself fed throughout the Retrograde.

The old man's head raised upwards, taking in the beastly figure in front of him. It had the head and body of a man, though there was hardly anything humane about him, given the fiery red glow of his eyes and the way his teeth protruded from his mouth like fangs. And then there was his skin—the veins beneath showing prominently, resembling thin black worms squirming just below the surface.

Too terrified to keep looking at the monstrosity before him, the old man trembled from head to toe. He lowered his gaze, noticing for the first time how dark swirls danced threateningly through the air, looking like ground-level storm clouds. Sickened, he realized the dark swirls had started moving towards him, encircling him as if blocking his path. Trapping him.

It hardly mattered anyway, since he was too petrified to move. The only thing he could do was scream.

His scream was short-lived, for Kek lunged at the man, grabbing him by the throat with one massive hand and lifting him right off his feet. The man sputtered, his thin legs dangling uselessly as the life was being choked out of him. His vision clouding over more and more by the second, he was unable to see how the dark swirls were now wrapping around his body. He could certainly feel them.

The Darkness spun around him, attaching to his skin and turning his complexion dark blue.

After he'd had enough of squeezing the man's throat, Kek tossed him to the ground, sneering with his fangs still hanging over his lips. He watched as the man squirmed on the ground, coughing in attempts to recapture his breath. The instant enough air returned to his lungs, he released another scream—this one long and soul-shattering as the Darkness penetrated his skin and sank inside of him.

The man exploded, his feeble body no match for the Darkness that had invaded it. The woods around him splattered with blood and bone, while Kek stood, soaking it all in with an eerie and jovial laugh.

And then he continued on his way.

* * *

Khalfani Abaza was miles away, as he and the other soldiers continued on their pilgrimage to the center of the city. Nonetheless, something stopped him dead in his tracks, apprehension making his spine tingle.

The others continued walking, and Isis had made it a few paces away before realizing Khalfani had come to a stop. She halted too, glancing over her shoulder before backtracking and making her way back to him. Staring for a few seconds, she noted the alarmed and disgusted expression plastered to his face. "Khal?" she said, stepping closer. "Khal, are you all right?" She glanced down at the communication device on his wrist—something all the soldiers had been given—wondering if he had received an unexpected call. But there was no telltale flash indicating that he'd received any calls. Subconsciously, she touched her own earpiece and glanced down at her wrist-device, double-checking that she hadn't unknowingly missed anything.

Khalfani shuddered and blinked several times before focusing his gaze on Isis. He cleared his throat and nodded. "Yeah...yeah," he said, though not entirely meaning it. Inwardly, he couldn't make sense of why thoughts of various townspeople being brutally murdered by the Retrograde had so unexpectedly sprang to mind. Granted, he knew the Retrograde was coming and that fatalities would happen; the reality of it was simply part of being a soldier. What he hadn't anticipated, however, was things feeling so personally close to him, for lack of better terms.

It was almost like, on some level, he felt responsible in ways he couldn't understand.

There was one townsperson in particular that weighed on his mind—a poor and elderly man with a kind smile. Khalfani had seen him on numerous occasions before, picking through fruit at various stands throughout the town. He always seemed to be in good spirits.

Khalfani squeezed his eyes shut for an instant and rubbed his temples, eager to rid himself of the troubling thoughts. But it was Isis's hand coming to rest on his shoulder that finally did the trick of soothing him.

"It's all right," she whispered, giving his shoulder a gentle squeeze. Her deep brown eyes locked with his brilliant green ones. "Khal, whatever got to him, there's nothing you can do about it now. He's dead. We have to keep going so that we can fight for those who are still living."

While Isis's presence had initially been soothing, Khalfani now tensed for an entirely different reason. He stared back at her, searching her face—her smooth bronze skin and dark eyes, surrounded by luscious, dark and unruly hair…

How could she have possibly known?

Stunned, Khalfani's mouth moved wordlessly, unable to formulate the question on his mind. Before he could manage to articulate anything, however, Isis had turned back around and trotted off, rejoining the rest of the group.

How he hoped she wasn't a mind-reader…

Still dumbfounded, Khalfani could only scurry behind her to catch up.

* * *

"Do you guys hear that?" Apple's tentative voice asked.

"Yeah, I do," Khalfani responded, frowning.

"Do we keep going?" Lia asked, as the sounds of fighting drew nearer.

"Of course," Tekem answered her and then exchanged glances with Khalfani. "This is nowhere near the worst of it, trust me…"

Walking beside Tekem, Lia grimaced.

They'd been walking for quite some time when the sounds of fighting slowly reached their ears. And then, the source of the commotion came into view. In the distance, a group of men brawled in the streets for no detectable reason.

"It's really about to start soon, isn't it?" Orsel muttered in a low voice.

"Well, what's there to be surprised about? We've all known for a while now that it was coming," Jacey retorted.

"Yeah, but seeing this now—it just makes it all more real," Orsel said.

"It's because we're at the outskirts of the city," Easton said. "It's like seeing the first symptoms of an infection."

"Do you always have to intellectualize everything?" Jacey complained.

"You might want to watch your attitude, Jacey," Lia chimed in. "People might be inclined to think you missed the inoculation."

Tekem snickered, and Lia shot him a grin. "Good one," he said.

"Thanks," Lia replied.

Jacey sucked her teeth. "Whatever," she muttered, and then moved to the other side of Farhad.

"Settle down now, children," Amam's voice boomed toward them. "Unless you want to pause and settle your little dispute right now. Might be good practice for what's to come."

Mirko laughed. "Yeah, I could use the entertainment."

"Hey," Khalfani said over the bickering. "Cut it out, guys. Now is not the time."

"Sorry," Mirko said. "Just trying to lighten the mood."

Orsel cleared her throat. "Kind of hard to have a lightened mood right now, don't you think?" she said, right as another straggler came into view. The young man bumbled about expressionlessly in the street, hardly even registering their presence—a good thing, considering how close he came as he passed them by. And while no one in the group needed to say it, they were all thinking it—with each strangler that crossed their path, they were looking into the faces of soon-to-be changelings.

The soldiers grew quiet, not wanting to bring unnecessary attention to themselves as they trekked on, getting closer to the city. Although these changelings were in the early stages of infection, they could still cause trouble if provoked, and the soldiers needed to preserve their strength for when it was truly needed.

Isis, who was completely new to the firsthand experience of seeing changelings altogether—even changelings-to-be, for that matter—did her best to follow the lead of the other soldiers, keeping her face neutral as she walked silently. Nevertheless, she couldn't help her fascination, seeing what the Retrograde did to people with her very own eyes rather than through a screen from the safety of her parents' home.

They crossed one woman's path, and Isis noted the deep scowl on her face. Breathing heavily, her teeth were clenched as if she was in pain, and drool ran down her chin. Her gaze turned to the group of soldiers, her eyes darting from face to face, as if looking for a reason to start an altercation.

Someone beside Isis cleared their throat.

Isis jumped.

"Best not to stare at them so hard. Don't want them taking it as a challenge, especially if they're already that far gone," Kaiden warned. "You're new to this, but trust me, some of these changelings are bound to be a more formidable opponent than Parr…" He smirked.

Isis swallowed, her eyes instantly finding the back of Parr Grixti's head walking several paces ahead of her, his gait appearing off-balanced due to the way his broken arm was bandaged. "Sorry," Isis whispered, refocusing her energy on keeping her eyes ahead and not on any of the stragglers as they stumbled about.

Kaiden cleared his throat. "No, I'm sorry. That was a bad joke."

"Yeah, because now's not the time for jokes, period," Khalfani said, shooting Kaiden a look.

Seeming to recoil under Khalfani's gaze, Kaiden fell back several paces behind Isis to walk beside Orsel instead.

Though the sky was already dark, it seemed to keep darkening. Occasionally, a flash of lightning appeared without warning, eerie in its absence of thunder.

All the while, the group of soldiers kept walking, their paces quickening in response to the trepidation saturating the air. Even though all of them had received inoculations and had been training diligently for this moment, actually being out in the city was definitely a wakeup call. They could all feel it in their bones that they were walking through the calm before the storm.

As they began hearing more screams, yells, swearing, and fighting, Isis tried to keep her cool. Still, each scream had her head involuntarily snapping in its direction, wondering if someone needed help and if there was anything they should be doing rather than ignoring them.

"Sad, isn't it?"

Isis turned her head to see that Aurora, with Apple in tow, had come to her side. She nodded, unable to speak at the moment due to the lump that had formed in her throat.

On, they kept walking.

Moving from the poorer areas into the richer areas was astonishing—and upsetting. They could tell when they reached the neighborhoods of citizens with more money, for the dwellings had grown larger and were noticeably boarded up with armor similar to what the Mahmoud complex and its surrounding houses had.

Isis glanced up at the houses, noticing that she could see some of their inhabitants. Some stood on their rooftops while others simply sat in their windows, watching the poor roaming the streets below. Others nodded appreciatively at them, obviously recognizing them as the army due to their gear.

Isis pressed her mouth into a tight line, honestly not sure if she appreciated their appreciation. It wasn't them that they were out risking their lives for, because as their houses proved, they were going to be fine. Isis was even willing to bet these particular citizens had also received inoculations.

Unable to stop the grimace on her face, Isis thought about how much better off they all would be if the rich citizens of Damara who could afford it had simply boarded up their houses and bypassed the inoculations. Had that been the case, there would have been enough of the inoculation to go around for those who couldn't afford house armor.

Wouldn't that have dramatically diminished the Retrograde's reach? Isis pondered.

But she knew it was sometimes too much to ask the rich to be less selfish. Her frown deepened, hating the injustice of it all. Being forced to see the contrast between those walking the streets, and those safely tucked away in their houses, simply waiting to watch the chaos ensue like a sporting event—it all put things into a harsh perspective.

"Some of the rich families consider themselves charitable," Aurora said, still walking beside Isis and clearly sensing the track of her thoughts. "They'll randomly open their homes to a lucky child from a working-class family—or sometimes a whole family, even—for the duration of the Retrograde. Only if they've had an inoculation though, of course. It's like a lottery. But as for those who aren't so lucky, well…" She gestured toward a group of women staring at each other with feral expressions, ripping each other's hair out in what looked like a fight over nothing.

Isis shook her head in frustration. "*Baan.*" *Ridiculous.* "There really has to be a way to keep everyone protected. It's just not fair, the way things are…"

"Yes," Aurora agreed. "Seems like since the beginning of time, the world has never been fair. But that's why we're out here fighting, right? To help even the score, even if just a little bit."

Isis nodded, and then looked toward Khalfani on the other side of her. He, however, was looking in the opposite direction. Isis followed his gaze, seeing that he was staring at another straggler trailing down the street.

There was something noticeably different about this particular strangler, though. He was clearly rich, judging from his expensive clothing and well-groomed appearance. Nevertheless, there was a gleam in his eye that looked fevered and deranged. Infected.

"What's he doing out here?" Isis muttered. Until then, she'd been convinced that all of Damara's wealthy citizens had locked themselves away to safety by now.

Khalfani frowned and spoke in a clipped tone. "If I had to guess, I'd say it looks like he went to run an errand a little too late, and obviously waited too long to get his inoculation. Now, he has the misfortune of getting himself caught up in this mess. Not part of his plan, I'm sure."

"Idiot," Tekem muttered.

Isis had to agree. She stared at the man a moment longer, simultaneously sorry for him and annoyed at him. She couldn't help feeling sorry for anyone who fell victim to the Retrograde's clutches. However, someone like this man, who had the means to keep himself protected—means that the working-class and the poor would kill for—should have known better than to take his privilege for granted. People like him just showed how some members of the upper-class fancied themselves invincible and consequently took unnecessary risks, assuming he was too important—too good—for misfortune to catch up with.

Most importantly, though, this man was solid proof that if there was an even playing field across all socioeconomic statuses, the Retrograde wasn't beyond discriminating against anyone.

Remembering that she wasn't supposed to be staring at the changelings-to-be too long, Isis finally averted her gaze and continued walking with the others.

A short while later, they spotted another member of the upper-class on the streets—a woman this time. Despite the slightly fevered gleam in her eyes, she was beautiful—a sight to behold in a stunning ball gown, her hair styled in intricate curls. She initially appeared to be wandering aimlessly, but upon spotting the group, she slowed her pace.

Isis tried not to stare, but this time, it seemed virtually impossible, considering the way the woman stared back at her.

To the whole group's astonishment, the woman began making a beeline towards them.

"Easy, everyone. Easy…" Khalfani warned, carefully watching the woman. His stance immediately grew cautious, and his hands tensed beside him, prepared to draw his weapon at any moment should the need arise.

Isis's breath hitched in her throat, seeing the way the woman stared at her so intensely. Parr, Farhad, and Jacey, who'd been walking slightly ahead of the group, dodged out of the way as the woman crossed their path. Like the rest of the soldiers, they all watched her, seemingly teetering between wanting to keep moving and wondering if they needed to prepare for attack.

"Isis, watch out," Kaiden said, taking several cautious steps in her direction, his hand instinctively darting out towards her.

But Isis had frozen on the spot, and the woman had stopped a mere foot away from her. They locked eyes, and a flash of lightning flickered across the sky as they stood face-to-face. In her periphery, Isis saw Khalfani watching attentively, sizing the woman up, and trying to determine if she was a threat. Isis didn't need to look at him to know the conflict that filled his green eyes. She could even sense the apprehension of the other soldiers—the uncertainty they all felt in trying to figure out why a changeling-to-be had stood so close to one of their comrades.

Staring back at the woman, Isis couldn't help noticing that what initially looked like crazed eyes were actually deeply saddened eyes. Nevertheless, there was still slight aggression lurking beneath her expression, indicating that she was indeed feverish with the beginning stages of disease. It was just a matter of time before she was thoroughly within the Retrograde's clutches.

"I don't want to live through this," the woman said, her voice surprising in its clarity. She may have already been marked by the Retrograde, but as for now, she was still lucid and of sound mind. She leaned forward to Isis, decreasing the already minimal distance between them. "Please, kill me. Kill me before it gets worse. Kill me…" she pleaded. She paused and suddenly raised her hand.

Isis flinched, stunned when the woman abruptly ran her index finger down the side of Isis's face. Although, the gesture was performed in a caressing manner rather than a threatening one.

"You are so beautiful," the woman breathed, her brow temporarily furrowing as if confused. She looked into Isis's dark eyes, and then took in her full lips and thick hair. Slowly, her feverish gaze trailed downward, over the rest of Isis's body before moving back up to her eyes. Then, without warning, she kissed her.

"Oh my god," Easton's shocked voice drifted to Isis's ears.

Meanwhile, Isis's eyes nearly bulged out of her head, feeling the woman's lips unexpectedly crashing down on hers, the kiss deep and somewhat aggressive. She panicked for a moment before remembering that she'd had her inoculation and therefore wasn't in any real danger—provided the woman didn't make any sudden dangerous gestures.

A shocked Khalfani watched, speechless for a moment. But then fury overshadowed his shock, and he lunged forward, ready to pry the woman off Isis. Once again, however, Aurora stopped him. She sprang after Khalfani, grabbing him by the arms and pulling him to halt, not wanting him to cause a bigger scene than what was already happening. There were still stragglers in the street, and if they sensed violence or aggression, they would be drawn over like moths to a flame.

Staying calm may have kept the stragglers away, but the same couldn't be said for the male soldiers standing about. With the exception of Khalfani, Tekem, and Kaiden, the others watched the kiss with amused eyes and stupid grins on their faces. Besides himself, Farhad wolf-whistled, prompting a sharp elbow nudge in the ribs from Kaiden, and snickering from Hyrdus and Garth.

Deciding it best to keep playing it cool, Isis remained calm, allowing the kiss to continue. Feeling the smudge of the woman's lipstick on her mouth, she understood the Retrograde had lowered the woman's inhibitions, permitting instinct and desire to take over.

Moving as carefully as possible while kissing the woman back, Isis discreetly reached for the gun at her hip. As she did so, she could sense rather than see the soldiers around her tensing up, Khalfani included. No one dared move, afraid to risk causing any disruptions that could potentially end in disaster.

Once her hand was securely around the gun, Isis quickly removed it from her hip, took a step back to break the kiss, and pressed the gun's barrel right to the woman's chest. The woman hardly had time to react before Isis had pulled the trigger.

The shot blasted through her, and the woman met Isis's gaze with a brief look of surprise. Milliseconds later, her eyes filled with gratitude, silently thanking Isis for her mercy. Then she fell to the ground, her body limp as the lights left her eyes and her life faded away from her.

Isis stared down at the woman, dead at her feet. Her heart pounded, her throat felt tight, and her eyes stung. But she knew what she'd done was necessary; it had been a kindness to put the woman out of her misery before her misery could fully kick in and harm others.

Khalfani cleared his throat, and Isis jumped, staring at the woman so intently that she hadn't noticed him trying to get her attention. He shook his canteen of water in front of her, a disgusted frown on his face. "Here. Have some water. Rinse out your mouth…"

Isis took the water, taking a gulp and swishing it around in her mouth before spitting it onto the ground. As she did so, she could hear the other soldiers behind her—Tekem and Mirko from the sounds of it—snickering and whispering to each other. Noticing the annoyed expression on Khalfani's face, Isis realized they were laughing at him more so than at her…

Because Khalfani was clearly jealous. The thought nearly made Isis want to laugh as well. Nonetheless, she couldn't help feeling a bit flattered, even though Khalfani's jealousy was unwarranted.

"Well," Aurora said, stepping forward with an embarrassed looking Apple at her side, "I think we need to get back moving before any more unplanned ordeals can catch up to us."

"Agreed," said Khalfani quickly.

Refocusing on the task ahead of them, the group gathered itself and continued on their way.

"Are you all right, Ninna?" Khalfani asked in a slightly strained voice, walking closely beside Isis.

She smiled at the nickname and nodded. "Yeah, I'm fine."

"All right," he said. After a moment's hesitation, he placed his hand on the small of her back as they walked. Although his touch was gentle, there was something possessive about it.

Isis found herself suppressing another grin. With anyone else, she would have minded such a touch. But with Khalfani, she didn't mind at all.

CHAPTER 10

If Rania tried hard enough, she could pretend that she and her husband were merely on vacation. The underground dwelling they'd taken refuge in was cozy and welcoming, complete with their own private living quarters, furnished with all the comforts of home. But it didn't matter, for there was nothing Rania could do to take her mind off the nightmare that was occurring above ground, where her daughter remained.

As the days passed by, Rania fought herself each passing second, torn between wanting news on how things were progressing in the war against the Retrograde, and being too terrified to find out. It ultimately didn't matter, though, for each day, it was as if her feet had minds of their own, leading her to the control room to await the city's live surveillance newsfeed for images of the war whenever reception was strong enough to permit it.

Unfortunately for her, the last images she'd caught had been too dismal for her liking. Seeing the Retrograde above, drifting through her city and taking hold of its first victims, had made her want to vomit. Unable to stand seeing any more, knowing her daughter was up there somewhere, Rania had retreated to a vacant corner of the control room, taking a seat facing away from the screen and letting her tears fall freely while the others watched. All the while, she just kept wondering why the gods had made it so that her daughter had to be around to fight the worse Retrograde to date.

Just thinking about it sometimes left Rania so consumed with guilt, she felt nauseous, wondering if it would have been better for her and Maat to stay above ground. How could they go into hiding when their little girl had been brave enough to stay behind? Perhaps, they should have stayed behind too, to face it with her.

Before arriving, the knowledge that their underground hideout was being prepared had been a source of comfort. Yet now, the thought of staying there for however long it took for the Retrograde to pass—while Isis faced it head-on, no less—seemed unbearable.

"Please, don't cry, *ti biyeh.*"

Rania looked up through tearful eyes, seeing her husband approaching her. Pulling up a chair, he sat down before her in the corner of the control room. "Isis is where she belongs. She's strong, and she's with Khalfani. She's going to be okay. Don't worry," he said.

Rania hastily rubbed her eyes, smearing tears on her beautiful face. "Don't worry? How can I *not* worry?" She narrowed her eyes at Maat. "And how can you be so *unworried*?"

He smiled sadly and shook his head. "Please, don't be mistaken. I *am* worried, but I know everything is in the hands of the gods at this point. I can only do my role." He reached forward and took Rania's hands into his. "All that's left for us to do is trust and pray for our soldiers, including our beloved daughter. We must keep positive spirits and pray they're successful in getting the situation contained before it too thoroughly takes over all three regions. Remember, our faith gives them strength."

Rania lowered her gaze to the floor, wanting to find solace in her husband's words, but not knowing how or what to say.

Understanding Rania was at a loss for words, Maat gently kissed her hands. "I know it's hard, but just have faith. And I think you could use some time away from here. Why don't you go to our bedroom quarters for a while to rest?"

"But what if I miss an update?"

"You know I'll report it to you. Now, please, go rest, *ti beyeh*." Maat leaned forward and kissed her forehead.

Not really ready to leave, but not wanting to argue any further with her husband, Rania reluctantly nodded and stood. She wrapped her arms around him in a quick hug, kissed his lips, and then exited the room.

In his wife's absence, Maat sighed heavily to himself. While he had done his best to comfort her out of her worries, he had some of his own he needed to sort out and mull over.

Slowly, he turned around, merely taking in the rest of the room for a moment. There were several others present, some of them anxiously pacing the floor while others kept their eyes glued to the screen as if expecting it to flicker on at any moment, eager for an update on the conditions above ground.

Whistling casually to himself with his hands stuffed into his pockets, Maat strolled into the center of the room, drawing attention onto himself. Several bowed their heads respectfully at him as they made eye-contact.

"Good afternoon," Maat greeted politely.

"Good afternoon, sir," they greeted in return.

"Do you need anything, sir?" Elias Onai, Maat's adviser, stepped forward.

"Yes," Maat said. "I don't mean to be an inconvenience, but I need this space to myself for a while. There are some patterns with the Retrograde that I need some time to examine in peace. I won't be long, and I promise to let you all return here in due time."

"Of course, sir." Elias turned towards the others in the room. "All right, soldiers, let's vacate the area. He needs a moment alone. Let's grant him his wish."

"Yes sir," the others muttered, bowing again before making their exit.

Maat tipped his head at Elias. "Thank you."

"No problem, sir."

Once alone, Maat pulled up a seat and placed it before the surveillance screen, his mind already racing.

For days now, a vision had been on the brink of his mind, and he had been impatiently waiting for it to show itself.

Too antsy to remain seated, Maat stood again and began pacing the floor, trying to clear his mind to make space for the vision to breathe and solidify. Yet, when nothing came to mind, he refocused on the screens, pressing buttons on the control panel to let previous images replay. Standing there, watching the chaos that had already unfolded, he felt the edges of his mind clouding over.

Finally, the vision that had been hiding from him pushed itself to the forefront.

Young Khalfani stood before Maat once again, looking distraught but determined to put forward a brave face as he asked for a spot in the army. It was not Khalfani that Maat was focused on this time around, though.

Behind the young boy, dark mist swirled. Maat narrowed his eyes, trying to understand what he was seeing as the mist thickened, looking like storm clouds at eye-level. They hovered, moving around behind an oblivious Khalfani. And then, they began to stretch, elongating into an abstract figure that eventually started to sprout feet, legs, arms, a torso…A head…

Not before long, they'd taken on the shadowy shape of a man.

Dumbfounded, Maat took a step back, observing as the shadowy figure disappeared altogether, leaving a fully visible man in its place.

Maat's jaw dropped. A chill ran down his spine, for he was now looking into the face of someone he'd seen too many times before to count. It was a face that had stood beside him so frequently in his youth.

A face that he saw traces of each time he looked at Khalfani, even more so now that the boy had become a young man.

It was the face of none other than Kek Abaza. Maat stared at it in confusion.

"Sir, please," young Khalfani pleaded, seemingly unable to see his father standing beside him. Mere seconds later, though, Maat could no longer see him, either. Kek's image vanished without a trace, and soon, the entire vision did as well.

Maat felt like he was swirling through the Darkness himself when all of his surroundings clouded over, the world around him becoming nothing more than a mist. However, as the mist began to clear, Maat realized he was landing in yet another vision.

For one brief moment, he thought he'd returned to the underground hideout. But he quickly realized the set-up of it was wrong, the surveillance screens unfamiliar and belonging to some sort of device he'd never seen before.

These screens, too, broadcast images of the war against the Retrograde—however, it did so through a noticeably different angle. While the surveillance screens Maat and his companions used were meant to provide updates on the Retrograde's progression, these particular screens seemed designed specifically for spying. Other screens appeared to be measuring tools used to strengthen the effects of the Retrograde. There was something very intrusive and dangerous about these screens, and standing directly in front of them, there he was again—Kek.

Kek wasn't the only thing that had returned to Maat's vision anyway. The dark swirls were present yet again as well, floating behind Kek. Maat stared, fascinated, and repulsed at the same time, attempting to make sense of what the dark swirls were and why they made him feel so uneasy.

All the while, Kek watched the Retrograde's devastation throughout Damara on his unusual device, absolute glee in his eyes. He gave an inhumane laugh, and the dark swirls behind him pulsated, matching the rhythm of that laugh.

Maat moved like a ghost through his vision, bringing himself closer to Kek. The eyes he had known so well as a youth now sat in the middle of a deranged man's face, fiery red and visibly tainted with evil.

Maat's stomach turned in knots, and the vision began to dissolve once more.

The next thing Maat knew, his daughter was before him, along with Khalfani. The two of them walked alone, fully dressed in their army gear and oblivious to Kek's darkened figure advancing on them. The dark swirls following Kek began to drift towards Isis and Khalfani, though neither of them noticed until it was too late.

Maat watched in horror, the fear on Isis's face almost stopping his heart.

The Darkness thickened and intensified, ghostly images of Kek materializing and dematerializing as he trapped Isis and Khalfani, smothering them and providing them no chances of escape.

They screamed helplessly as the Darkness latched on to them, pulling their bodies into its misty clutches, attempting to swallow them whole until they no longer existed separately from it.

Khalfani let out one final cry before the Darkness overtook him and then set its sights, consuming the rest of Isis.

The last thing Maat saw was his daughter's anguished face, her eyes wide and tearful as she screamed for help. She squirmed and fought, but her attempts were useless. And then she, too, was gone.

The space around Maat came back into view as he snapped out of the vision, trembling and panting, his heart racing. The surveillance screens were still blank, giving him consolation that the images he'd just seen of Isis and Khalfani being consumed by the Darkness hadn't actually happened.

At least, not yet.

But they never would, if he could help it.

Though still shaken, Maat sprang into action, lunging from the control panel. His hands flew over various buttons, entering the codes to access the surveillance screen, pulling up the feature designed to track the Retrograde's movement where it was strongest.

Frantically, his eyes darted around the screen, searching the results. Finally, he spotted the black and red swirls representing the Retrograde moving along the heart of the city. He pressed another button on the control panel, zooming in to locate the eye of the Retrograde.

He narrowed his eyes, trying to identify the spot he was seeing. It appeared to be a large building of some sort, resembling a castle—almost similar to the complex up above that he and his family called home. Nevertheless, the Darkness so thoroughly casted shadows over it that the building remained difficult to decipher. It was like trying to see through a pitch-black cloud.

Thinking for a moment, Maat decided to retrieve satellite images of that location from the past, before the Retrograde's arrival. His fingers proceeding to fly over the control panel again, he searched images captured several months beforehand.

His jaw dropped.

Clearer images of the massive building displayed on the screen, along with video footage showcasing a man coming and going on a regular.

The man was none other than Kek Abaza, of course…

Maat took several steps back, bringing his hands to his head in disbelief as the pieces to the puzzle finally came together in his mind. He had the full image now. He understood his visions, and the warnings and hints the gods had been giving him.

The building so thoroughly engulfed by the Darkness was Kek's home…

*I keep seeing Kek intertwined with the Darkness because…*Maat swallowed, his mind reworking what he knew of his former best friend's past. He thought of the defeated and sorrowful look on Khalfani's face when he had sought Maat's help as a young child…

He knew the boy's mother—Kek's wife—had passed away. But how?

In light of current revelation, Maat did a search for Tije Abaza. The system's results flashed onto the screen, showing that she was deceased. However, her cause of death was marked as unknown. What caught Maat's attention most was the year of her death.

It was the same year Khalfani had shown up on his doorstep.

Khalfani ran away from home because his father, Kek Abaza, killed his mother. Kek killed Tije. Maat thought to himself, bewildered. *Kek must have been on a mission to strengthen the effects of the Retrograde. Tije must have found out and then Kek killed her. Perhaps, he was on some kind of deranged quest for power or control. Somehow, though, his actions must have recently caught the attention of the Darkness. The ancient evil force that no doubt contributed to Ximxija's downfall.. And now, Kek has literally become the Darkness. Those dark swirls encircling Kek appeared to be an unholy biproduct of The Darkness itself, a force that Maat knew all too well.*

It all seemed too much to be true. Yet, the more Maat thought on it, the more he realized it probably wasn't so far-fetched, after all. Even when they were young, Kek had always had unusual ways about him. In fact, Maat could recall the hostility that often flickered over Kek's face—something he had always ignored for the sake of their friendship.

But now, it all made sense. Kek was the perfect host for the Darkness…

Maat's astonishment turned into panic when he strictly reflected on the last part of his vision, in which he'd seen the Darkness attacking Khalfani and Isis. The image practically made the blood drain from his face. He worked over the control panel again, this time in attempts to reach Isis and Khalfani.

They needed to know the truth about what they were up against.

* * *

Isis and Khalfani walked side-by-side, the center of the city looming ahead of them.

"What is it?" Isis asked, looking sideways at Khalfani when his steps began to slow down before eventually coming to a stop altogether. She halted as well, letting the rest of the group bypass her.

Khalfani looked up at her, his eyes wide. Before he could answer her, though, Isis noticed the buzzing at her wrist. She glanced down at her communication device, seeing that her father was calling.

"He's calling me too," Khalfani said.

They answered their calls at the same time.

"*Poje*?" Isis said.

"Yes, sir?" Khalfani greeted.

"Isis, Khalfani," came Maat's voice through both of their earpieces, "are the others around you?"

"Yes," Isis answered.

"Can you separate yourselves? I don't want any of this to be overheard."

Right at that moment, Tekem happened to glance back at them. He stared for a second, giving them a slight smirk. Likely thinking they were trying to get a moment alone, he turned back around, presumably giving them privacy.

Not wanting to draw anyone else's attention, Isis and Khalfani slowed their pace until they lingered behind the group, but made sure not to fall too noticeably far behind.

"What is it? What's wrong, *Poje*?" Isis asked, her skin starting to tingle with panic.

"First, how are the two of you doing?" Maat asked. "Have you encountered any changelings yet?"

"No, sir," Khalfani replied in a low voice. "We've been seeing some who are on their way to becoming changeling, though. The signs are definitely out here. It's started, and it won't be long—"

"Okay. Well, I take it that you both are being careful," Maat said.

"*Poje*," Isis interjected, preoccupied with the distress she heard in her father's voice, "What is it? What's wrong? I know you didn't call just to tell us to be careful."

Maat sighed. "Look, there's no easy way to say this," he began. "I'm calling because I had another vision. A very important one…" He paused, and from the corner of her eye, Isis saw the confusion on Khalfani's face; not everyone was aware of her father's visions. "Khalfani," Maat continued, "you've told me about your mother, Tije, but you have never spoken to me about your father. Is your father Kek Abaza?"

Khalfani was taken aback by the question. He suddenly felt a nauseating pain in his stomach. He could only imagine what news confirmation of this fact would bring.

"Yes, sir." Khalfani admitted.

"I hate to tell you this, Khalfani," Maat continued, "but I've come to the understanding that the reason this Retrograde is different from those of the past is because there is a Darkness, an ancient evil in our Universe, and it is working through someone to strengthen the Retrograde. I saw this person and the Darkness become one. There's no easy way to put this, but it's your father, Khalfani. Kek—he was chosen by the Darkness to help extend the Retrograde's reach and ultimately destroy our planet, Damara. It was drawn to…to what was already inside of him…"

Isis's skin prickled further from the shock of the news. Despite how startling it was to hear, however, her primary concern was for Khalfani. She looked at him, closely observing his reaction.

His eyes had become wide and unblinking, and a muscle worked in his jaw as he clenched his teeth. Though he was still walking, trailing behind the rest of the group, his movements had grown tense. He hardly even seemed to be breathing, clearly struggling to take in all that he'd just heard. He'd initially been caught up in trying to understand what Maat had meant by visions. But that curiosity very quickly got overshadowed by the news Maat had followed up with.

"I…I'm sorry, sir," Khalfani said, "but did you just say…" He cleared his throat. "Did you just say that my *pa* was behind the Retrograde? A part of the Darkness?"

*It was drawn to what was already inside of him…*Maat's words echoed through Khalfani's head. Yes, he knew exactly the implication behind that statement. His father was a murderer. Of course, the Darkness would be drawn to someone like him.

"I saw it, Khalfani," Maat said grimly. "I'm so sorry, son."

Khalfani swallowed, his eyes stinging, overwhelmed from both the news regarding his *pa* and from hearing Maat refer to him as 'son.' He would have given anything for someone like Maat Mahmoud to be his father, rather than the one he actually had. "I…I have to go find him then," Khalfani stammered, trying to gather his thoughts.

"Mark my words," Maat replied, "he's your *poje*—he'll find you. Just stay cautious. In the meantime, you need to focus on your plan once you get to the city's center. I have reason to believe things are going to get very bad, very quickly. The last thing you want is to let the changelings get out of control and gain the upper hand. There's going to be a lot of them this time around."

Khalfani nodded, though his expression was blank, still stupefied by the news he'd just been given.

Sensing his distress, Isis gently grabbed his hand and gave it a squeeze.

Khalfani, however, pulled away from her touch. Knowing what had become of his father—the type of man whose blood ran through his own veins—had him feeling like the Mahmoud family was too good for him. He was tainted; he didn't deserve them.

Feeling him pull away, Isis fixed her gaze on him. She reached for his hand again, only for him to move out of her reach once more.

"Khal?" Speaking a bit too loudly, Kaiden and Lia turned around and glanced at Isis. Wanting to deter their attention, she rearranged her features to look as if it was nothing serious. When they turned back around, she leaned in to Khalfani and lowered her voice. "You know this doesn't change the way I feel about you, right?"

He lowered his eyes to the ground. "Well, it should…"

"Well, it doesn't," she countered sternly.

Khalfani swallowed, his throat constricting. He looked into Isis's deep brown eyes. They blazed with such intensity, yet somehow felt so comforting. It hardly made sense. "I love you, Ninna," he said, the words slipping out of his mouth before he had any hopes of stopping them.

"I love you too," she replied without hesitation.

So caught up in the moment, both of them had forgotten Maat was still listening. And they had no way of knowing about the approving smile that had slipped onto his face at having overheard them. He firmly believed those two were the strongest beacons of light during these dark times.

Not wanting to embark on their privacy too much, he cleared his throat, reminding them that he was still on the line.

Both of them jumped, their faces warm.

"Whatever you do," Maat resumed, carrying on as if he hadn't overheard such an intimate moment, "I need you both to stay extra cautious."

"Of course," Isis said quickly.

"And I need you both to know about the Dark Order—" Maat said, but right that instant, their connection broke.

"*Poje*?" Isis said, pressing the earbud farther into her ear as if it would bring him back. "*Poje*?"

"He's gone," Khalfani said, fumbling with his own earbud and staring at the device on his wrist. "Dammit."

"What was that?" Mirko asked from up ahead, he and several of the other soldiers glancing back at them again.

"Nothing," Khalfani said. "Tripped on a branch."

Mirko and the others chortled and turned back around.

With the others' attention off of them again, Isis turned to Khalfani, confused. "What's the Dark Order?" she asked.

He frowned and shook his head. "I wish I knew."

Meanwhile, back at the underground hideout, Maat uttered a stream of swears, trying to restore his connection to Isis and Khalfani. There was still so much he needed to tell them. But he couldn't reconnect, the device before him continuing to flash signals about them being out-of-range.

He slammed the control panel with his fist in frustration.

Hearing slight movement across the room, he looked up to find Rania standing in the doorway. Her eyes were wide with worry, and she fidgeted with her nails—one of her nervous ticks. For a moment, he just stared at her, wondering how long she'd been there and how much she'd heard.

He received his answer when she rushed into his arms. "I'm so scared for our daughter," she whispered in his ear. "And Khalfani too. I love him like a son, just as you do."

Maat held her tightly. "I know, *ti biyeh*. I know…"

* * *

Isis and Khalfani picked up their speed, rejoining the rest of the group and trying to keep their appearance casual. While they were still reeling from the shock of Maat's news, the rest of the soldiers were simply grappling with the fatigue of their journey. The overall pace of the group had slowed considerably, and everyone struggled to keep moving.

"What's that?" one of the soldiers whispered, garnering curious and confused glances from the others. She took a quick look around. "I thought I heard something. No one else heard it?"

"Have some water. You're delirious," Farhad replied, tossing her a canteen.

A few chuckled, and she muttered in return, but accepted the canteen nonetheless.

They resumed walking in silence, the brief interruption forgotten…

Until they rounded a corner and stopped dead in their tracks.

A changeling had appeared.

Unlike the misfortunate souls they'd previously encountered, this one was a full changeling, not someone just in the early phases. Immediately seeing them, the changeling growled ferally, its teeth bared and drool spilling down its chin. His eyes were bloodshot and fiendish, his clothing filthy and carrying a stench that reached their noses despite the distance between them. His hands clenched and unclenched into fists at his sides, his fingernails bloody and torn.

As frightening as it was to encounter a changeling in person, Isis hadn't anticipated how sad it would be. Even given what had become of this person, it was clear that he had once been normal—attractive even, given his shiny dark curls, hazel eyes, and high cheekbones. Now, however, the Retrograde had turned him into nothing but a shadow of his former self, and there would be no returning to normalcy for him.

He practically looked like a walking corpse.

As if trying to speak, gibberish began leaving his mouth, faster and louder by the second. Then, without warning, he ran off to the side, raised a trashcan over his head, and began charging towards them.

"Line up! Arm yourselves!" Khalfani ordered.

The soldiers lined up, creating a wall of defense with their bodies while drawing their various weapons. Without waiting for Khalfani's additional instructions, Amam open-fired, a look of relish on his face. And then, following suit, Mirko joined in. The changeling's body jerked and convulsed before he fell to the ground, releasing one last growl before the life went out of him. The trashcan he'd been holding above his head fell with a loud clatter that coincided with a flash of lightning across the sky.

Snarling, Tekem rounded on Amam and Mirko. "He said arm yourselves, not fire!" he yelled, gesturing to Khalfani.

"That was a full-blown changeling!" Amam argued. "What were we supposed to do? Wait for it to attack? Actually *let* it attack?" He turned towards Mirko for reinforcement. But instead, Mirko lowered his weapon and looked away, guiltily.

"It was just one changeling," Khalfani said, fixing Amam with a stern gaze. "We could have killed it with quieter means." He looked down at the dead changeling. "Now, we know full changelings are out there—and near. And you've potentially alerted them to our arrival. Thanks a lot."

"Oh, so it was okay for Isis to shoot that lady, though?" Parr said, an eyebrow raised.

Isis clenched her jaw as Khalfani turned towards Parr. "Isis had no choice," he retorted icily. "That woman was literally on her."

"Oh—I'm sorry. Is that supposed to mean a quiet stabbing wouldn't do?" Parr titled his head sideways. "Or perhaps she could have just broken the woman's bones and incapacitated her. Let's not pretend she isn't skilled and deranged enough to do it." He turned steely gaze towards her.

Isis stammered angrily. "I…I acted on instinct. I just happened to grab the gun first…I…"

"You don't think. That much is obvious," Parr spat. "Too emotional and impulsive."

"All right, that's enough," Khalfani interjected. "Drop it. And from now on, nobody fires without being given the order to do so first. Understood?"

"Oh, so if a changeling is about to kill me—"

"Then you use your common sense," Aurora said, stepping forward and positioning herself between the arguing soldiers. They immediately fell silent, with Parr even stepping back. "So," she said, "are we ready to resume and get back to business?"

"Yes, of course," Khalfani answered, with the other soldiers muttering in agreement. No one dared argue against Aurora, not even Parr.

Aurora smiled. "All right. Let's carry on then," she said, patting Amam on the back and moving along.

The other soldiers exchanged glances with one another, and then wordlessly followed behind Aurora, quietly accepting that the Retrograde had officially begun, and full changelings were out there awaiting them.

* * *

"So…how many of them do you think are out there now? The changelings," Lia asked tentatively, falling into step beside Khalfani, Tekem, and Isis.

Khalfani cleared his throat. "Depends on how…how strong the Retrograde is, this early on…" Although he tried to keep his voice steady, Isis could hear the concern lurking in it. And judging from the way Tekem sighed, she supposed he heard it too.

"I guess that's something we'll be finding out very soon then," Tekem said.

Lia wiped her brow and bit her bottom lip, giving an expression that very clearly showed she wasn't exactly ready to find out. And as Isis looked around, she saw that Lia wasn't at all the only one.

Isis's stomach clenched nervously, so keenly feeling the heavy sense of foreboding in the atmosphere. Glancing around again at her fellow soldiers, she saw that they were all in varying degrees of exhaustion. When their apprehension was added to the mix, it was abundantly obvious that Cairo's army wasn't in the best condition at the moment.

Isis nudged Khalfani's arm.

He looked sideways at her, one eyebrow raised.

"I think we should take a break," she leaned over to whisper to him.

He bit his bottom lip and then shook his head. "I don't think we have the time, Ninna..."

"Khal, look at them." Isis gestured to the other soldiers, right as one of them tripped and stumbled over his own feet. Another was asking his neighbor for a sip of water because his canteen was empty. Orsel and Easton were walking so closely together their shoulders touched as if physically using each other to stay upright to keep walking.

On the other side of them, Tekem was rubbing a crick out the back of Lia's neck as they walked. And up front, Aurora walked alongside Apple, encouraging her to remain strong and reserve her strength. "We aren't going to make it much longer if we keep going like this. In this state, our army won't stand a chance. The changelings will wipe us out so quickly there won't even be a war. We need to rest and reboot, Khal, or we're not going to win this battle."

Taking another look at the soldiers, Khalfani realized just how worn out they looked. He sighed and nodded his head. "Guess you're right." Looking ahead, he pointed to an abandoned building. "Maybe we can stop there."

They walked a few paces farther, until getting closer to the building. "All right, everyone," Khalfani said, positioning himself in front of the group, "we're going to stop for a minute. Take a breather." He pointed over his shoulder to the building. "This place up here should do, but it needs to be checked out first."

The group all muttered appreciatively.

"I'm going to ask some of you to stay back and keep watch for a second out here," Khalfani said. "As for Amam, Mirko, Tekem, Farhad, Jacey, Aurora, Kaiden, Isis—you guys come with me."

Those called by name stepped forward and tentatively entered the building behind Khalfani, holding their weapons at the ready. Inside was dark, musty, and covered in dust.

The very second they entered, Isis suppressed the urge to sneeze. Jacey hadn't been so fortunate, however. She turned her head to the side, sneezing into her sleeve to muffle the sound, but still noisy nonetheless.

Everyone came to a cautious halt. Their eyes scanned every inch of the building, listening and waiting for any disturbances or signs that their presence had been detected. Fortunately, though, the building appeared to be empty.

"Looks like the coast is clear," Khalfani said, looking at Tekem. "Get the others."

Tekem returned to the entrance and poked his head out. "Coast is clear, guys. Come on in."

The remaining soldiers filed inside, immediately spreading through the building and stretching out on the floor to rest.

Some pulled out water and food, while others lied on the floor with no concern about the dust covering it, desperate to squeeze in a power-nap.

Khalfani looked toward Isis and jerked his head to the side, gesturing for her to follow him to a corner of their own, where they settled down for a quick snack and some water. All the while, they consciously avoided discussing the elephant in the room—Khalfani's father.

Isis stared out at her fellow soldiers, her eye accidentally catching Parr's again before she quickly looked away. Chewing thoughtfully, she instead watched Aurora and Apple sharing a sandwich. "Can I ask you something?" she said to Khalfani.

"Sure," he said, albeit hesitantly.

"What do you think our chances are?" she said, keeping her voice low to avoid being overheard. "You know…" her voice trailed off, but she hoped he understood the unspoken thoughts behind it.

You know your pa better than anyone. Do you really think we can defeat him?

Khalfani's shoulders tensed for a moment, and then he shook his head. "I wish I knew. Hopefully, our chances are whatever they need to be to win this thing. I like to believe that good always prevails in the end…"

They quietly finished their snacks, and then sat in companionable silence for a bit longer. Isis looked at Khalfani, realizing that he seemed to be in some kind of trance, off in his own world. He stared off into the distance, his chest gently rising and falling with the breaths he took. Studying him, she realized that she had seen him go into such a state before. Meditating.

Turning away and giving him his moment, Isis began to look at the other soldiers, her gaze settling on Lia, who'd been talking with Tekem. Perhaps it was just female intuition, but Isis thought she saw something in the way Lia looked at Tekem. But before she could think any further on it, Lia had turned her attention away from Tekem and approached Orsel, who'd isolated herself from the others and was pacing the floor, singing quietly to herself.

Noticing Lia standing behind her, Orsel came to a halt, a look of startlement on her face. Isis watched them, though too far away to hear their conversation.

"I'm sorry," Lia said to Orsel. "Please, don't stop on my account. Your voice is gorgeous. You sing like an angel."

Blushing, Orsel brushed her shiny black hair behind her ear and awkwardly cleared her throat. "I didn't realize anyone could hear me."

Lia smiled. "If I had a voice like that, I'd want everyone to hear me."

Orsel chuckled. "Well, thanks, but umm…I'd appreciate it if you don't tell anyone." Orsel swallowed. Of all the soldiers, she was the most petite and sometimes felt like she had more to prove to make up for her size. Singing wasn't exactly a skill she presumed would impress most soldiers.

Lia held her hands up in surrender. "All right. Your secret's safe. Just know that it shouldn't have to be a secret, though…"

Meanwhile, Isis continued watching from across the room, simply wondering what her fellow soldiers were discussing. But shortly thereafter, Khalfani stretched, coming out of his trance.

"Welcome back," Isis teased.

"Huh?" he said.

Isis laughed and shook her head. "Oh, nothing."

Khalfani smirked at her for an instant, before his expression grew serious. "Well, thanks for this—pointing out that we needed a break. It's been nice. But time is wasting, unfortunately. We need to get back out there."

Isis nodded solemnly. While she didn't want the moment to end, she knew it had to. And when Khalfani stood, all the other soldiers seemed to immediately recognize and accept that the break was over.

They all knew that with each passing second, the Retrograde was spreading. And the farther it spread, the more damage it did, and the stronger it would become, making it even harder to defeat.

"Time to get moving again, guys. We're almost there. It's time to meet this thing head-on and let it know that we won't let it take Damara."

* * *

Isis and Khalfani walked side-by-side, and soon, found themselves coming to a screeching halt. Several soldiers behind them gasped, and the rejuvenated state they'd all just been in quickly turned into pure dread.

None of them had been prepared for how close they were. But now, there was no denying that they'd reached their destination, whether they were ready or not.

They had walked into Hell on Earth.

Isis blinked, her eyes tearing, and her nose burning from the stench around them. Everywhere they turned, buildings were either crumbling or covered in graffiti. Bodies littered the street—so many of them appearing to have suffered self-inflicted wounds in attempts to escape the Retrograde on their own terms. Their blood seeped into the ground, turning the pavement into sordid decorative tiling.

As for those who were still standing…

A collective shudder went through the entire group of soldiers as an army of changelings stared back at them. Their undead eyes glared with bloodlust, the very air itself charged with their aggression.

"It's showtime," Mirko said grimly.

CHAPTER 11

For an instant, it felt like time stood still. The changelings were far too many to even comprehend, let alone count. Maat had warned Khalfani and Isis of what was coming, but this was more than they could have anticipated. They exchanged panicked glances with one another, both of them feeling a sense of guilt for not giving the others a full heads-up regarding what they were walking into.

The soldiers shifted uncomfortably on their feet, several of them muttering while others swore under their breath. The eeriness of the situation increased tenfold as the changelings, looking like an army of their own, practically began to growl in unison. The sound started off as a low rumble, like distant thunder, but grew, creating the illusion that the soldiers were surrounded by hungry mythical beasts, for none of them could even think of anything they'd ever encountered in life that sounded remotely like what they were currently hearing. Their vocalizations charged the air with their malevolence.

The hairs on the back of Isis's neck stood on end. While the soldiers and changelings all stood eyeing each other for what felt like forever, in reality, it couldn't have been any more than a few seconds.

Listening to the changelings and watching the similarities in their hateful expressions, Isis wondered if there was still some form of intelligence that resided in them, after all. How else could they move and act in such perfect unison? However, as the thought crossed her mind, she realized their actions probably weren't consciously planned. More than likely, it was simply the Darkness inside of them guiding their behavior. Hence, in a sense, they were an army—an army of evil and chaos with their commander-in-chief being the Darkness itself.

Or Kek, in other words.

Beneath her fear, Isis's heart ached for a moment for Khalfani. She couldn't fathom what it was like for him to be seeing this, knowing his own flesh and blood was influencing it.

As the changelings' growls intensified, they started moving closer, inching towards the soldiers.

"STAND GUARD!" Khalfani yelled, his voice strong and steady as he screamed over the changeling cacophony. "ARM YOURSELVES. PREPARE TO FIGHT. THIS IS THE MOMENT WE'VE BEEN TRAINING FOR. LET'S MAKE DAMARA PROUD!"

Khalfani's voice, so brave and resolute, was the kick-start the army needed. His conviction and determination proved to be contagious. And while it went unspoken that they all knew some of them probably wouldn't make it out of this ordeal alive, this was what they signed up for, and backing down wasn't an option.

Isis took a deep breath, trying to force away the trepidation that she felt. If Khalfani could be brave under such unconventional circumstances, then so could she. Thinking of what he had to be going through at the moment made thoughts of her own parents fill her mind, and she found herself wishing more than anything that she could hug them both one more time before the battle began. Her *pa's* voice rang through her ears, and her *eva's* pretty face drifted through her mind.

Then, she remembered her reason for being there—she was fighting for those who were less fortunate. For those who couldn't sufficiently hide or protect themselves from the Retrograde. She remembered that once, her own mother had fallen into this category.

Isis began to look at the changelings in a new light, understanding that so many of them were just people who simply didn't have the means to prevent what they had become. This war was about making sure others didn't suffer the same fate, and putting those who'd already been victimized—the changelings—out of their misery.

It was a war she was determined to help Damara win.

She looked sideways at Khalfani, and he returned her stare with his blazing green eyes. Without saying a word, they somehow seemed to give each other the strength they needed.

Khalfani gave Isis a single nod, and she did the same to him. From that moment on, they were both ready.

Their whole army was ready.

A battle cry sounded through the air, piercing over the growls of the changelings. A split-second later, Aurora sprinted forward, reaching for the rope at her belt. Seconds went by in which the other soldiers could only watch in awe—Isis included. While Aurora's fighting prowess was well known throughout Damara, it was the first time Isis was actually seeing Aurora in action outside of practice.

Aurora's rope practically had a life of its own. The instant she unhooked it from her belt, it split into two whips. Aurora swung her arm in a maneuver that almost made it look as if she was dancing, and each whip flew in opposite directions. The edges of the whips were made of poisonous spiked blades. Flashing through the air, the blades headed straight into the crowd of changelings. Hit simultaneously from the right and the left, the herd of changelings began falling like demented dominoes as the blades sliced through them before meeting in the middle and becoming one solid rope again.

Aurora made another arm maneuver, sending the rope swinging above her head, waiting to attack again. "*For Damara!*" she bellowed.

Her yell awakened the rest of the soldiers. Instantly, they sprang into action, energized by Aurora's quick thinking to give them the upper hand. Many of the changelings were still knocked off balance, which gave the soldiers the perfect opportunity to strike.

A flash of silver flew through the air as Aiari unleashed one of his homemade weapons into the herd of changelings, hitting the first few who managed to get back on their feet after Aurora's rope-attack. Right on his heels, Mirko charged forward, aiming guns at the changelings still squirming on the ground. And then, Amam was there, reaching for changelings with his bare hands when his battle axe was not quick enough to get the job done.

Isis unhooked her gun from her belt, the feel of the cold metal in her hands triggering the memory of the beautiful woman she'd had to kill not long ago. For a moment, she trembled, choking on the reality in front of her.

Her hands unsteady, she fired a shot at a changeling coming in her direction and missed, the bullet only grazing him. He continued charging at her, looking like something straight out of a horror picture show. Her heart pounded, seeing how quickly the changeling moved. Before she knew it, he was within feet of her, his filthy hands outstretched and ready to seize her. He growled, his hot putrid breath reaching her nose.

She squeezed the trigger again, this time getting the shot through his chest right in the nick of time; he'd been seconds away from attacking her.

Watching the changeling fall dead to the ground flipped a switch in Isis's brain. She refocused, remembering that these were people who needed to be put out of their misery.

People who would only bring more devastation to her beloved planet if they were left to roam freely, infecting those who couldn't defend themselves.

How many people had her *eva* lost in her youth due to changelings?

Isis spun around, seeing more changelings heading towards her. She fired again, this time without hesitation, the warrior inside of her thoroughly awakened. As another came for her, she swung her leg, kicking it square in the chest to create distance—a move that Aurora had taught her. She then fired again, shooting it in the head.

Turning around again, she saw Khalfani nearby, launching himself at a group of changelings, using a mixture of shooting and hand-combat to fight them off. Though it made her nervous to see him surrounded by so many, he was handling his own, proving to be just as efficient a fighter out on the field as he'd been in training. And right beside him was Tekem, mixing martial arts into his shooting.

Isis jumped, hearing something swish past her ear and realizing it was an arrow. It landed swiftly in the temple of a changeling that had been sneaking up at her. She turned around, seeing one of her fellow soldiers with a crossbow. She nodded in gratitude, but he was already firing at the next.

Gunfire rang through the air, shots being fired left and right. Yet, the changelings kept coming, seemingly multiplying by the seconds, the sounds of the fighting drawing more and more of them to the city's center.

Isis twirled on the spot, keeping a lookout in every direction that she could, shooting at any changeling she could get a decent aim at.

But there were just so many…

In her periphery, Isis saw Aurora brandishing her whip, charging at swarms of changelings in quick succession. Isis yelled, seeing a changeling behind Aurora and fearing the worst. However, Aurora abruptly jumped into the air, spun around, and kicked the changeling. It tripped backwards, stumbling into another changeling. When Aurora landed back on the ground, she snatched an arrow from her belt and threw it, killing both changelings in one go. The arrow flew straight through the first changeling's throat and exited out the back of its neck before landing in the chest of the one directly behind it.

Aurora clearly needed no help.

Staying close to her was Apple, who was taking out plenty of changelings in her own right. Crouched low and keeping alert eyes across the field, she shot any changeling that actually did manage to escape Aurora and her spiked whips. Additionally, she kept an eye out for changelings attempting to catch any fellow soldiers off guard. Witnessing the stealth in which Apple worked, Isis found herself suspecting that so many of them had been underestimating her all along; the girl was an impeccable sniper, and they were lucky to have her fighting alongside them. Gentle nature or not, she definitely showed the signs of being raised by Aurora.

Isis jumped, her attention refocusing when a changeling abruptly launched at her, having taken advantage of her blind spot. With a startled cry, she shot it in the chest. Yet, the very second it fell, another snuck up beside her. She spun around, finding it too close to shoot safely. Moving quickly, she pulled one of the two knives from her belt and swiped it across the changeling's face and then ducked to the right to avoid its splattering blood. Its head snapped sideways, and she gave him a powerful shove in the chest before shooting it.

Hardly having time to catch her breath, she turned around, open-firing at a group of ten or more heading her way.

Sweat ran down her forehead, and her hair clung wildly to her face. She gritted her teeth, astounded by the fact that no matter how many changelings they killed, more showed up. It was as if each one they killed caused three more to avenge it.

Isis continued shooting as many as she could, when suddenly, a piercing, masculine scream penetrated the air. She instantly spun around, her heart leaping into her throat and her mind on Khalfani. However, she quickly deduced the screaming wasn't coming from him. Scanning the premises, her eyes landed on Parr Grixti.

Too stubborn to bypass fighting in the war, there was no doubt he had to be regretting his decision now. A group of changelings had him swarmed, and he struggled to defend himself. Isis's stomach churned, watching the changeling closest to him knock the gun out of his one good hand.

Parr tried to run, but the changelings had him too thoroughly surrounded. Hearing his screams growing in intensity, Farhad, Jacey, Garth, and the rest of the soldiers in his vicinity tried to help, but it was too late. In the center of the swarm of changelings, Parr fell to the ground and couldn't regain his footing. For an instant, he couldn't even be seen through the wall of changelings around him. But eventually, Isis was able to glimpse one of the changelings straddling him. The changeling lowered his head to Parr's chest, biting, scratching, and ripping at his flesh.

"HELP!" Jacey screamed on Parr's behalf, while the soldiers around her continued shooting at the herd that had descended on him. But their efforts were of no use. Even as Tekem, Lia, and Kaiden made their way over, there was little that could be done.

Parr's screams grew muffled as yet more changelings descended on him, thirsty to get a piece of him. The metallic scent of his blood tainted the air, and Isis had to grit her teeth against the bile rising in her throat. She didn't want to see, but couldn't seem to look away…

Something white poked through Parr's chest, sticking out from the mess of gushing blood. With a sickening swoop in her stomach, Isis realized it was his broken rib cage, protruding out. Additionally, she noticed a red mass clutched in the hand of the changeling straddling him…

"No," she groaned, feeling close to vomiting. Finally, she turned away, trying to suppress her urge to heave. Yet, she couldn't block out the sounds…

The sounds of changelings gnawing, slurping, and devouring Parr. One of them was eating his heart…

Parr's screaming had long since come to a stop, and his body lay on the ground, serving as a human buffet for the bloodthirsting fiends hovering over him. Soldiers cried and shot, trying to put an end to the grotesque scene. But it wasn't until Aurora's ropes came whipping through the air, eliminating the remaining changelings around Parr, that the brutality stopped. Unfortunately, by that time, there was hardly any of Parr left; there wasn't even enough of his body to dignify his remains with a burial.

Never in a million years could Isis have imagined a more unbecoming death.

Nevertheless, the shock of it all increased her adrenaline tenfold, seeing just how dangerous the changelings really were. Seeing what they were capable of made it all the more necessary to win this war.

Gritting her teeth and releasing a war cry of her own, Isis began to plow through the changelings nearby. There were too many of them, but she didn't care, as long as she killed as many as she could. Her knife in one hand and a gun in the other, she sliced and shot. Sliced and shot.

A changeling unexpectedly clawing at her shoulder, Isis's knife dropped out of her hand. She spun around the seized the changeling by its collar, placed her gun to its temple, and pulled the trigger. Then, instead of letting it fall to the floor, she maintained her grip, holding the changeling in front of her like a shield against the others coming her way. From over the dead changeling's shoulder, she aimed and shot. Aimed and shot. Aimed and shot…All the while, screaming out her frustrations.

Hearing her cries, Khalfani turned on the spot from where he fought, terrified that she was in trouble. Yet, when he spotted her with her changeling-shield, he saw that was far from the case. Isis was fighting more fiercely than he knew she could, doing more than she had even done in training. Despite the hellish pandemonium around them, his heart swelled with pride for her, which encouraged him to fight harder.

It was crystal clear to him now that they had to survive this. It was absolutely necessary. Because once it was over, he had to take Isis into his arms.

A changeling darted at him from his right, and Khalfani caught it in the throat. Gritting his teeth and looking into its deranged eyes, he squeezed the monstrosity with all his might, strangling it with his bare hand. With his free hand, he aimed at a changeling he saw in his periphery, efficiently shooting it right through the forehead. All the while, he could hear several others sneaking up behind him. As the one he'd choked collapsed to the ground, he turned around and shot through the swarm behind him. Somewhere during all of this, Khalfani registered that his senses seemed to be heightened. Though he couldn't explain or understand it, he could feel that his senses were keener. Even the hairs on his arms seemed to prickle in a way that detected motion around him, alerting him to the direction of the most immediate danger.

As valiantly as Cairo's army fought, though, they seemed to hardly even put a dent in the number of changelings that kept coming for them. All around, the growls and grunts of the Retrograde's army filled the air, as well as the screams—both of terror and battle cries—from the soldiers. Guns fired, bullets whistled, and arrows swished and exploded their poison into their targets, causing blood to splash through the air like rain showers. Falling bodies, racing feet, and gunfire made the ground shake, the earth trembling in despair.

Rotting flesh, unwashed bodies, sweat, and blood perfumed the air, working together to create a nauseating aroma of death and destruction.

And through it all, changelings stretched on as far as the eye could see. Panting and fighting, the soldiers could literally taste their own despair. Still, giving up wasn't an option.

The muscles of Isis's arm ached, straining with the effort of holding on to her changeling-made shield. Unable to endure it anymore, she reluctantly tossed the changeling to the ground.

Yet, doing so only gave her a better view of just how many still remained. Ignoring the trepidation running through her, as well as the achiness of her muscles, Isis kept going. She kicked and shot the changelings closest to her, all the while regrettably realizing the battle was too big to win. Cairo's army was in over its head, and it was getting increasingly more difficult not to feel overwhelmed.

They were outnumbered, plain and simple.

Looking around, Isis didn't know if it was just her imagination or not, but she could have sworn she was drawing more attention from changelings than the other soldiers. Seeing changelings coming at her from every direction, the fight quickly left her and got replaced with panic. Suddenly, all she could feel was her own sense of self-preservation.

Moving backwards, Isis stumbled over something at her feet. Gasping, she just barely maintained her balance. When she looked down, there was a changeling just inches away from biting her ankle. She kicked it in the face, breaking its nose. Then, she turned around and broke into a run, her flight reflex overpowering her fight reflex. As her feet pounded the pavement, she could feel a horde of changelings hot on her heels.

Pausing just for an instant to wipe sweat out of his face, Khalfani was abruptly hit with a feeling of dread right in the pit of his stomach. A chill ran over him, letting him know something other than the obvious was wrong.

"ISIS!" a voice cried out. Kaiden's. Through the changelings surrounding him, he saw Isis running, her thick wild hair catching in the wind behind her.

Hearing Kaiden scream Isis's name, Khalfani's mouth instantly grew dry, and his heart stuttered. Frantically, he searched the premises, his blood running cold at realizing he didn't see her. Spinning on the spot, his frantic eyes finally located her retreating into a nearby building with a herd of changelings in uncomfortably close pursuit.

His first instinct was to follow her, but the number of changelings around him had grown so thick, he lost sight of her. Frustrated and feeling that things were getting too far out of control, he reached behind him, freeing his secret weapon—a bladed boomerang that Aiari had designed specifically for him.

He squeezed it in his hand for a moment, activating its thought-control feature. Once the weapon tuned into his thoughts, Khalfani opened his hand. A weapon like this was powerful, but took a lot of concentration to operate—and this kind of chaos could easily hinder one's focus. Fortunately, the meditation techniques Tekem had taught him came in handy at times like this.

Thinking about losing sight of Isis, Khalfani, for a millisecond, closed his eyes and trained his thoughts on slicing the throats of the changelings around him to clear his vision field. When he opened his eyes, the boomerang set to work, doing exactly as he wished.

Meanwhile, a panting Isis reached the building and made her way inside. Once through the door, she hastily looked around, searching for something—anything—she could use to barricade herself inside until she got her bearings and felt capable of rejoining the war. While she searched, she realized the dimly lit building appeared to be a ballroom of some sort.

As her eyes darted from left to right, up and down, she was in the center of the ballroom when she realized she'd possibly made a grave mistake…

There was no escaping the changelings. Their trademark stench permeated the building, and Isis's stomach twisted in knots as she began to spot them. It was like they were appearing out of thin air. And now, Isis was all alone, having separated herself from her fellow soldiers.

She recalled hearing Kaiden calling out to her but wondered if he had actually seen where she went. Would he come looking? Would he alert the others?

While she wanted to hope that help would arrive, she doubted it. All of the other soldiers, including Kaiden, had been too caught up with the fight and wouldn't be able to help her even if they wanted to…

Not even Khalfani.

After all, she had witnessed firsthand what had happened to Parr, and that was even with people trying to help.

She breathed hard, a stitch forming in her side, wondering what had made her take such an action.

What had she been thinking? Why had she run? Why had she doomed herself like this?

She closed her eyes and covered her head with her hands as the changelings drew nearer, encircling her just as they had done outside with Parr. Suddenly, her heart began to pound, louder and louder until the sound became deafening. Her breathing began to shallow. And that was when the building's already dim lights flickered out, leaving her in darkness.

Khalfani clenched his teeth so hard he thought he might shatter his own jaw. He held out his hand, catching his boomerang as it circled back to him. Then, holding it like a knife, he began wielding it, stabbing through a nearby group of changelings, determined to make it inside the building to check on Isis. Resending his boomerang out to work on his behalf again, he resumed his attempt to clear a path for himself through the changelings. The boomerang sliced through the changelings nearing the building, and Khalfani used his gun to handle any that it missed. All the while, his heart throbbed painfully with anxiety, wondering why Isis had taken off running in the first place.

Had she been hurt? He looked around, wishing he could ask Kaiden. But he couldn't even see him anymore, either. There were so many changelings. They practically obscured his vision all around.

No, she's not hurt, he thought, not even wanting to entertain the idea. Isis couldn't be hurt. He couldn't accept that. He wouldn't accept that.

Using all of his strength, he shot the last few changelings in his immediate vicinity, caught his boomerang, and then took a deep breath, preparing to make a mad dash toward the building Isis had disappeared into. Yet, he'd barely even managed to take a step towards the building when an explosion assaulted his eardrums.

He stood, momentarily deaf and dumbfounded, trying to figure out what had just happened. Fear swept through his body, realizing the explosion had come from the building Isis had been running towards.

Moving on autopilot, he broke out, dashing toward the building, feeling as if his own head would explode in any second if Isis wasn't okay. He ignored the rubble and smoke filling the air, the war and changelings momentarily gone from his mind. All he could think of was Isis.

He'd halfway made it to the building when he came to an abrupt halt, seeing a figure emerging through the smoke. He would know that figure anywhere—tall and strong, yet beautiful and feminine…

His heart throbbed with relief this time, but also, with quite a bit of confusion.

There was something different about her…

Khalfani squinted, trying to make sense of what he was seeing. Though he would recognize Isis anywhere, there was a foreign look in her eyes, which likely had something to do with the fact that they were glowing red, resembling dancing flames in the middle of her face where her soulful brown eyes should have been…

He stared, thinking—hoping—he was just seeing things. Wondering if the dust and debris were affecting his vision. But before he could focus on Isis any longer, she'd taken aim at the changelings mobbing her. Yielding a bow and arrow this time, she instantly rejoined the fight. Changelings dropped before her, splattering under the assault of the exploding arrows that she fired off, one after the other, moving so quickly her body became all but a blur.

Losing track of things around him, Khalfani was startled back into action when he suddenly sensed a changeling sneaking up behind him. The changeling was crouched low, its yellowed teeth bared, ready to pounce. How Khalfani knew this, he didn't know; it was as if he could literally see this particular changeling with eyes in the back of his head that he didn't know about.

Swiftly turning to meet it, Khalfani stretched out a murderous hand right before the changeling reached for him. Grabbing both sides of the creature's face, Khalfani efficiently snapped its neck and tossed it to the ground.

He briefly looked down at his own hands, feeling the strength running through them. Despite being stunned by Isis's transformation, he knew something was indeed different about him, too, though he couldn't place his finger on what. Regardless, whatever it was—it felt good.

Knowing that Isis was all right and reveling in his own newfound strength, Khalfani's adrenaline kicked into high gear. With the cry of a warrior escaping his mouth, he charged for a group of changelings, plowing through them so quickly, they hardly had time to realize what hit them. He turned around, prepared to work his way through another group, only to find that Isis had gotten through them first. They exchanged a brief smirk before continuing the fight—a deadly duo.

Off to the right of them, Aurora fought an intense battle of her own, with Apple still in sniper mode nearby, moving strategically but never straying too far away. Apple kept her watchful eyes quickly scanning the premises, setting her sights on a changeling that appeared to be seconds away from surprise-attacking Easton. Crouching carefully and taking aim, she prepared to shoot the changeling.

"*HELP*!"

Apple stuttered for a second, hearing the scream drift towards her and immediately fearing the worst. Her heart pounded, hoping she hadn't missed anyone else being attacked…

Hoping they didn't have another Parr situation on their hands…

Quickly firing the shot and saving Easton at the last minute, she turned around in search of the voice.

Her eyes landed on a girl—a young woman who looked no older than her—running her way. The girl's clothes were in tatters, and her face was a mask of pure terror. Apple wondered how the girl had ended up there, and then concluded she must have just been in the wrong place at the wrong time. Perhaps, she had been out on her own, seeking shelter from the Retrograde, and had been unsuccessful in finding it.

As the girl drew nearer, Apple lowered her gun, trying to think fast about what she could do to get the girl out of harm's way. Without knowing her, she already felt a kinship towards her. Apple was aware of her background; had Aurora not taken her in as a baby, she could have very easily been in this girl's shoes.

Apple glanced towards Aurora, seeing that she was so engulfed in fighting that she hadn't noticed the young woman.

Apple frantically waved her arm at the girl. "Come here, hurry!" she yelled, wanting to at least shield her from the flying bullets and arrows. With quick hands, she shot at a changeling that had started running behind the girl.

Moments later, the young woman was finally within arm's reach. Apple grabbed her, pulling her close.

Suddenly, a horrible sharp pain went through Apple's abdomen. She doubled over. For a moment, she thought she'd been shot by either a stray bullet or one of the exploding poisonous arrows. Lowering her gaze, she blinked, trying to comprehend what she was seeing…

The girl's hand—there was a blade in it. And on the other end of the blade was Apple's stomach.

The girl had stabbed her.

Apple looked up, stunned.

Slowly, a deranged smile spread across the girl's face, dark shadows lurking through her eyes. Her mouth opened, a sickening laugh escaping her parted lips. And in that moment, Apple suddenly saw the girl for what she really was—a fresh changeling.

Apple staggered back in disbelief, her vision blurring, and her surroundings dimming. Lightheaded, she moved backwards enough for the girl's hand to finally slip off the blade. Breathing laboriously, Apple clutched the blade protruding from her stomach with one hand, and her gun in the other. With the last of her strength, she aimed at the girl's head and pulled the trigger. Shortly thereafter, Apple's legs buckled beneath her, unable to support her weight any longer. She collapsed to the ground, where she lied, trying to blink away the tears in her eyes, but the pain kept them forming.

Scanning the premises, she saw Aurora twelve yards away, not yet aware of what had just happened as she continued battling changelings. Very soon, however, Aurora came to an abrupt halt, and it was evident that she knew something was wrong…

After killing one more changeling, she stooped down, clutching her chest as if in pain.

Watching through blurry eyes, Apple's already labored breaths caught in her throat, fearing her mother had been hurt too. But she had been watching Aurora the whole time and therefore knew no physical harm had actually come to her. No stray bullets, no arrows, no unexpected attack from a changeling...

It was a different kind of pain Aurora was feeling.

She stood on the spot, a look of pure terror on her face. Her hands falling limp to her sides, her whip condensed into one rope again. Then finally, she turned around, her eyes darting the premises until spotting Apple lying on her back, a pool of blood seeping through her clothes and spilling onto the ground beneath her.

The sight nearly made Aurora collapse. A scream left her mouth, so shrill it nearly stopped everyone—soldier and changeling alike—in their tracks. Her own legs feeling like spaghetti beneath her, she ran towards Apple, tripping and stumbling the whole way while her rope dragged the ground.

In that moment, the war no longer mattered to Aurora. If it came between winning the war or saving Apple, she selfishly knew what she wanted to choose.

"*Imma...*" Apple said breathlessly, her voice a strained whisper, inaudible in all the chaos around her. Nevertheless, Aurora heard her as if she had yelled it in her ear.

Her legs moving numbly beneath her body, Aurora reclipped her rope to her belt and reached under her shirt, pulling out her necklace and clutching its amulet. The amulet heated in her palm before suddenly vanishing, disintegrating into thin air.

In a low voice, Aurora began chanting in her native language, briefly closing her eyes as she did so. When she reopened her eyes, a force exploded all around her…

This explosion was invisible, and no one knew what had hit them.

Confused, Isis and Khalfani looked towards each other, their hands outstretched but unable to clasp as they both shot upwards into the air.

Lia screamed, her vivid red hair whipping over her face as she was blasted into the air. Hearing her cry, Tekem turned around, only to find himself suddenly suspended in air, as well.

Mirko swore as he too found himself suddenly shooting off the ground, staring in shock as Amam's massive body, too, began to hover above the earth.

Jacey grabbed Farhad at the last minute, the two of them suddenly floating together. Orsel, Easton, and several other female soldiers screamed and tried to grab hold of each other, but all floated out of each other's reach.

Not before long, all of the soldiers found themselves floating, abruptly blasted off their feet and suspended in mid-air. It was like gravity had unexpectedly stopped working and gotten replaced by another force…

A force that was pushing them—sucking them away like a vacuum—to the outskirts of the city. The ground whirled blurrily beneath them as they moved farther and farther from the battle site, their cries of protest useless and ignored.

The whole time, Aurora kept heading towards Apple, unaffected by the force that was clearly under her control, to begin with.

The closer she got to Apple, the more changelings charged for her, drawn to her urgency and anguish. But she couldn't be thwarted. She pushed through them, determined to reach the girl whose blood didn't stop from being her daughter.

Nevertheless, the more Aurora pushed through the changelings, the more that came after her. Angrily snapping their necks like twigs and dropping their bodies to the ground like refuse, she could not seem to kill them fast enough, as they continued to block the way to her Ra, her *iva.*

And the more precious time ticked away from Apple's fleeing life…

The thought sent fury like no other through Aurora. Her body began to tremble so hard from the force of her fury that she began to tremble, a fire-like flame encircling her legs and thighs until her whole body vibrated…

And then she began to separate from herself. Transparent clones—like astral projects—pulled out of Aurora's body until there was an army of Auroras on the ground, attacking every changeling who dared get in the way of the real one.

Cairo's soldiers—still hovering at the city's outskirts—watched in shock at the display beneath them. Astral-projection Auroras were squashing out changelings left and right until the area around her and Apple was finally clear.

As abruptly as it had occurred, the multiple Auroras blurred together until they became one once more.

Finally, she had a free path to reach Apple. She stumbled towards her, vaguely registering that there were still quite a lot of changelings about, but they were moving around in confusion toward the city's outskirts, attempting to reach the dumfounded soldiers hovering out of their reach.

Meanwhile, Apple felt worse witnessing Aurora's anguish than she did, feeling her own pain. She didn't like the idea of Aurora bringing the war to a halt on her account. They all needed to stay focused…

Finally at Apple's side, Aurora knelt down and gathered the girl into her arms. Feeling Apple's weight against her, another cry of despair left Aurora's mouth.

"I shouldn't have let you come. I shouldn't have let you come. I shouldn't have let you come!" Aurora cried, shaking her head as she cradled Apple in her arms.

Apple looked up at Aurora with her bright blue eyes and blinked away tears, managing a small smile for her surrogate mother. Her *imma.* Her breathing had become too unsteady to speak, but she hoped—knew—Aurora could still sense her unspoken gratitude.

Sniffing back tears, Aurora gently stroked Apple's blond hair. She then leaned down and pressed a kiss to her forehead.

Though she was beyond the point of talking, Apple opened her mouth as if she had something she wanted to say, after all. But of course, no words came out.

"Shh," Aurora said soothingly. She gave Apple a wobbly smile, letting her know that anything she could have possibly wanted to say, she already knew.

Knowing her feelings were understood, Apple relaxed in Aurora's arms. Slowly, her eyes began to glaze over.

A lump formed in Aurora's throat, but she lifted her hand and placed it over Apple's still parted lips. Feeling Apple's last breath leave her body, Aurora clutched it in the palm of her hand, savoring the bittersweet beauty of capturing such a lovely soul upon its release.

Seeing the light officially leave Apple's eyes, Aurora delicately closed the girl's eyelids with her fingertips.

Without warning, another anguished cry left Aurora's throat, triggered by the thought of never looking into the bright blue eyes beneath her fingers again. She wailed, the pain too much to bear.

The more Aurora cried, the more she drew the attention of the changelings who'd been making their way to the outskirts of the city, trying in vain to reach the soldiers hovering far above them. Seemingly refocused on a more immediate target, they changed courses and began heading back toward Aurora, hungry for the taste of her despair.

Crying and rocking Apple in her arms, Aurora watched as the changelings headed back towards her. Looking down at the girl in her arms, she hated that she'd caved in and gone against her better judgment by letting Apple fight in the war. Every instinct within her had warned that Apple wasn't meant for battle, but she'd ignored her gut in favor of Apple's wishes…

It just wasn't fair.

Her sorrow was suddenly replaced with fury. Watching the changelings—the Retrograde's soldiers—sputtering, drooling, and growling on their way over, Aurora clenched her teeth, knowing her emotions were beyond her control and would explode out of her again in any second. Her blood felt like it was literally boiling, waiting to bubble out of her veins.

Her mouth dropped open, releasing a roar that put the growling of the changelings to shame. Her voice dropped low into an unnerving pitch as she began to chant again, her words filled with fury.

"Halla-ah 'arshilhum 'isla aljahim. Yursilun ruhahum 'iilaa alzalam," Aurora chanted, her words somehow echoing through the sky, louder and louder, although her intonation had not changed.

And as the chants left her mouth, the ground began to tremble, starting from the outskirts of the city and moving inwards. Aurora was calling upon the Universe to avenge the blood of her daughter. She begged it for blood, for death, for revenge.

Everywhere the ground's quaking touched, changelings began to explode—their blood, bones, and limbs blasting through the air as if they'd stepped on landmines.

All the while, her fellow Damara soldiers remained out of harm's way, still suspended in the air at the city's outskirts. While Aurora's main reason for forcing them away was for their own protection, another factor was simply that she hadn't wanted them attempting to assist her, as she knew many of them would have been prone to do so.

Aurora continued rocking Apple in her arms, now satisfied that her wish had been granted as she watched the quaking ground's movement get closer to them. Soon, the changelings within their vicinity were struck by it. Aurora momentarily closed her eyes against the blasts of blood and bone flying through the air near her.

And then she felt the ground directly below where her knees rested began to shake. She clutched Apple's lifeless body closer and squeezed her eyes shut more tightly, ready for the inevitable.

The explosions hit them. Despite her hold on Apple, the girl was blasted from her lap. Aurora's last glimpse of Apple was shrouded in blinding light before darkness overtook her own vision. Her body went numb, and she felt herself no more as she disintegrated from the world.

Cries of protest spread among even the toughest of the soldiers suspended in air, helplessly watching the events transpiring down below. And then, quite abruptly, Aurora's spell broke. The soldiers crashed back to the ground, and for several long seconds afterwards, they just lay, sprawled on grass and pavement, trying to wrap their minds around what had just occurred.

Khalfani and Isis were the first to move. Thoughts of Aurora and Apple fought through the stupefied hazes of their minds as they climbed back onto their feet.

Isis's eyes stung, but she was in too much shock to cry. She wanted to scream. To run towards where Aurora and Apple had been. But instead, she froze and merely stared. And then wordlessly, she pointed.

Khalfani and the others silently followed her finger, seeing that she was pointing toward the space Aurora and Apple had last occupied.

The soldiers all collectively gasped, freezing to a standstill just as Isis had done.

At the precise location where Aurora and Apple had last been seen were two bright balls of light. One, a brilliant and rich purple; the other, a bright and jovial yellow—Aurora's and Apple's favorite colors, respectively. The purple matched the color Aurora so frequently wore, and the yellow looked like a literal representation of Apple's sweet and sunny disposition.

Directly beside each other, the two lights shot off into the sky, looking like a two-colored rainbow.

CHAPTER 12

It was as if time stood still, and no one could take their eyes off the spot where Aurora and Apple had last been.

Isis blinked, her eyes still stinging. And then, her body reacting on instinct, she began to move forward, taking small steps at first before breaking into a run.

"No!" Khalfani cried out, rushing after her. He reached out and grabbed her by the wrist, bringing her to an abrupt halt.

Her teeth gritted in a snarl, she stopped and turned back to him. In that moment, however, she found that she could no longer speak. Her throat felt like it had constricted on her. Silently, she met Khalfani's gaze and understood perfectly what he was wordlessly telling her.

Aurora and Apple were gone. There was nothing they could do for them now…

The tears finally fell from Isis's eyes, hot and fast. Sniffing, she hastily wiped them away and looked up to the sky, shaking her head. The time she'd spent around them felt so brief, yet so long ago at the same time. She remembered when she first realized Aurora knew who she was. She remembered the one-on-one training Aurora had given her. She remembered meeting Apple for the first time…Learning the story of how the two of them had become each other's family.

Things weren't supposed to turn out this way…

Khalfani released Isis's wrist. As bad as he felt for Aurora and Apple, in that moment, a bulk of his despair simply came from seeing Isis cry. He wanted nothing more than to console her. To wrap his arms around her…

And he was about to do just that when something stopped him right in his tracks.

His mind hadn't even fully registered what he was hearing. Nevertheless, it sent chills down his spine. When his mind finally comprehended it, he felt sick to his stomach. The voice was dark and sinister, calling out to him…

A voice that had haunted him for his whole life, even after he'd run away from it in the hopes of never having to hear it again.

Kek.

Khalfani clenched his teeth, his skin crawling. His eyes darted around the premises, terror sweeping through him at the thought of his *pa* materializing before them at any second.

Isis stared back at him with equally wide and dumbfounded eyes. Her tears dried as she froze on the spot, listening. "What's that?" she said.

"What?" Lia asked, stepping forward and narrowing her eyes at Isis.

But Isis was too preoccupied listening. The voice was low, but felt like an assault on her ears nonetheless, like nails scraping against glass.

Khalfani flinched, hearing it again. "All right, we have to keep going." He turned on the spot, discerning the direction Kek's voice was coming from. "Follow me...I think it's coming from there."

"What's coming from where? What are you talking about?" Tekem asked, confused. The other soldiers stood around him, looking equally dumbfounded.

Khalfani blinked.

"Khal?" Tekem said, his brow furrowed as he stepped closer to his best friend. "What is it, man?"

Isis took in the faces of the other soldiers, noting their collective visible confusion. She moved towards Khalfani and whispered in his ear. "I don't think anyone else can hear it..."

After a few seconds pause, Khalfani nodded, realizing she was right. He swallowed, feeling guilty under Tekem's gaze. As his best friend—the only other person who had known the truth about his *pa*—it dawned on Khalfani that Tekem was one person who deserved to know the whole truth. But unfortunately, now was not the time to fill him in on it.

Beneath the guilt, though, Khalfani also felt preoccupied, wondering what it meant for him and Isis to be the only ones who could hear Kek. Staring at Isis, he wondered if she could hear too, simply because she did know the whole truth…

Or, he wondered, if it was another reiteration of that strange instance where she could sense his thoughts, like when she had somehow known what he'd envisioned regarding the tragedy that had befallen one of the old townspeople at the hands of the Darkness?

He thought back to their last contact with Maat. Hadn't he mentioned something about visions?

Looking into Isis's deep brown eyes—so much like her father's—Khalfani suspected that she had much more in common with her *pa* than either of them even realized.

But in that moment, he knew there was no explaining the situation to the other soldiers. "Listen," he said to the group at large, "I need you all to just follow me, okay?" He hesitated, unsure of how to proceed. He simply knew it would probably be detrimental for them all to know exactly what was going on at the moment. Looking at them each one-by-one, he could so easily see their confusion and frustration. However, he was almost positive that their mere befuddlement would become outright disdain if they found out that Kek—his own *pa*—was the one behind their misery. And that disdain wouldn't just be for Kek—it would be for him too.

How would they ever trust him as their leader if they knew that he was the flesh and blood of the enemy? He couldn't expect them all to take as kindly to the news as Isis and Maat Mahmoud had.

Truth be told, Khalfani wasn't even sure he would trust himself if he were in their shoes. And the reality was, he needed them. All of them. They had to stick together if there were any hopes of defeating this Retrograde. Of defeating Kek.

Just at the thought of his name, Khalfani heard the horrific voice calling out to him again. He turned his head in its direction. "We have to go that way," he said, looking out into the distance. Resolute, he took several steps forward. "Come on."

But to his surprise, none of the others budged.

"No," one of them said. Khalfani turned around, turning a startled gaze toward the soldier who'd spoken—Farhad. He looked back at Khalfani with a deep frown on his face and shaking his head.

"Excuse me?" Khalfani said.

"No," Farhad repeated.

"No what?"

"No, I'm not following you."

A long and intense silence ensued, in which everyone suddenly seemed unsure of what to do. It was Khalfani who finally broke the silence again. "Listen," he said, "we need to finish this war. Am I missing something here?"

"Yeah," Farhad said, meeting Khalfani's gaze with a challenging stare. "You're missing a logical way to continue!"

"There is no way to continue!" Jacey interjected in a strained voice. "There's nothing to finish." She gestured helplessly to where they'd just watched Aurora's and Apple's demises.

All the while, Isis had been standing by, watching the exchange. She could feel the other soldiers' despair, and it suddenly struck her how deeply the loss of Aurora and Apple had impacted the group as a whole.

They may not have realized it at first, in the aftermath of their shock—but now, it was abundantly clear that losing Aurora was proving to be the army's undoing. She had been such a stabilizing force for them all; even those who didn't particularly like her still respected her. Watching one of Cairo's greatest warriors become a casualty at the hands of the evil around them had unraveled and unnerved them all—some of them, apparently, to the point of no return.

And deep down, Isis didn't exactly blame them. If one of Cairo's greatest had been driven to sacrifice herself but still hadn't been able to bring the whole horrifying ordeal to an actual end, what hope did the rest of them have?

And to make matters worse, Apple's death had only added insult to the injury. It made sense that after losing such a sweet and innocent soul, some of them were feeling too crushed to continue, even if it was at Khalfani's request.

Perhaps, thinking along the same lines, Khalfani's voice grew softer. Gentler. "She was important to me too, you know," he said, looking from Farhad to Jacey. "I've known her for years. I've known—knew—both of them for years. So, I know the last thing they'd want is for us to give up. They died trying to help us...Trying to save us. You all should know that. Conceding and accepting defeat is not how this is supposed to end. It can't. We're better than that."

"Then what is it that you want us to do?" Garth asked, eyeing Khalfani.

Khalfani looked at Garth for a second and then turned back towards the direction he'd heard Kek's voice. "To keep moving," he answered. "This thing, this Retrograde—we can't let it win. We can't even let it think it can win—or that it's already won."

Jacey gave a condescending laugh. "You speak as if it's a person."

A cold chill ran down Khalfani's spine, and he clenched his fists to keep himself from shuddering. "It's…it's an entity…"

"Oh whatever, Khal," Garth muttered, waving his hand dismissively. "Now, tell us, where is it that you want us to go?"

Khalfani pointed and swallowed, yet trying to keep his expression determined and resolute. "Out there. That way…We need to go that way," he said, gesturing in the direction where he'd heard Kek's voice.

Garth folded his arms across his chest. "You know what? I'm with Farhad. I'm not going, either. *Out there* does not sound like a decisive plan."

"Glad someone else has some sense," Farhad said approvingly.

"What bright ideas do you two have, then?" Tekem said, a deep frown on his face.

"Well, take a look around," Farhad said, gesturing to the changeling bodies and destruction in the city below. "Going out there," he then pointed towards where Khalfani had suggested they go, "is like willingly walking into more disaster. We'd be out in the open, where more changelings could easily spot us, like they did just now. Obviously, we need coverage." He turned and gestured to the woods. "I say if we're going to keep moving, we need to travel through the woods. That way, at least we're concealed and won't be blindly ambushed."

A muscle worked in Khalfani's jaw as he locked eyes with Farhad, considering his rationale. While he knew there was some reasonable logic to what he'd said, Khalfani's gut told him it was the wrong move. The woods wouldn't be providing them coverage from the Retrograde; instead, they would just be hindered from keeping track of Kek.

Khalfani knew his *pa* well enough to know that the man sometimes felt all-knowing. How he managed to keep track of things—people—so keenly was something Khalfani had yet been able to figure out. But he knew for certain the man would use the skill to his advantage if they were obliviously trekking through the woods under the false pretenses of being hidden.

He shook his head. "No, we can't go that way. It'll make things worse. If we don't stay out in the open, we can't see anyone—anything—sneaking up on us. We need to keep a clear view of what's coming." As he spoke, he sought Isis's gaze, exchanging a meaningful look with her. She nodded in return, showing that she understood.

"Yeah, maybe we'll see what's coming right before it slaughters us all," Jacey countered. "I'm sorry, Khalfani, but I'm with them on this one." She nodded to Farhad and Garth.

"Traveling through the woods sounds like a better plan to me. Who else agrees?"

A long, pregnant pause spread across the group. For a moment, no one moved, apart from their eyes silently darting around at each other.

"I'm going through the woods," Hydrus said, practically to no one's surprise. If Farhad, Jacey, and Garth were all going one way, he was sure to follow, completing the clique that was so well known throughout the soldiers.

Khalfani swallowed. "Guys, I have a bad feeling about this," he said, eyeing the four of them. "Please don't do this. We shouldn't be separating."

"Yeah. Well, we've got a bad feeling about your plan too," Farhad said. "But we know it's useless to convince you to do otherwise. So, suit yourselves. Just don't be surprised if you end up like Aurora and Apple." He then turned to the others who hadn't decided to join him. "And that goes for the rest of you too." Then, turning towards his loyal clique, he set off for the woods. "Come on."

Khalfani sighed, running an agitated hand through his hair.

Isis immediately came to his side, placing her hand on his shoulder. "It's their choice. There's nothing you can do. You tried, Khal. You tried…"

Khalfani nodded absentmindedly, though he was too distracted by the sight of the four soldiers leaving, heading into the woods. His stomach clenched.

"Khalfani?" He turned around, seeing Tekem stepping forward. "Forget them. We're staying with you, man." He moved forward, clasping Khalfani's hand in a firm shake and then slapping him on the back. "If President Mahmoud entrusted you to lead this army, it was for a reason." He then turned towards Isis and bowed respectfully.

Softly, the others remaining— including Kaiden, Lia, Aiari, Mirko, Orsel, Easton, and Amam—all murmured in agreement, nodding and bowing at Khalfani and Isis.

"So, what's next?" Kaiden asked, standing to his full height and meeting Khalfani eye-to-eye. It was a strange moment, for Isis could literally feel Kaiden's effort to not look at her. However, she could also tell his restraint was out of respect.

"Well, same as I said before," Khalfani responded. "We need to head that way, out in the open…" His voice trailed off as he refrained from adding *'out where I heard my poje's voice.'* He waited with bated breath, fearing another would speak up in protest. But none did.

"Lead the way, then," Lia said, smiling briefly at Khalfani.

He nodded and clasped his boomerang in one hand, and his gun in the other. "All right, guys. Follow me. Stay alert.

And most importantly, stay ready." He cast one last glance toward the woods where the other four had disappeared to, and then brought his eyes to Isis beside him.

She gave him an encouraging nod.

And then they were off.

* * *

"Farhad? Hey, wait. Where are you? Where are we going?" Jacey said, holding her hands out in front of her.

"I'm right here," Farhad replied irritably.

"Right where? I can't see you, either," Garth said.

"Yeah...it is getting darker in here," Hydrus stated nervously.

"If you guys would just shut up and follow me, there wouldn't be a problem," Farhad shot back from the front of the small group.

"We have no problem following you, that's why we're here," Jacey retorted. "However, it would be nice if you would tell us where the hell we're going!"

"Listen here," Farhad snarled, but was cut short by Hydrus's gasp. "What is it?"

"Guys?" Hydrus said. "This isn't funny anymore. I really can't see anything. Where are you...I...What is this? Fog?"

But the only answer he received was Jacey's scream.

"JACE!" Farhad screamed, automatically grabbing his gun in panic. "Jace! What happened? Where are you?" But in that moment, he realized that he, too, couldn't see anything.

None of them could see beyond an inch from their face, for dark mist had surrounded them, cutting them off from each other.

Farhad stared, his eyes growing wide as the mist began to swirl around him. If he didn't know any better, he would have thought his eyes were playing tricks on him, because there was no way the mist was sprouting arms and legs. He swore. "Are you guys seeing this?"

This time, it was Garth's scream that answered him.

Farhad swore again, at the top of his lungs as the mist figure leapt towards him. Instinctively, he fired his weapon. But unbeknownst to him, a stupefied Hydrus had been standing right in the bullet's path. He collapsed to the ground. But the mist continued to hide him from Farhad's view.

Jacey, however, had a perfect view of Hydrus, for she had dropped to the ground in fright, trying to escape the suffocating mist. Yet now, she looked into the dying eyes of her friend. He stared back at her, blood spilling out of his mouth—or at least, that's what Jacey initially thought it was…

She'd been screaming his name in denial when she finally noted that the blood oozing from his mouth looked more like tar. And instead of spilling onto the ground, it floated and took on a mist-like form. Bewildered, Jacey's mouth twisted open in horror…

And the Darkness propelled itself into her mouth and down her throat. Convulsing, she flipped over onto her back, clutching her throat and trying to breathe, but the pressure was too immense. She felt the Darkness expanding in her throat, and her very last memory was the unbearable pain ravishing her body as the world around her faded away.

Meanwhile, Garth stood just a few yards away, still unable to see his friends. But feeling the need to save himself, he spun around, trying to determine which way to flee. He settled on a slightly lit pathway before him, but only managed to take a few panicked steps before crashing to the ground, a pressure hitting him square in the middle of his back. Falling on his face, dirt filled his nostrils, and the wind was knocked clean out of his lungs. Determined to get away, he got on all fours, attempting to crawl to safety.

But there was no escaping the Darkness.

In a humanoid form, it sprouted legs and feet and stood on Garth's back. He collapsed onto the ground again, squirming under the pressure. He tried to move, to slide forward, but to his horror, he realized he couldn't. All the while, the pressure on his back grew stronger and stronger. The Darkness's misty-foot grew, covering all of Garth's body, pressing him into the ground until it squashed him like a bug.

And then there was Farhad, also just a few yards away, still unable to see anything that had just happened. He stood with his gun poised, ready to fire, regardless that his enemy remained elusive. His head snapping from side to side, he tried to detect any sounds of movement. Any traces of his friends. But there was nothing but mist around him.

Gritting his teeth, a fury built up inside of him. "YOU WON'T TAKE ME!" he shouted to his unseen enemy. "YOU HEAR ME? YOU WON'T TAKE ME!"

But then his screams grew silent upon seeing the mist swirling before him take on a humanoid shape once again. He aimed his gun and fired, but the mist could not be penetrated. Then, in the blink of an eye, the mist was on him. With a cold and dark hand that somehow felt like both liquid and air, the Darkness seized Farhad by the throat. Weakened by his oxygen supply suddenly being cut off, he dropped his gun. He reached for the Darkness, attempting to seize it in his hands, but it was like grasping thin air.

Farhad sputtered, his mouth gaping open in attempts to gather breath that kept evading him.

With its free hand, the Darkness reached inside Farhad's open mouth.

Farhad's eyes bulged as the hand went down his throat, then the entire arm—and soon, all of the Darkness. He dropped to the ground in agony, feeling as if his whole body was about to explode. Blood oozed from his ears, mouth, nostrils and eyes as pressure continued building into his throat. And mere seconds later, the Darkness, satisfied with the havoc it had just wrecked on the small group of four soldiers, exploded out of Farhad's throat, splattering the trees around him with his blood.

"Khal? What is it now?" Tekem said, noticing that his friend had come to a stop.

Beside him, Isis had stopped as well. But unlike the others, she already knew what was wrong. She could sense it. A cold chill ran down her spine, and she was fairly certain the air was tainted with the scent of blood.

She and Khalfani exchanged glances, intuitively knowing the other soldiers hadn't made it.

"Do you think the others are okay?" Orsel asked. It was the question that was on all of their minds—and a question they all deduced the answer to, judging from the expressions on Khalfani's and Isis's faces.

Isis turned away from the group to face Khalfani and spoke in a hushed tone. "Maybe we should retreat for a while," she said uncertainly. She bit her bottom lip and shook her head. "Khal, I think we're in over our heads right now. Things aren't going right…" Her voice trailed off as Tekem came to stand beside them, his brow narrowed.

"Don't mean to intrude," he said, "but umm…what the hell is going on, guys?"

Isis cleared her throat. "I was just saying I think we need to take another break. We need to…to reorganize and re-strategize. Before anything else has the chance to go wrong."

Tekem nodded. "Certainly doesn't seem like a bad idea to me."

"But where?" Khalfani asked. "Where do we go?"

"I've thought about that too," Isis chimed in. "We could go to one of my family's safehouses for a little while. It's an underground hideout, not far from here, we'd just need to follow this same path a short while longer." As she uttered the suggestion, however, Isis couldn't help briefly worrying about what her parents would think. If they showed up to the safehouse, she knew her parents were likely to find out about it.

How would they react, knowing Cairo's army—or what was left of it, rather—had retreated to a safehouse for respite? Would they think the army had failed Damara? Would they think they had all thrown in the towel regarding the Retrograde?

Would she eventually have to endure her eva saying, *'I told you so'*?

The thoughts left a bitter taste in Isis's mouth. She bit her lip. Yet, as quickly as they sprang up, they disappeared. She knew her parents' primary concern would always be her safety, along with the well-being of the army. If they needed a break, the Mahmouds would understand, especially after finding out how many soldiers they'd lost.

*How many we've lost...*The thought gave Isis a pause. There had been causalities in the war, like with Parr. And they had all seen what happened to Aurora and Apple. But the soldiers she'd been thinking about in that moment had been Jacey, Farhad, Garth, and Hydrus. Without knowing exactly what had happened to them, she simply knew they were gone. It was a fact she could feel in her bones.

She shuddered. She then locked eyes with Khalfani. "I don't know about you, but I've seen enough blood for one night."

"We all have," Lia said, stepping forward to stand beside Tekem. "So, what do we do now?"

"Isis says we should stop by her family's safehouse for a while to regroup. I personally think it's a good idea," Tekem said.

Immediately, the remaining soldiers all began muttering their agreement.

Khalfani simply stood for a moment. But eventually, he nodded. "All right, then," he said, tapping Isis on the shoulder. "Lead the way."

Isis took a deep breath and looked up to the sky, where a silent but angry flash of lightning pierced through the darkness. "All right. Come on, then," she said, and moved to the head of the group.

It was only a matter of moments before the trek proved that it was going to be more arduous than any of them had hoped—a gruesome sight greeting them to prove it.

"Oh God…" Easton whispered, coming to a halt. She averted her eyes, her stomach twisting with nausea.

"Is that…? No…" Kaiden whispered. "Damn…"

Isis saw it too. Bile rose in her throat. Soon, all the soldiers had come to a stop.

Khalfani rubbed his temples in distress, and Orsel abruptly turned around, heaving and retching onto the ground.

Ahead of them, perched on a tree, was the head of a befallen soldier. Farhad, to be more precise. Blood and sinew hung down from his severed neck, and his head was almost unrecognizable, staring at them with empty sockets where his eyes should have been. It was a message of what was to come.

Isis turned around and rested her hands on her knees, willing herself to not be sick. In her periphery, she could see that Khalfani was literally shaking with anger. He and Farhad had never been particularly close, but it was still unsettling to lose an army member. Farhad, like the others, had been one of theirs.

And his life had been taken…

By Kek.

Feeling the need to be strong for Khalfani's sake, Isis forced herself to stand upright. "Hey," she said, grabbing Khalfani by the shoulder and giving it a reassuring squeeze, "don't worry. We're going to stop this thing. I promise. We're going to stop *him…*"

Wordlessly, Khalfani nodded. He turned his head to the side and gave Isis's hand a quick kiss. "Let's keep moving," he said.

Anxious to leave the horrific sight behind, the soldiers continued walking, all of them picking up their paces now. And the farther they walked, the more they began to notice animals scurrying out of the forests, running for cover from the evil they felt lurking about.

And though no one else seemed to hear it, as they continued on their path, Khalfani and Isis could hear the eerie laughter occasionally drifting through the air, letting them know that Kek was out there—watching and waiting, making the hairs on the backs of their necks stand on end.

CHAPTER 13

Khalfani stared down at the ground as he walked, listening to his footsteps as well as the footsteps of the other soldiers around him. He tried to focus on the rhythm of their walking, letting it soothe his troubled mind as he worked his way into a meditative state. He knew there was so much that lied ahead of them, but in the moment, he just didn't want to think about it. He simply wanted a break from it all, at least for a little while.

Nevertheless, that proved to be a difficult feat. Every time he thought he'd succeeded in putting himself into a much-needed meditative trance, he was snapped back to reality by the sounds of soldiers sniffling behind him. Listening to their sniffs and knowing that tears were falling from their eyes made the harsh conditions around them impossible to escape, no matter how much he wanted to retreat from them. Some of the soldiers even sobbed outright, in obvious despair over what had recently happened and the peers they'd just lost.

Khalfani looked sideways to Isis, who walked silently, matching his pace. He wanted to reach out and take her hand, but another thought stopped him from acting on the inclination. Quite abruptly, he remembered the abject terror he'd felt when he hadn't been able to locate her during the fight—and how that terror had increased tenfold when the building she'd run into exploded.

But that wasn't what preoccupied his mind at the moment. Instead, he was thinking about what happened after she'd resurfaced unharmed—and different.

He could still see the way the deep brown tone of her eyes had temporarily been replaced with the color of red flames…

Sensing his stare, Isis turned to look at him.

Khalfani glanced around at his fellow soldiers, seeing the way they were all in their own worlds, wiping away tears, staring at the sky, or simply walking through emotional numbness. Convinced none of them were paying him any attention at the moment, he moved closer to Isis. "Ninna," he said quietly, "what's happening to us?"

She furrowed her brow. "What do you mean?"

Khalfani hesitated for a second. "I saw you after the building exploded…I saw when you reappeared. You were… *different…*"

Isis swallowed, for she knew exactly what he was referring to. She had felt different herself. Stronger. More powerful. And it had happened so abruptly that she wasn't even entirely sure how it had occurred. She simply knew that one moment, she'd been trapped inside the building, scared out of her mind and not knowing what to do, feeling as if she had doomed herself and failed her peers. But then, quite suddenly, everything around her had exploded. She'd felt the heat on her skin—and then, she'd felt it *inside* her skin. Shortly thereafter, she'd ended up back outside in the open, fighting changelings with a renewed strength that felt simultaneously foreign yet innate.

"You know it," Khalfani said. "And I know it, because something is different about me too..."

Isis looked at Khalfani and shook her head. She sighed, turning her gaze back to the path before them. "Khal, if I knew, I'd tell you. But after seeing what just happened with..." She paused, her voice trailing off and her throat suddenly feeling tight. Farhad's head impaled on the tree, Parr's gruesome death, and Aurora's and Apple's demises all flashed through her head in quick succession. As horrible as all of that had been, she compared it to the immense power she felt and knew that somehow, all hope wasn't lost. "Listen, all I know is that the gods are involved. This is beyond us now, Khal. Something more—

something *greater*—is happening here. We just have to see it through. The *Hallah* has something planned. I can feel it."

Khalfani nodded his head, his expression contemplative.

"What are you doing?" Isis asked, watching as he reached for the communication device on his wrist.

"Calling your *pa*. I've been meaning to mention it to you. He probably needs an update..."

Isis nodded and swallowed. "Yeah, you're right," she said, though she dreaded giving her *poje* the bad news.

They continued walking, staring at the back of the heads of the soldiers in front of them while waiting to be connected to Maat.

"Khalfani!" Maat said when the connection was finally made.

Khalfani cleared his throat as he slowed his pace and adjusted his earpiece. "Hello, sir."

"Hi, *Poje*," Isis said, tuning her own device into the call and adjusting her earpiece as well.

"How are you? We've been so worried," Maat said.

"We're...okay..." Khalfani answered, his voice somewhat quaking.

"What's wrong?" Maat said immediately.

"We can't speak for long, sir," Khalfani informed. "But regretfully, I have to tell you—we've had some major losses."

He swallowed. "During the battle, Parr, Apple, and…and Aurora didn't make it, sir." He paused, letting the information sink in. Hearing him say Apple's and Aurora's names, some of the other soldiers glanced over their shoulders, noticing that he was on a call.

"And after the battle," Isis said, seeing that Khalfani was having difficulty resuming, "Farhad, Garth, Jacey, and Hydrus separated from us and…it…they…They didn't make it, either…*Poje,* we can't even bring them back for a burial. There's nothing…"

"I'm so sorry to hear this," Maat said, his voice thick after a prolonged pause. He sighed, and Isis could envision him closing his eyes and rubbing his temples.

Khalfani forced himself to continue. "Aurora—she sacrificed herself after Apple was killed by a changeling. Her sacrifice—it bought us some time and killed a lot of them. I don't think the rest of us would have made it without what she did for us."

"Sounds like Aurora was herself right up to the end, then," Maat said, his voice mixed with pride and sorrow. "How are the rest of you holding up?"

"As best as we can, sir."

"Well, that's all I can ask of you, son," Maat replied. "Please, keep me posted."

"Will do," Khalfani replied. "As for now, Isis is taking us to one of the hideouts so that we can recuperate and regroup."

"Good idea," Maat said. "Take care of yourselves, the both of you."

"Yes, sir," Khalfani said. He was just about to end his connection to Maat when Isis interrupted.

"Wait, *poje*," she said, a thought reoccurring to her.

"Yes, *iva*?"

"What is the Dark Order? You didn't get a chance to explain the last time we spoke," she said.

Khalfani's eyes widened, surprised that he had almost forgotten about this.

"Yes, right," Maat said. "The Dark Order is basically what Kek has embraced. It means that he has joined forces with the Darkness to fight against the Light."

"In other words, he's joined evil to fight against good," Khalfani said, a deep scowl forming across his brow.

"Yes, my son," Maat said. "Our gods are part of The Light. They fight for truth, justice, and love. They protect the innocent and those kind at heart. But The Darkness and its Order or organization are against The Light. Its mission is power, destruction, and pain. It wants nothing more than to enslave Damara and every other planet to carry out its wishes. Everyone working directly with the Darkness has joined the

Order to wage war with the Light. Unfortunately, The Darkness wants you both, and it will be relentless in trying to get you. It knows how special—how powerful—you both are."

"*Poje*, are you saying this…this thing…wants us to fight against The Light and the very gods that we worship?" Isis stammered.

"Yes, and—" But Maat was interrupted. Khalfani and Isis listened, eager for him to continue, but hearing voices in the background clearly trying to catch his attention. "I'm sorry, you two, but I have to go," he said once his voice returned on the line. He spoke quickly. "But let me finish by warning you both, be careful. The Darkness can easily disguise itself as just about anything, including all that is good. So, do not be easily fooled. Trust your instincts so that you do not succumb to its treachery. This will be the greatest battle of your lives. Stay alert. Stay vigilant."

"We will, sir," Khalfani said. "*Ose.*" *Thank you.*

"Stay strong, son."

"*Sahha, Poje.*" *Goodbye, Papa.* "I love you," Isis said.

"*Sahha, iva.*" *Goodbye, baby.* "I love you too."

When they ended the call with Maat, Lia glanced back at them. "Feels like we're in some kind of dream, doesn't it? Especially…" her voice cracked, "especially with Aurora and

Apple not being here…" Tears welling in her eyes, she turned her head. "Or a nightmare is more like it, I guess."

Tekem pat her on the back in a consoling gesture. "They gave us a fighting chance, though. So, let's not dwell on their demise. Let's focus on making sure their deaths weren't in vain. We have to keep finding the bright side in all of this," he said wisely.

A brief silence passed over the group as they walked, until a sudden bout of snickering broke it. The soldiers all looked around at each other, trying to figure out who was laughing and what could possibly be funny at a time like this.

"Sorry," Mirko said, shaking his head and still wearing a slight grin. "It's just, I remember meeting Apple for the first time. She was just this bright-eyed sunny-looking kid, really. And she told me she was joining the army. I thought she had to be kidding. I mean, the girl looked more like a beauty pageant contestant than a soldier." At this, several other soldiers laughed in agreement. "She must have known that I wasn't taking her seriously…She walked away, and I ended up thinking to myself, *'Not only is this little girl physically weak, but she must be mentally weak as well if she just got so offended by me. She's never going to make it in Cairo's army.'* I turned around, heading to get my dumbbells, and all of a sudden, I heard a whistling noise and felt my hat flying right off my head. I turned around, and there Apple was, standing with a bow and arrow. She had literally shot the hat off my head! It was such a close and clean shot. I think she probably gave me a haircut along with it! Right then and there, I learned to not judge a book by its cover."

A few of the soldiers started laughing, and not before long, all of them were laughing—their tears of sorrow morphing into tears of hilarity, envisioning the young and sweet Apple besting a big, muscle-bound guy like Mirko.

"That girl was trained by the greatest, and it showed," Khalfani said.

"You got that right," Kaiden agreed.

"Just being around Aurora made all of us stronger," Orsel commented. "So, just imagine being raised by her, like Apple was." She looked up to the sky, squinting her narrow eyes as if she could still see the yellow and purple rainbow going across it.

"We all would be toast right now if it weren't for them," Aiari said. "Both of them had some pretty vivid imaginations. They inspired a lot of the weapons I made. As a matter of fact," he turned toward Khalfani, "I once heard Apple talking with Jacey one day about how cool it would be to control weapons with your mind. That's how I got the idea for your boomerang, Khal."

Khalfani raised an eyebrow. "Really? I never knew that."

"Sorry, I'm stuck on the part about you overhearing Apple talking to Jacey. I didn't know the two of them were friends," Lia said, pushing her red hair behind her ear as she turned to look at Aiari.

It was Easton who replied, though. "Well, it's *Apple* we're talking about. Even the hard-headed soldiers couldn't find it in their hearts to dislike her. Not really. And it also helped that she was known as Aurora's daughter. Everyone respected Aurora, even the tough guys. Look at how Parr or Farhad used to back off whenever Aurora intervened. They might have talked their trash to her every once in a while, but they would never dare outright disrespect her."

"Yeah. Some of them wouldn't have met such a harsh fate if…" Lia's voice quivered again, "if Aurora had been here to intervene when they decided to leave us…"

"Well, we don't necessarily know that," Kaiden said softly. "I mean, look at what happened to Parr. Who's to say, you know? Those changelings—they could have gotten to any one of us."

Isis shuddered. Somehow, she didn't think it was changelings that had gotten to Farhad, Jacey, Garth, and Hydrus. Yet, it didn't seem like the time to share that opinion.

"Aurora was pretty torn up about that," Kaiden resumed quietly. "I saw her when it happened. I was nearby. There were so many changelings around us, it was hard to see what was going on with everyone else. By the time she saw Parr surrounded and sent her whip after the changelings swarming him, it was too late. I could see it in her face how devastated she was that she hadn't helped sooner…I think it left her distracted. That's probably why she didn't notice Apple…"

The group fell silent again, Kaiden's recollections weighing heavily on their minds. They had all shared Aurora's frustration, in that moment. Parr may have been far from the most well-liked soldier, but none of them had wanted to see him meet such a horrible fate. At the end of the day, he was still one of them.

Isis, who had been listening appreciatively to the soldiers reminisce about their fallen, gave a sad smile. "We just have to keep faith that everything happens for a reason."

"Right," Tekem said. "Like I mentioned before, as much as it sucks to lose Aurora, I just try to keep things in perspective. Had she not sacrificed herself, there wouldn't be any of us in Cairo's army left. And then where would that leave our city?"

"Yeah," Amam said, speaking up for the first time in a while. "I hate to say it, but those changelings were kicking our asses."

Though the mood had grown somber again, there was something in the tone of Amam's voice that sent several of the soldiers snickering again. They covered their mouths, trying to stifle it at first, but their attempts proved useless. Their snickers burst into the air, unable to be restrained. Not before long, another round of laughter broke out among the whole group. And for those few blissful seconds, the surviving members of Cairo's army were able to forget the weight of the world was on their shoulders.

"Well, here we are," Isis said sometime later, announcing their arrival to the secret hideout.

The group slowed to a halt, confused as to what Isis was talking about. They stood before a stretch of land that looked barren, save for the rocky formation before them.

Isis smirked at their stupefied expressions. "What? You didn't think it would be out in the open for everyone to see, did you? What good would a hideout be if it was so easy to find?"

* * *

Back at the hideout located under the Mahmoud palace, a brooding Maat sat silently in the control room, watching those around him cheer.

The surveillance screens had detected something major going on above-ground—an earthquake of sorts. Although it seemed things had been too chaotic to get a strong signal to showcase the actual battle, once things calmed down, they were able to capture images of the aftermath. And as far as the eye could see, the ground was littered with the bodies of dead changelings. Hence, it appeared that Cairo's army had made quite a victory—or at least, that was the impression everyone had been under.

But then, Maat heard from Khalfani and Isis, and consequently had to face the harsh reality that appearances had been deceiving; they had no real victory to celebrate—not with all the soldiers that had been lost during the battle, the great Aurora in particular.

He sighed again, remembering his first time meeting Aurora as a young woman. She'd always had a fiery spirit, and even from their first encounter, he'd known she was going to amount to something special. Losing her from Cairo's army felt like a loss almost too much to bear. And considering the soldiers were planning to retreat to one of the hideouts for a while, Maat knew that it clearly was too much for them to bear as well.

"Sir, is there something wrong?" Elias Onai said, approaching slowly with a concerned crease marking his forehead. While the others continued celebrating what they thought had been a victorious first battle, Elias was the only one to notice that Maat looked less than thrilled.

"All is not as well as it appears, Elias," Maat said heavily and then stood to his full height. "I need to address everyone. I've got some important updates."

Now that Maat was standing, the others began paying him more attention, some of them finally noticing his demeanor. Elias silenced the group. As Maat made his way to the center of the room, smiles began to fade. When he cleared his throat, you could hear a pin drop.

During that silence, Rania appeared in the doorway, crossing her arms and leaning back against the wall, waiting just like the others, to hear what her husband had to say.

"Good evening, all," Maat said grimly, a sad smile flickering on his countenance. "I hate to be one to destroy the celebratory mood in the atmosphere, but I have necessary information to relay to you."

In his periphery, Maat saw Elias Onai shifting on his feet, just as eager and apprehensive to hear the news as everyone else.

"Now, don't get me wrong," Maat continued, "I am as happy about the small victory Cairo's army has had as the rest of you are, as well as the people of Zahara and the remaining population of Illyian. But it has to be noted that the victory was not without a tremendous cost... Not long ago, I spoke with Khalfani Abaza, and my daughter, Isis Mahmoud. They were in the battle, fighting bravely alongside their fellow soldiers. And they informed me that the army suffered great losses." He paused to clear his throat again, and then took a deep breath as he glanced at the faces surrounding him. Everyone stood around the control room, their stances, stiff and tensed. "Among the fallen in Cairo's army are Parr Grixti, Jacey Burnell, Farhad Spinks, Hydrus Rode, Garth Sturla, Apollonia Imamu…and Aurora Imamu."

There had been surprised gasps here and there as Maat recited the names, but the outright cries of disbelief did not sound until he'd said Aurora's name. Near the doorway, he saw Rania clutch her chest in shock.

"*Sik*," someone swore. "How did this happen? Didn't the soldiers all receive their inoculations?"

Maat nodded. "The inoculations prevent one from becoming a changeling, but it cannot protect one from being attacked by changelings and the Darkness." There was more muttering, but Maat held up a hand, silencing the room once more. "I know this news hits heavily on all of our hearts. But we must keep our soldiers, the fallen and those still fighting for us, in our thoughts and prayers. Those we've lost—let the gods know we appreciate their sacrifice. These brave men and women put their lives on the line to help ensure our safety during these troubled times. And please, know that the great warrior Aurora Imamu made the ultimate sacrifice; she sacrificed herself so that so many of the others could stand a fighting chance." He paused again and raised his hand in salute. "To Aurora," he said. "*Ose*." *Thank you.*

The others followed suit, making the same saluting gesture. "Aurora, *ose,*" they all said in unified, strong voices.

"Now," Maat resumed, "after much deliberation, I've decided the next steps that need to be taken, and I want to discuss them with you, as well. But first, I have some integral information that needs to be shared with you, just so that you all have a better understanding of what we're up against.

"I know it's been confusing, but I've been able to gain some clarity in the distinguishing factors between the actual Retrograde, and the Darkness. You see, it's become apparent to me that the Darkness is an entity of itself. It always has been. It is a force in the universe—the *Hallah*—whose main purpose is to work against The Light. It is The Light's opposite or Antimatter. Therefore, as The Light seems to preserve all that is good, The Darkness seeks to destroy it. It thrives on power, fear, and violence. The Retrograde, on the other hand, is a naturally occurring plague of destructive chaos. Hence, it's not difficult to see why The Darkness would trail the Retrograde, seek to strengthen it and use it as a tool to bring entire planets to their knees or even to their demise. Evil and chaos go hand-in-hand. The two are a perfect match."

Maat paused for an instant, furrowing his brow. "However, there is definitely something complicating matters this time around—or exacerbating them, I should say." He turned around, making eye-contact with Elias, who stood to the side of him. "Listen carefully," he said, and then turned back to the audience before him. "It was a little while ago that I learned precisely what is making this Retrograde so different from those that came before it. And that reason happens to be one man in particular. Regretfully, it is someone I know—someone I've known—for quite some time." He looked back at Elias again. "The person I'm referring to is a former friend of mine by the name of Mr. Kek Abaza."

Murmuring broke out among those in the room, some of them recognizing the name, and some not. Maat looked towards Rania, only to find her staring at him in disbelief; she knew very well who Kek Abaza was.

"Mr. Abaza was always a genius. But unfortunately, he has always been a misguided man, and the Darkness has been using him and his genius to maximize the chaos The Retrograde intends to spread. I have learned that Kek Abaza has a tracking system that even outmatches our own. I believe Kek designed it to somehow harness the power of The Retrograde. He likely thought it would serve as a tool for him to ascend to power and somehow eventually take control of the regions of Damara. In his quest to do so, he attracted the attention of the Darkness, who also shared his plight." Maat gestured towards the machines and surveillance screens surrounding them. "Kek calls the machine The Sharir Device. That, my friends, is what we must focus on to put a stop to the Retrograde's control and to help even the battlefield for what's left of our army. Kek's Sharir Device has been strengthening the effects of the Retrograde, and in turn, working directly with the Darkness. What we're dealing with is Kek Abaza, the Retrograde, and the Darkness, all forming a trinity of evil, determined to destroy us all. And if these forces succeed in destroying Damara, our neighboring planets won't stand a chance...

"I simply cannot let that happen. Elias," Maat turned toward his adviser again, "you and I must go to Kek's fortress. I located it recently using our surveillance equipment. We must get ahold of his tracking system. It took some time, but I managed to interfere with the device's signal, scrambling it and hindering its ability to track our soldiers and strengthen the Retrograde for the time being. That means that its effect will be halted for a little while. But Kek, he is a smart man, so this temporary fix will not hold for long. That's why we need to act while we still can, while we still have the slight advantage."

"What is it precisely that we need to do with the Sharir device, sir?" Elias asked.

Maat nodded. "I'm glad you ask. My plan is to reverse the device's signal. As of now, it seems that it's programmed to intensify the Retrograde's effects and can even pinpoint areas to reach and cause the most damage. Additionally, it has uncanny surveillance capabilities to confirm whether or not its targets have been compromised. If we can reverse the device's effects, we can literally weaken the Retrograde so much that it will no longer be a threat to Damara or any other planet. We can obliterate it, once and for all."

"Are you sure that's going to work?" Rania stepped farther into the room, her voice full of concern—and opposition. She shook her head. "Maat, I won't have you going out there for a plan if you aren't one-hundred percent sure it will work."

"Rania, *ti biyeh,* you know I cannot make any guarantees. However, I feel that this is our best shot. I know how frightening this all is, but I need you to be strong. Our army and our nation need you to be strong." He gestured around to the room at large. "We need to have faith that The Light will prevail over Darkness."

Rania locked eyes with her husband. When she spoke, her voice quivered, and she practically forgot that she and Maat weren't the only ones present. "Maat, is it not bad enough that our daughter is out there? And that we've lost so many soldiers? Cairo's army has been out there to witness the Retrograde first-hand. And if what they've been through is enough to make them retreat to one of the hideouts, why on earth would you risk going out there at a time like this?!"

"Because if things are as bad out there as we believe them to be, it's that much more important for us all to do our share in winning this war," Maat said sternly. "For our army's sake, for our daughter's sake—it's up to us to act now in a time like this, to do what we must for the greater good. Sometimes, we just have to accept that responsibility can involve significant sacrifice."

Rania's lips quivered, but she said no more.

Maat kept his eyes focused on her, almost as if he too had forgotten there were others in the room. "You have a role in all of this, too, you know, *ti biyeh*."

She pressed her lips into a tight line and gave her husband a questioning look.

"You, Mrs. Mahmoud, will be needed to keep watch of things here. In my absence, you're in charge—along with someone else who I think will be of great assistance to you, and who has arrived just in time." He looked towards the doorway and smiled appreciatively.

The others in the room followed Maat's gaze, seeing the man who had just arrived on the premises.

Immediately after hearing the news from Khalfani and Isis, Maat had made another important call. In light of what they were facing, he knew they needed the help of one of the most skilled and intelligent warriors he knew—someone who just happened to be considered the greatest friend he had.

"Everyone, this is my dear friend, Mukhalas. He's from the region of Zahara. He and my wife will be in charge during my and Elias's absence. I implore you all; please, show them the same respect as you have shown me."

Rania looked towards Mukhalas, who had given her a small nod in greeting. Meanwhile, everyone else had turned to eye Mukhalas, nodding respectfully at him before bowing towards Maat. "Yes, sir," they all muttered.

CHAPTER 14

Isis stepped forward and studied the rock formation before them, tuning out the confused whispers behind her. Squinting her eyes, she finally located it—the very fine lining in the rocks that outlined the hideout's entrance. Even though she'd known what she was looking for, she still found it impressive how well hidden it was; outsiders would never stand a chance of finding it.

Now that she'd located the doorway, she stared at it, remembering the instructions her *pa* had given her regarding how to get it to open. She brought her gaze precisely to the hidden door's center, staring keenly at it for ten seconds. Subsequently, a tiny dot that she was sure the others hadn't even noticed, flashed, letting her know she'd successfully activated the retina scan. Quickly, she thought of the access code, silently reciting it three times in her head.

The hidden door began to rumble, finally making itself visible as it creaked open amid the rocks.

"You've got to be kidding me…" Easton said, moving forward right along with the rest of the soldiers, in awe.

Isis looked back at them and smirked. "Told you it was right here," she said, and then stepped forward, squeezing her body through the small opening that had been revealed. Immediately, she was engulfed into darkness, save for one glowing red button on the other side of the door she'd just squeezed through. "Come on, guys," she called out to the others.

Though it was dark, she could see that Khalfani was the first to come through after her. Then came Tekem and Lia. Soon, the others were all there, crowded onto the landing with Isis.

"There are rails along the walls," Isis informed. "Hold on." She then pressed the glowing red button. The door closed, and the landing lowered, taking them underground.

An amazed silence spread across the group as they came to a stop, the intense darkness around them slowly lifting until they could make out a long corridor stretching beyond them.

"This looks like the entryway to the Mahmoud complex," Kaiden observed.

Isis nodded. "Yeah, that was the idea. The comforts of home." Without further ado, she led them ahead. As the corridor came to an end, the soldiers found themselves in a large opening that looked just like an underground mansion.

People walked by here and there, many of them whom Isis recognized as working for her *pa.* Upon seeing the soldiers, several of them nodded respectfully, bowed, or saluted them—making it obvious that Maat had alerted them to their upcoming arrival.

"Make yourselves at home, guys," Isis said. "There's plenty of rooms, beds, showers, and food for everyone."

"Ugggh, I so need a shower!" Easton exclaimed, wasting no time hurrying forward in search of one.

Tired, hungry, and also wanting showers, the rest of the soldiers rushed forward, eager to search the facility for whatever suited their most urgent needs.

Isis stared after them, a bittersweet feeling coming over her. A part of her felt grateful for suggesting they come to the hideout, glad to be able to offer her fellow soldiers some respite, even if just for a little while. Another part of her, however, was already anticipating the dread of when they would have to return above ground and face the additional horrors that awaited them.

How many other causalities would there be when that time came? She shuddered, not even wanting to think about it. After all the losses they'd just suffered, the remaining soldiers had all become even more of a family than before. The thought of losing any of them now made Isis nauseous.

It wasn't until then that she realized while all the other soldiers had scurried off, Khalfani had stayed. She turned around, finding him standing behind her, simply watching her.

"Are you all right, Ninna?" he asked gently, coming to stand beside her. But before waiting for an answer, he gathered her into his arms. Holding her, it dawned on him just how long he'd been waiting to do so.

In return, Isis practically melted in his arms. Her eyes closed, she relaxed her head on his shoulder, basking in the feel of his strong arms and the warmth of his skin. There had been so much on both of their minds, but suddenly, none of it seemed to matter anymore.

Remembering Khalfani had asked her a question, Isis lifted her head to answer him. Instead, however, she was stopped by his lips colliding onto hers. The kiss was urgent, intense, passionate…

A kiss as if Khalfani hadn't been sure he'd have the opportunity to give her another one.

How long it lasted, Isis couldn't tell. All she could do was respond to it, letting it momentarily drown out her worries.

Finally, their lips parted. They were both panting slightly, though still clinging to each other, standing with their foreheads pressed together. Isis closed her eyes again, feeling the warmth of Khalfani's breath on her face, while they breathed in each other's scents…

"Marry her, Khal."

The two of them jumped apart, startled by the sound of another voice—having temporarily forgotten other people even existed. They turned around, finding Tekem walking towards them, a playful yet serious expression on his face.

Khalfani cleared his throat awkwardly, but Tekem spoke again before either he or Isis could say anything. "Life is too short to wait, guys. We've learned that lesson in abundance today."

"Very true," another voice chimed in. It wasn't until then that Khalfani and Isis noticed Lia had been lurking behind Tekem—his tall, lean figure having initially obscured her. She grinned at the two of them and then looked around. "We could do a beautiful wedding right here. This place is perfect!"

Khalfani laughed, running his hand over his head and glancing sideways at Isis, checking her reaction. A bit surprised, he saw that she didn't appear particularly bothered by the idea.

His heart pounded…

She looked at him and shrugged her shoulders. "Honestly, I don't think I really want a big, fancy wedding anyhow. I'd be okay just using the poor man's method. Who needs all the extra fanfare? The only thing I need is you." She locked eyes with Khalfani.

"Are you…are you serious?" he stammered.

Isis nodded. "I am…"

"Good," Tekem said, smirking, "because it was a serious suggestion."

Now, Isis laughed, looking back at Khalfani's best friend. She thought she'd seen it before, but now she was certain that there was something intimate—longing, even—in the way Lia was looking at him. For a moment, Isis worried Tekem didn't notice—that he was so focused on the war and on his best friend, that he was missing what was right in front of him. But then, he looked at Lia, just as she tucked a lock of luscious red hair behind her ear. His gaze lingered, and it quickly became evident that Tekem was indeed aware, and that the attraction was mutual.

"So, what's this poor man's method you speak of?" Khalfani said, one eyebrow raised.

Tekem and Lia stood nearby, eager to listen in.

Isis paused for a moment, recalling how her *eva* had explained it to her. She glanced down at her arm and rolled up her sleeve. "Are you familiar with how wedding vows are activated through the arm-chip?"

Khalfani nodded. "Yeah."

"Well, that's all it takes. No fancy ceremony is really needed. You just say your vows to the person you want to marry and then touch arms. This is enough to activate the wedding vows, and announcements get sent out to your hometown, alerting everyone of the nuptials."

"Hmm," Lia said, tilting her head sideways. "So all this time, I've thought a wedding officiant had to be involved."

Isis smirked. "Yeah, I thought so too, until recently."

"I guess you learn something new every day," Tekem commented. "Now, I think that's enough stalling." His eyes flickered from Khalfani to Isis. "So, what's it going to be, guys?"

Isis felt her cheeks warm as she saw Khalfani squirming in her periphery.

Lia laughed and hit Tekem on the arm. "Oh, stop it. I think they deserve privacy to discuss this on their own terms. Stop pressuring them."

Tekem playfully grabbed at her waist, causing her to squee. "Oh, *I'm* pressuring them? Seems you were just chiming in with your agreement with my thoughts not too long ago…"

Lia shrugged her shoulders. "I'm not saying that I don't agree with you. I'm just saying, they need time to discuss amongst themselves, that's all…"

"Mmmhmm."

Lia sighed. "It still would be awesome to have a little ceremony, though, you know? Give us something happy to look forward to after losing Aurora and—" Her voice stopped abruptly. Caught off guard by her own emotions, Lia abruptly turned around to face away from the others.

Tekem, however, was there instantly, wrapping a consoling arm around her. “It’s all right, honey. Come here,” he said gently.

Isis lightly touched Khalfani’s arm and nudged her head, indicating that they should leave. She had a feeling that Tekem and Lia, too, needed some privacy.

* * *

As night fell across the land and the surviving members of Cairo’s army preoccupied themselves with taking refuge in the hideout, the Darkness outside continued with its own plans.

It lurked about, moving in the form of a dark black mist, eagerly seeking its next victims.

Despite the safety of the hideout and the recent malfunctioning of the Sharir device, emotions ran high among the soldiers, making it easy for the Darkness to sniff them out. Drawn to the chaotic feelings running through them, the Darkness began to creep towards the secret hideout…

It slithered like snakes made of mist, hovering closer and closer to the hideout’s entrance, searching for a way inside. Yet, just when it was starting to get close enough to pose a real threat to those inside, a bright purple glow formed right outside the hideout’s entrance.

Confused, the Darkness came to a halt and shifted into the shape of Kek Abaza. He stood, a figure of solidified mist, eyeing the purple glow before him. His head tilted, feeling simultaneously curious and annoyed. He was so close—the Darkness inside of him practically salivating at the scent of the army inside, wanting so badly to feed on their fear and despair.

Yet, with every step closer he took toward the entrance, the brighter the purple light grew…

It took a moment for Kek to realize that he had suddenly started to feel dizzy. Lightheaded.

The purple light was draining his energy.

For the first time since the Darkness had joined him, Kek felt a prickle of fear. He moved backwards, the dark swirls around him shifting away from the hideout's entrance. And then, miraculously, the Darkness itself grew cold with apprehension at the sound of a disembodied voice.

"The gods have decided the appointed time and place, and this is neither, Kek Abaza. On behalf of the gods, I will not permit you to seek anyone inside the protection of this dwelling until that time has arrived. Enough blood has already been shed."

If Kek had known better, he would have recognized the voice as that of none other than Aurora Imamu. Nevertheless, the simple thought of anyone telling him what he was or wasn't allowed to do immediately made his short-lived fear turn into rage.

He was the Darkness. He controlled the Retrograde. He was the ultimate power and authority. No one or nothing told him what to do.

In response to his fury, the black mist began to swirl around Kek like a tornado until he was swept along with it. Morphing into one powerful gust of wind, Kek and the Darkness charged for the hideout's entrance, intending to push through the purple glow.

As he reached the purple light, however, it was like running into an impenetrable brick wall. Kek bounced off of it, pain running through his body from the collision. Taking on his humanoid form again, he gritted his teeth and clenched his fists, cursing the gods.

"Remember this day," he growled, "because soon, you will learn who's the most powerful. Nothing can stop the Darkness, and I'm going to make you regret ever trying!"

"You are right. We will see who is strong and who is weak but only at the appointed time," Aurora's voice said, the purple light pulsing with each word she spoke.

Kek listened, his every instinct wanting to fight back right then and there. But instead, he retreated, recognizing that this was a battle to resume on another day.

Moving away from the hideout's entrance, Kek dematerialized into the mist around him and drifted away, heading back to his home.

As Kek and the Darkness retreated, the purple light dimmed and darkened, turning into a mist of its own, resembling a sort of shiny crushed obsidian stone. The mist grew solid and sprouted limbs. Soon, in its place, a sable colored she-wolf appeared. It looked into the sky with eyes like glowing amethyst, following the last of the Darkness as it drifted away through the air.

Purple eyes sparkling in the darkness, the wolf settled itself by the hideout's entrance, ready to keep watch while the oblivious soldiers rested inside.

CHAPTER 15

Maat sat in the backseat of the caravan, his heart heavy with the goodbye he'd had to exchange with Rania. It felt horrible to leave her behind, but he knew that she had finally come to an understanding of what he was doing and why he had to do it. After he'd finished addressing the rest of the crowd, the two of them had snuck off to talk some more in private.

"Whatever you do, schvak se." Be careful. *"Come back to me, and make sure our daughter is safe,"* Rania had said once she'd finally reached the point of acceptance.

"I promise you, ti biyeh—I will do just that if the gods are willing," had been Maat's response.

After that, the others residing in the hideout had bid him, Elias, and the small entourage accompanying them farewell and safe travels.

As the caravan left the premises of the Mahmoud palace, though, it was not without notice from the rest of the town. First, there had only been a few onlookers. But they grew in size until a whole crowd had left the safety of their homes—some of them even having walked over through word-of-mouth—just to see what the President was up to and to find out where he was going.

Looking out at the people—the people who counted on him—Maat felt a deep sense of responsibility towards every single one of them. "Stop the car," he said, leaning forward in the backseat to address Elias.

Elias glanced at Maat through the rearview mirror, his eyebrows raised. "Are you sure about that, sir?"

In the passenger's seat, a guard turned around to eye Maat as well.

"Yes, I'm sure," Maat said, somewhat irritably. "I cannot leave like this. I need to address the people."

With that, Elias slowed the caravan to a stop. Immediately, the crowd began to swarm around it, yelling, knocking on the windows, and attempting to get a glimpse of Maat inside.

"Hold on, sir," the guard said, and then proceeded to exit the vehicle himself. Maat watched as he and some of the other accompanying guards traveling in subsequent vehicles began pushing the crowd back, creating some distance between them and the vehicle.

Elias then took a deep breath and exited the caravan next, rounding to the backdoor and opening it for Maat.

"Thank you," Maat said with a nod and climbed out of the caravan.

His presence was met with a hush, and the crowd eagerly awaited what he had to say.

"Good evening, everyone," he prefaced, his voice projecting over the large gathering before him. He glanced into the faces surrounding him, seeing the deep fear and confusion in their eyes. Though they were outdoors, and the weather was comfortable, their trepidation permeated and stifled the air.

It was in that moment that Maat Mahmoud realized it would be detrimental to tell the people precisely what he was doing, for that would only intensify their apprehension. Still, he knew he had to say something.

He had to leave them with some kind of hope and peace of mind.

"I know these are troubling times we are living in," he resumed. "And believe me, I share all the same concerns and fears as you all do. As many of you know, my very own daughter—my one and only child—is out there fighting this Retrograde. And while I cannot divulge too many details, I know it has been difficult on our army. That being said, I remain confident that this Retrograde can be stopped." He paused, letting the confidence and authority in his voice resonate through the crowd. "I also want you all to know that as your President, I will do whatever it takes to see that we succeed in bringing this Retrograde to a successful end."

Maat paused again, taking in the crowd and pleased to see that many of their faces had gone from frightened to optimistic, just as he had hoped.

He was just about to bid the crowd farewell when he caught sight of a middle-class woman forcing her way forward through the crowd, pushing and shoving her way to the front with a deep crease sketched across her forehead. Her eyes were blazing and bloodshot, and even though she wasn't speaking, her lips were quivering.

Maat felt a pang go through his chest, immediately recognizing the woman.

"Sir," she cried out, unflinchingly meeting his gaze.

"Yes, ma'am?" Maat said, though he already dreaded what was to come next.

"You say your very own daughter is currently fighting in Cairo's army, so I know that means you are carefully tracking the army's progress. My son—Parr Grixti—is fighting alongside your daughter. But there have been terrible rumors..." She paused, her lips quivering more than ever now. "I need to hear the truth from you. I want to know...Do you know what has become of my son?"

Her question sent their surroundings into stony silence, and Maat's heart felt heavy. As a parent, he knew the fear of losing a child was second to none, and he felt that fear himself, knowing that his daughter was out there too.

Actually losing a child, however—that was a pain Maat felt too harsh to even comprehend.

As the mother of Parr Grixti continued to stare at him, demanding a response, he knew the only respectful thing he could do was give her an answer.

He bowed his head at the woman, lowering his gaze to the ground.

"Although Parr fought valiantly, he was unfortunately killed in battle." Maat said.

"No," the woman breathed in despair.

Maat righted himself again and looked the woman in the eyes. "I am so sorry for your loss, ma'am. We all are. Your son was a valuable member of Cairo's army, and he showed great bravery even in the face of adversity. You have my word that he will always be remembered as a war hero and that we will ensure your needs are cared for moving forward."

The woman had fallen to her knees, while concerned citizens surrounded her, patting her shoulders in attempts to console her. But she was beyond consoling.

"His body! Where is his body?! Is there anything left of my son?! Please!" she screamed hysterically, her voice so shrill it made the hairs on Maat's arms stand on end. His throat tightened. From what Isis and Khalfani had described to him, those who'd been killed didn't even have bodies left to honor with burials.

"What about my daughter?" another concerned parent spoke up. Soon, voices shouted from all around, asking about the statuses of their children serving in the army. Their voices reached a feverish crescendo, parents everywhere fearing the worst about their children.

Maat raised his hands, trying to silence the crowd. "Please," he said, speaking over them, "my information is limited at the time. I'm sorry. As more information becomes available, I promise to relay it to you all. But for now, all we can do is stay strong and keep our children in our prayers." With that, he waved to the crowd and dodged back into the vehicle behind him.

The guard, moving quickly, shut the door behind Maat, and then made his way back to the passenger's seat. "Let's go," he said to Elias. He then cast a concerned look back at Maat Mahmoud, who sat in the backseat, his face filled with sorrow for the mother of Parr Grixti and the other parents he'd yet had the heart to tell that their children had also been killed.

With a sigh, Maat rested his head in his hands and closed his eyes.

* * *

As Maat and his entourage embarked on the journey to find Kek's Sharir device, the hideout of his daughter and the remaining soldiers of Cairo's army had been transformed for a small, intimate celebration.

Khalfani stood, dressed in white linen pants and a matching linen shirt, looking at the modest decorations around him, appreciating the beauty of their simplicity. His heart swelled, thoughts of his *eva* crossing his mind, wishing she could be there. For him, her absence was the main thing missing, but he wholeheartedly believed she was still there in spirit.

His heart pounded as he turned around and caught Tekem's eye, who was looking at him with a proud yet goofy grin. He appeared to want to say something, but stopped and glanced at a spot over Khalfani's shoulder.

Khalfani turned around, finding Lia and Orsel approaching them with pnina flowers in tow. Lia looked stunning in a simple yellow dress, most likely to honor Apple's memory.

"Where did you find those?" Khalfani asked, stunned.

Lia winked. "Never you mind. Just know that I've heard you call Isis 'Ninna' a time or two, so I thought it would add a nice touch."

Khalfani smiled, accepting a flower from Lia and pinning it onto his shirt.

She then approached Tekem, a sly grin on her face. "Thought the best man should probably wear one too," she said, and then proceeded to pin a flower onto Tekem's shirt.

He bowed his head at her and smiled. "Why, thank you," he said. The two of them stared at each other for a moment until Orsel began to squirm, looking slightly embarrassed in her short white dress embroidered with lace.

"Well," Lia said after clearing her throat. She looked towards Orsel and grinned. "We'll have another surprise coming for you soon. Right, Orsel?"

Orsel glanced away shyly. "I suppose," she muttered. "Umm, I think I'm going to go take a seat now."

Lia placed an arm around Orsel's shoulder, and the two of them walked off, heading to the chairs that had been arranged in rows in the center of the room.

"What was that about?" Khalfani asked.

"No idea," Tekem said, staring after the girls. "Anyway, how are you feeling, man?"

Khalfani took a deep breath and then smiled at his best friend. "Like this is right…Like this is perfect."

Tekem chuckled and slapped Khalfani on the back. "Told you so."

The two of them then stood in companionable silence, watching the room fill up. Kaiden walked in, nodding respectfully at them, although he had a somewhat pained look on his face that he was trying unsuccessfully to hide. He took a seat beside Lia and Orsel.

Not long after that, Amam arrived, looking bored but immediately perking up after seeing one of the cooks walking by with a delicious cake. Then came Aiari, Mirko, and Easton, among a small crowd of additional soldiers and Mahmoud employees who'd also been residing in the safehouse. One of them had a device for taking digital photographs. They took their seats, smiling amicably at Khalfani as they waited for the ceremony to begin.

A hush fell over the room, and Khalfani's heart pounded so furiously, he thought he could see it beating right through his borrowed shirt. The doors to the room opened, and in walked Isis.

She took Khalfani's breath away.

Lia, Easton, and Orsel had spent quite some time on her hair, pinning it up in an elegant design so that the natural beauty of her face was on full display. And though there had been no chances of finding an extravagant wedding dress under such short and impromptu notice, the area of the hideout reserved for Rania had turned up a simple white dress that fit Isis perfectly, despite the height difference between her and her mother. The sleeveless white dress hugged her figure while still preserving some modesty, and fell just below her knees. The neckline plunged ever so slightly to reveal a glimpse of her delicate collarbone. In her hands, she carried a makeshift bouquet of pnina flowers, matching the flowers that Lia had arranged in her hair.

Her eyes met Khalfani's, and quite abruptly, it was like everyone else in their presence had disappeared. She took in his tall and strong form, his proud stance, and his handsome face. Gliding through the room, she stopped before him, the two of them saying more to each other with their eyes than words could ever express.

"Please be seated, everyone," Tekem said from in front of the couple.

The onlookers sat, varying degrees of smiles on their faces. All the while, Isis and Khalfani continued to have eyes for only each other.

Tekem, who'd researched wedding vows on his communication device, served as the wedding officiant, though it had taken some time for Isis and Khalfani to permit him to do so after being sold on the idea of a poor man's wedding.

"You're still having a poor man's wedding," Tekem had argued. *"I'm not a real wedding officiant, and this is going to be a cheap and impromptu ceremony that no one even knows about yet. Isis, you're the President's daughter. C'mon, an underground mansion is as poor as it's going to get."*

"Welcome, everyone," Tekem said. "Thank you for coming to this last-minute gathering. As you all know, we are here to witness these two—Khalfani Abaza and Isis Pnina Mahmoud—join each other in matrimony." Tekem was forced to pause when the room broke out in applause and cheers.

Isis and Khalfani grinned, laughed, and joined hands.

"You look beautiful," Khalfani mouthed to her.

Though she rarely did so, Isis blushed. "Thank you," she mouthed back.

"We may not have a fancy or extravagant wedding ceremony planned," Tekem said once the room was quiet again, "but that hardly matters. The love these two have for each other is more than enough. So, without further ado, Khalfani, do you take this incredible hottie, Isis Pnina Mahmoud, to be your wife?"

Stuck in the deep brown of Isis's eyes, Khalfani nodded. "I do."

"And do you, Isis, take this dude here—my best friend, Khalfani Abaza—to be your husband?"

"I do," Isis said with a joyful chuckle.

"All right," Tekem said, grinning. "Well, you two know what's next."

Simultaneously, Isis and Khalfani exposed their forearms to each other. They then pressed their arms together and held each other's elbows, both of them gazing into each other's eyes, elated and in disbelief over what they were doing.

"I promise to love you forever, Ninna," Khalfani whispered.

"And I promise that you are my forever, Khal," Isis whispered back.

And then, before Tekem could even give the instruction to do so, the newlywed couple kissed. Each of them felt warmth radiating through their forearms, signifying that their marriage vows had been activated and immediately the announcement went out alerting Maat and all of the other citizens in Cairo that Khalfani and Isis were now husband and wife.

"Well, I guess that makes it official," Tekem said, beaming at the couple before him. "Ladies and gentlemen, presenting Khalfani and Isis Abaza!"

The crowd erupted into cheers, applause, and whistles so loud it sounded like far more people were there than really present.

Khalfani and Isis smiled and laughed, with Khalfani lifting Isis right off her feet and spinning her around in circles. When he placed her back on her feet, they kissed again.

"And now—one last surprise," Tekem announced, looking into the crowd towards where Lia and Orsel stood.

Lia nudged a nervous-looking Orsel with her arm. After a pregnant pause, Orsel stood. Her shiny black hair was tied back into an elegant bun, and her eyes shone with anxiety. Yet, she slowly made her way across the room, coming to stand before Khalfani and Isis, who smiled back at her curiously, wondering what she had in store.

Orsel looked at the couple and bowed. "Congratulations," she said, before turning around to face the crowd. Standing as tall as her petite figure would allow, she squared back her shoulders and glanced upwards to the ceiling, and then a beautiful note soared up from her throat and out of her mouth.

Orsel began singing with the eyes of a stunned crowd glued to her.

Isis smiled through her shock. She turned her gaze to Khalfani, prepared to ask him if he'd known that Orsel could sing. But when she looked at him, she saw that he was smiling back at her, with his hand outstretched, silently asking for a dance.

Her smile widening, Isis let Khalfani take her hand and draw her in close. She rested her head on his shoulders, and the two of them began to sway gently, sharing their first dance as husband and wife to Orsel's lovely singing.

When Orsel finished her first song, the celebrating continued. Several of the cooks residing in the secret hideout had prepared food and snacks that they set out for the wedding guests. Amam helped himself to a huge chunk of cake. All the while, Orsel, who seemed to have gotten over her shyness, continued to sing, providing the perfect soundtrack for the guests to dance and laugh to.

Isis and Khalfani stood huddled together, laughing and sipping wine they'd been provided with when they noticed Kaiden approaching them with a tight smile.

He stopped before them and nodded his head at Khalfani. "Just wanted to personally say congratulations." He held out his hand.

Khalfani stared at him for a moment, clearly sensing the tension, but appreciating the respect. He clasped hands with Kaiden, the two men shaking firmly. "Thank you," Khalfani said.

Kaiden then turned towards Isis. "And congratulations to you as well. You make a beautiful bride. I'm happy for you." He gently kissed Isis's hand before hurriedly moving away to retrieve himself a drink.

Khalfani and Isis quickly exchanged glances, but said nothing, for Kaiden's actions had started a trend. Before they knew it, everyone present was approaching them, wanting to offer their own well-wishes before rejoining the makeshift party that had broken out in the room.

"I don't think this could have been any more perfect," Isis said, after she and her new husband had completely lost track of time amidst all the laughing, dancing, and hugging they'd been surrounded by. "I just wish my parents could have been here."

Khalfani pulled Isis close, wrapping her into a loving hug. "I know," he said. "As soon as this is over, we'll have to have another celebration that they can enjoy with us."

Isis sighed. *As soon as this is over…*the words reverberated through her mind, reminding her of the reality all of them had pushed away for the time being. But eventually, they would all have to accept that they were still at war, and the happiness was bound to be short-lived.

They wouldn't be able to hide out forever; there was a city out there counting on them.

"What is it, Ninna?" Khalfani asked in her ear, obviously sensing a slight change in her mood.

"Nothing," she sighed, feeling a blush coming across her face. "I umm…just really want to be alone with you right now, while we still have time…"

Now, it was Isis who sensed a change in Khalfani. She felt his arms tighten around her, his fingers digging into the small of her back. He glanced out at their friends and hideout housemates. "Looks like everyone is enjoying themselves…" he said, his voice trailing off.

"Yeah," Isis agreed, murmuring into his shoulder.

"I don't think anyone would really notice if we snuck off to have some time to ourselves for a little while…"

"And who cares if they do?" Isis challenged. "We're married now."

Khalfani looked into her eyes and grinned. "Well, what are we waiting for, Mrs. Abaza?"

Isis laughed and pulled away from him. "For you to catch up," she said, quickly darting for the door and leaving him to chase after her.

The sounds of the celebration growing distant as they left the room and darted down the hall, Isis and Khalfani made their way to the quarters that had been serving as their bedroom. Giggling, they stepped inside and checked around, ensuring they were alone. They then closed the door.

For a long moment, the two of them merely stared at each other, letting their minds wrap around what had just happened…

With a sly smile, Isis slinked over to Khalfani, stopping just inches away from his face, letting her brown eyes stare into his brilliant green ones.

Unable to resist her beauty, Khalfani gently ran his hand down the side of Isis's face. "You are so *harika*, Ninna," he murmured. *So beautiful.*

As his hand trailed down her cheek, she turned her head to kiss the palm of his hand. "I love you, Khal."

"I love you too."

They rested their foreheads against each other's again, their eyes now closed, and their breathing matching each other's. Slowly, Isis's hands wrapped around Khalfani's neck, and he encircles her waist with his muscular arms. They pressed their lips together, the kiss starting off slow, sweet, and romantic before growing passionate and lustful, the two of them getting lost in each other.

Their bodies pressing into each other's, they stumbled across the room until Khalfani backed into the bed.

Hearts racing, their kiss broke.

Isis pressed her hands to Khalfani's chest, pushing him onto the bed. And then she stood for a moment, relishing the sight of him staring up at her with so much yearning.

His heart fluttering and unable to withstand another second without having her body next to his, Khalfani reached forward and pulled Isis down on top of him. Their lips descended on each other again, and they rolled over onto the bed so that Khalfani hovered above her. His kisses trailed from her lips, to her cheeks, and then down her neck. And for the rest of the night, the two did not exist outside of each other.

* * *

Just as Isis had predicted, the remaining soldiers didn't even seem to notice her and Khalfani's absence—and if they did, they seemed unconcerned about it for the time being.

As the overall wedding celebration died down, the soldiers set off to explore more of the secret hideout, reveling in how big it was and how many hidden rooms they kept stumbling across.

"Whoa, guys—come here," Amam's voice cried out from farther down the hall, having discovered yet another room. With a wine bottle in hand, he beckoned the others over.

"Wow…" Mirko said and then let out a low whistle as he came up behind Amam and peered into the room. "Jackpot!"

"What is it?" Tekem said, hurrying over with Lia moving alongside him.

Soon, all the soldiers huddled around, peering into the room in awe before entering and closing the door behind them.

"So, before we leave here, we should seriously ask if we could use some of this stuff," Aiari said.

The walls of the room were covered from top to bottom with shelves, and on those shelves were weapons. Guns, boomerangs, crossbows, rifles, knives, machetes, and on and on it went.

Lia sighed, causing Tekem to look back at her. "What's wrong?"

She wrapped her arms tightly around herself, suppressing a shudder. "Just don't want to think about fighting right now, I guess. This was supposed to be a day to take a break from it all, you know?"

"I hear that," Easton said, glancing around at the weapons with a mixture of fascination and dread.

"Well, we're in luck," Kaiden said, stooping down to pick something off the floor. He turned around to face the group, holding up a deck of cards. "Anyone wants to play?"

"That's more like it," Lia said, smiling. "And pass some of that along, too, will you?" She gestured to Amam's wine bottle.

Amam turned the bottle upside down. "Sorry, babe. All gone." He grinned. "Although, maybe we can find another use for it later…"

Tekem cleared his throat by way of interruption, and then took the deck of cards from Kaiden. "All right, who wants in on the first game?"

The soldiers broke into pairs—Tekem and Lia, Orsel and Easton, Mirko and Amam, and Kaiden and Aiari—to play several rounds of card games and share plenty of laughter before growing bored and looking for something else to do.

"Hey, Amam—what did you mean about finding another use for that empty wine bottle?" Kaiden asked.

Amam smirked. "There's this ancient game called 'Spin the Bottle.' Ever heard of it?"

"No," Kaiden said while the others all collectively shook their heads.

"Well," Amam continued, grabbing the empty wine bottle and laying it down on the floor, "you do just as the game says—spin the bottle." He demonstrated. "Thing is, everyone has to sit around the bottle in a circle, and the person who spins the bottle has to kiss whoever the bottle points to once it stops spinning."

A silence followed Amam's instructions of the game, only broken when Lia stepped forward and grabbed the bottle.

"Hmm," she said, suppressing a grin. She then placed the bottle on the floor and gave it a twirl.

Everyone watched the bottle with bated breath, wondering what the outcome would be. Yet, as the bottle began to slow down, Tekem discreetly moved about the room, taking advantage of the fact that everyone else was too busy staring at the bottle.

When it stopped, everyone looked up to find Tekem conveniently standing right where the bottle pointed.

"Funny," Amam commented, his head tilted sideways. "I thought you were standing over there?"

"What?" Tekem scoffed, glad that his dark brown skin concealed his blushing.

Another silence engulfed the room as Lia slowly sauntered over to Tekem. Stopping just inches before his face, the two locked eyes. And then Lia separated the distance between them with a kiss. The kiss was a light peck on the lips, though she ran her hand gently down the side of Tekem's face afterwards. His eyes bore into hers with such intensity that the others began to feel they were invading on a truly private moment.

Kaiden coughed, breaking the stillness of the room. "Yeah, so, I'm not sure I'm really feeling this game. No offence, guys, but uhm…anyone else got any other ideas?"

Nervous, yet relieved laughter filled the room, and Lia and Tekem finally put some space between them.

"How about 'Truth or Dare' then?" Amam suggested.

Easton raised an eyebrow. "Is that another one of your ancient games?"

Amam shrugged. "Well, I don't hear anyone else coming up with anything."

"Fine. How do you play that one?" Kaiden asked.

"It's simple. You just pick truth or dare. If you pick truth, someone asks you a question, and you have to answer it, telling the truth. If you pick dare, you get dared to do something, and you have to do it."

Easton shrugged. "Sounds easy enough. Me, first. I pick truth. So, what is everyone's greatest fear?"

"That's not exactly how it goes," Amam interjected. Yet, when everyone proceeded to stare at him, he sighed and waved a dismissive hand. "Whatever. Never mind…"

"My biggest fear," Orsel said, looking around the group as they all suddenly looked back at her, "is not being taken seriously as a warrior simply because I'm female."

"Why would you fear something like that? Aurora was female and one of the most respected warriors ever," Aiari said.

"Everyone isn't Aurora, though," Easton said, looking at Orsel and nodding. "I understand how you feel."

"Me too," Lia said quietly.

"Well, for me," Tekem said, "I'm afraid of not having what my *pa* had…" He swallowed, suddenly feeling awkward but continuing nonetheless. He resumed, staring at the floor as he spoke. "My *poje* was in the army, so I always grew up under the impression that I needed to be the kind of man he was. I *want* to be the kind of man he was. But...I mean, now—after seeing all this death and destruction..." He shook his head. "I'm afraid I'll never make it. I'm scared that I'll meet my end before getting the chance to have a family of my own..." He paused and furrowed his brow. "I understand now that this Retrograde really is different from what they dealt with in the past. You just don't know how much time you have left these days..."

Lia brought her hand to his shoulder, giving it a comforting squeeze.

"I can understand that a bit," Mirko said. "I'm afraid of dying before building my legacy...Can't say I've really given having a family too much thought. Honestly, I just want to be remembered as an incredible warrior."

"Well, I can understand the fear of not getting the chance to have a family," Kaiden said. "I mainly fear never being able to find true love..." His voice trailed off, his expression growing far away as it finally dawned on him that Isis and Khalfani were missing. He bit the insides of his cheeks, trying to keep himself from grimacing too noticeably.

There was a pause, as they waited for the next confession.

"Well, for me," Easton said, "my biggest fear is ending up like my mother." She shuddered and sighed. "She was basically a prostitute."

Amam tried to disguise his snicker as a cough, and Easton shot him a dirty look. "Sorry," he muttered.

"Anyway," she resumed, "she ended up marrying a complete creep." She cast her eyes downwards to the floor. "Abusive, you know? To me and to her. That's why I wanted to become a soldier, so that I could find…protect myself. Not end up like her, letting someone treat me any kind of way…"

Another heavy silence ensued, the remaining soldiers seeming too nervous to speak up now.

"You know what?" Aiari said. All eyes turned his way, waiting to hear his greatest fear. "I think this game is stupid."

The others laughed and jeered at him.

He held up his hands innocently. "I'm just saying—we still have to fight this Retrograde. The newlyweds might be off…err…taking a break. But as for the rest of us, sitting around talking about our fears isn't going to help anything. We need to be discussing a plan and trying to figure out how this thing is going to play out. It's been nice, but playtime is over."

"Can't argue with that," Mirko said, while the others muttered their partial agreement.

CHAPTER 16

Maat sat in the backseat of the vehicle. He was in somewhat of a daze, thinking about how proud he was of the fact that his daughter and Khalfani decided to marry despite their challenging circumstances. He imagined that although the war had been brutal, their wedding must have at least brought a bit of joy into the tense atmosphere that they and their comrades had endured over the last few days. And although he would have given anything to have been there with Rania watching his only child take her nuptials, he hoped that soon enough they would be together again to celebrate their union, even if it was after the fact. He smiled to himself, briefly absorbed in thoughts of how beautiful Isis must have been walking down the aisle, how much she reminded him of Rania especially as of late and how precious happy moments now proved to be in a world with so much uncertainty. Reflecting on these things gave Maat even more impetus to destroy Kek's Sharir and defeat the Retrograde once and for all. They reached the center of the city. And though no one had spoken, the atmosphere itself snapped Maat out of his thoughts.

He leaned forward, an icy chill running down his spine. His now alert eyes staring out the window, he literally felt the despair in the air—along with the scent. The putrid aroma of evil and death invaded his nostrils as he saw all the bodies lying in the street—dead changelings as far as the eye could see. Even where there weren't whole changeling bodies, there were body fragments—limbs, hands, torsos, decapitated heads…

The road itself was stained mahogany due to so much blood having seeped into it. Its metallic scent mixed with the earth and pavement, drifting through the car vents as they continued to move along.

Maat had always known how devastating Retrogrades could be, but he had to admit he had never seen anything quite like this before. His chest felt tight, thinking about his daughter having to experience such gruesomeness firsthand. He was abruptly hit with images of her as an infant, and then as a young, innocent child. Never in a million years could he have predicted that the small girl who'd loved it when he gave her piggyback rides would be on the frontlines, fighting the evil of the world on their city's behalf.

Glimpsing Elias through the rearview mirror, Maat could see the disgust on his face. Even the guard in the passenger's seat sat with his jaw clenched, afraid to breathe in the stench and looking as if he was in danger of being sick.

"Stop the vehicle," Maat said, his voice quiet but commanding nonetheless.

Elias met his eyes through the rearview mirror. "Sorry, sir?"

"Stop the vehicle," Maat repeated, knowing he'd heard him the first time.

Elias's hands tightened around the steering wheel, his expression uncertain, although he didn't dare disobey his boss's order. As he slowed the caravan, he regretfully rolled down the window beside him, his stomach churning as the stench outside drifted more freely into the caravan. He then held his hand out, signaling for the entourage driving behind them to stop their vehicles as well.

"Thank you," Maat said. "Unlock the door, please."

Elias pressed the button, and Maat sprung out of the caravan before the guard in the passenger's seat could climb out to open his door for him.

"Sir, wait." "Hold on, sir." "Please, sir." The entourage of guards accompanying him for the journey all rushed out of their vehicles, nervously approaching Maat and trying to assume their protective stances around him before he ventured too far off. Yet, even as they attempted to protect Maat, the scenery proved to be too much for some of them. They held their noses and breaths as

best as they could—one unfortunate soul retched, unable to hold back the bile that had risen in his throat.

But Maat was unconcerned, his eyes too busy taking in the sights around him. His senses were on overload, and though everything was still and quiet around him—save for the fuss that his entourage was making—he could practically hear the sounds of the battle that had occurred. He could sense the screaming, the yelling, the crying, the blasting and whistling of weapons…

Hear the blood splattering and feel the cold chill of the Darkness…

Still, his legs carried him forward. "Out of the way! Fall back!" he commanded when the guards attempted to surround him.

Frowns on their faces, they reluctantly did as they were told. With great apprehension, the guards—Elias included—trailed closely behind Maat Mahmoud, permitting him to lead the way and survey the damage around them. Their movements were awkward, stepping over changeling bodies the whole way. But on they went, determined to keep Maat within reaching distance at all times.

His eyes flickering here and there, Maat's heart thudded when he saw something silver glinting on a particularly disturbed spot of the ground. His legs automatically carrying him towards it, he realized precisely what he was seeing…

It was one of the digital dog tags often worn by soldiers as a sign of their loyalty and dedication to the people they served. The necklace lay in an exceptionally grisly puddle—blood, bone, skin, and muscle surrounding it. Once again, Maat could hear his guards protesting as he moved closer, but he ignored them. He didn't stop until he stood directly before the necklace, a strong wave of grief coming over him at seeing the digital initials, 'P.G.'

Parr Grixti.

Maat lowered his head and closed his eyes, internally uttering a prayer. The guards, finally realizing what Maat was standing in front of, all watched with bated breath and grief of their own.

Maat carefully picked up the necklace, thinking of Parr's mother. His ears had not forgotten the fear in her voice as she'd asked about her son, nor the despair in her cries after receiving the news that he was no more…

"Sir," Elias said, coming to stand beside Maat.

Maat looked up, seeing that he was being handed a white handkerchief. He nodded. "Thank you." He took the handkerchief, wrapped Parr's necklace in it, pocketed it, and vowed to get it to Parr's mother as soon as he possibly could.

He then stood and continued walking, his skin prickling with unease. Once again, he felt as if his body knew better than his mind regarding where he was going, some sort of unconscious instinct guiding his direction, bringing him right to the spot of Aurora's and Apple's demises.

He stared at the ground, not fully understanding how he knew this was the location, since unlike with Parr, there was nothing left behind of neither Aurora nor Apple.

Maat's throat suddenly felt tight, and his eyes stung. He just barely registered the guards around him repeatedly asking if he was all right, undoubtedly wondering why he had suddenly frozen.

Though he wanted to answer them, to tell them that they were standing at Aurora's and Apple's final resting places, the words never made it out of his mouth. Without warning, he felt winded, like someone had punched the air out of his lungs.

Doubling over until his knees hit the ground, his surroundings faded until he was swept away with another vision.

Maat's eyes were lowered to the ground, where the dark earthy colors of soil, grass, leaves, vines, and tree branches passed by him in a blur. Wind whipped across his nose, keenly filling it with a variety of scents from all directions. And beneath his body, he could feel the fast and frantic movement of his limbs, expertly navigating over the uneven grounds.

It was then that he realized he was running.

Lifting his gaze up from the ground to see ahead of him, Maat stared, dumbfounded; his vantage point was unnaturally low…

Too low…

On top of that, a strange panting filled his ears. He listened carefully, recognizing that there was something canine about the sound of it. Yet, he also could feel his own lungs expanding and restricting, coinciding with the panting.

Hence, though it seemed impossible, he understood the panting was coming from him.

Trying to make sense of the sensations going through his body, Maat felt his legs—four of them in total—moving faster and faster. Despite not knowing where he was going or what his destination was, he automatically came to a stop upon noticing a beautiful sable she-wolf resting approximately ten yards away from him.

Intrigued by the wolf, he stared in awe, recognizing a sense of protectiveness about her. Raising his head as high as it would go, he finally noticed his location—he and the she-wolf were right before the entrance of the secret hideout that Isis, Khalfani, and the rest of Cairo's army had retreated to. He stared at it longingly, wanting nothing more than to go inside and see his daughter…

Wanting to see her with his own eyes, to know that she was all right.

But the she-wolf guarded the door, blocking it. Noticing his presence, she lifted her head and looked at Maat with stunning bright purple eyes. The she-wolf stood, a purplish glow surrounding her muscular body, growing brighter by the second until every inch around her was obscured by the glow.

Maat squinted his eyes, the sudden brightness too intense to behold. But slowly, the glowing subsided, and in place of the she-wolf stood none other than Aurora Imamu.

A man like Maat Mahmoud was rarely astounded by anything, but the vision of Aurora was breathtaking enough to leave him thunderstruck. He raised his head to take in the full length of her, her figure so tall and willowy, yet strong—seemingly stretching into the starlit sky above her from Maat's lowered vantage point. He wanted to speak, feeling compelled to say something to her. But he noticed no voice would leave his throat. If he didn't know better, he would have described the sound he made as reminiscent of howling…

Aurora smiled down at him, her face brilliant and even more beautiful than it had been in life. She then nodded her head down towards him, and her voice rang out, "Hello, my King."

"Sir?"

"Mr. Mahmoud?"

"Sir, are you all right?"

The frantic voices of the guards and Elias surrounded Maat, all of them alarmed from seeing him unexpectedly crouching down on the ground, his expression zoned out.

Maat blinked, coming back from his vision and readapting to the world around him. Feeling the firm ground on his hands and knees, and feeling the hands of the guards attempting to help him back to his feet, Maat finally stood.

Sometimes his visions were so difficult to interpret; he wouldn't figure them out for days—weeks even. But that wasn't the case, this time around. He found the meaning of this particular vision clear as day—the great Aurora Imamu was still fighting on their side, even if she could no longer do so from the world of the living. So dedicated, she was, that she was spending her time in the afterworld watching over and protecting her peers.

Still ignoring all the questions being thrown his way, Maat Mahmoud smiled, feeling more comforted than he had been in a long time.

* * *

Isis listened to Khalfani's heart beating under her ear, her head rising and falling with each breath he took, while savoring the feel of his skin on her cheek. With his arm curled beneath her, he traced gentle circles on her bare back with his fingertips, feeling content from the warmth of her body pressed next to his.

The setting Ra cast an orangish glow on the bedsheets haphazardly covering them.

Isis raised her head, kissing Khalfani's chin. He glanced down at her and smiled. With his free hand, he took her hand in his, their fingers intertwining. They kissed again, slow and lingering on each other's lips, both of them wishing the moment could last forever.

But they knew it couldn't.

Khalfani sighed. "I think we should probably contact your *pa* again."

Isis nodded. "Yeah," she agreed, hoisting herself up on her elbows to look Khalfani in the eyes. "But I think it can wait just a little while longer." She smiled, and pressed her lips to his again.

* * *

Kaiden found himself standing in some kind of residence that appeared familiar and foreign to him at the same time. He realized that he must be dreaming, but everything felt so real.

Shadows shrouded the entrance of the residence, leaving only a small ray of Ra's light shining in as it was setting. He turned his back to the entrance and looked out the window into the dusk, feeling a longing for the woman that he now knew could never be his. At this point, however, Kaiden had resolved in his mind that perhaps that was his fate. He should just get used to it. He felt tears welling up in his eyes. "Why couldn't she love me?" he questioned. "I would have been just as good of a protector and husband as Khalfani." He thought. His heart sank as he began to ponder the notion that perhaps he would never be able to love again. Suddenly, a voice from behind him, as if reading his thoughts, answered the questions that had been plaguing him ever since he watched Isis being bound to Khalfani in matrimony.

"Because Isis was never meant for you and never has been. I am the one that you are seeking. Isis and I are similar, but not the same."

Kaiden turned suddenly in the direction of the soothing voice coming from the opposite end of the room. He could not make out the face of the person he was seeing, but the body looked so eerily similar to Isis. The figure continued steadily walking toward him, and little by little, the woman came into view.

"Your heart longs for me, Kaiden, just as my heart has longed for you. I never thought the moment would ever come when I would see you again. I have searched our entire galaxy for you. And now, I've finally found you. It won't be long now. You and I are destined for so much."

The figure continued walking slowly toward him. Kaiden blinked hard three times, trying to either snap himself out of the dream or to make sense of what was happening. Finally, the young woman's face became visible. She was a vision with a stunning similarity to Isis. It was almost as if they could be sisters, but Kaiden knew for certain that Isis was an only child. He wondered how this was possible.

"I am Ehe," the woman said. Even though she looked like Isis, her mannerisms confirmed that she was indeed someone altogether different.

"For now, I can only visit you in dreams, but soon, that will change. Hold on, ti biyeh. I'm coming for you." Ehe closed the space in-between her and Kaiden. His heart pounded. There was something so mysterious about her. Was she dangerous? Where had she come from, and how did she seem to know him so well? He was too astonished to even question her. Yet somehow, he knew he was helpless against her charms. He would never be able to resist her, not in the state that his heart was in now. He breathed her in with his hands trembling,

unsure of what to do with them. Her sweet perfume hinted of jasmine and rust wood, leaving a permanent memory of her scent in his mind. He looked into her intense amber-colored eyes, and before he knew it, she had pressed into him. With her fingers running through his hair, she began kissing him with such passion and intensity that he began to feel weak. As perplexed as he may have been about what was happening, he made no plans to escape from her. He eagerly returned her kiss. When their lips parted again, she smiled and looked him directly in the eyes, willing him to believe her.

"Wait for me, ti biyeh," Ehe said. And just as suddenly as she appeared, Ehe vanished.

Kaiden woke with a start. He wished the dream could have continued longer. He had so many questions that he wanted to ask. Nevertheless, he could rest easier now, knowing that there was someone that loved him greatly, someone like Isis. He would not be alone for long. Remembering her words, he touched his bottom lip to see if any of it was real, and strangely enough, it felt damp, as if he had really been kissed. Desperately needing the dream to be true, he thought of another confirmation. Quickly, he grasped the collar of his shirt with his free hand and smelled it. Sure enough, there it was, the sweet jasmine and rust wood scent of his newfound love. Kaiden smiled, delighted in the knowledge that he now also had someone just for him that no one would be able to take away. He determined to keep this new revelation a secret from everyone and looked around the room to make sure that all were fast asleep. Still touching his lip and smiling to himself in keen anticipation of what would happen next and what this all might mean, Kaiden drifted back off to sleep, remembering the name of the woman, his love, that was searching so desperately for him – Ehe.

By the time Khalfani opened his eyes again, he saw that their bedroom was completely shrouded in darkness. It was the middle of the night, and Isis's deep breathing let him know that she was still sleeping soundly. They had yet to contact Maat again, but he knew they needed to do so soon.

Carefully climbing out of bed not to disturb Isis's slumber, Khalfani stretched, dressed, and quietly exited the room.

He felt content, happy, relaxed, curious, yet energized. Needing to redirect his energy, he decided to explore the hideout.

Treading lightly, he walked down its many corridors and twisting paths, taking in the sights. Finding one door cracked open, he approached and peered inside, his jaw dropping for an instant. In awe, he looked around the walls, amazed to see so many weapons.

He then lowered his gaze, and a grin stretched across his face, his amazement at the weapons temporarily put on hold. He chuckled softly, seeing his fellow soldiers stretched out across the floor, sleeping. He spotted Tekem first, who was sleeping propped up against a wall with Lia in his arms, her head resting on his shoulder.

Not far from them, Orsel lied curled in a ball, her head resting in her hands. Easton lied beside her, a crease in her brow while she slept as if distressed from a dream.

Mirko lied spread eagle on the floor, snoring with his mouth wide open and making Khalfani struggle to fight back a boisterous laugh.

Kaiden, with his hair tousled, was sleeping peacefully in a corner alone with a small smile on his face. He had not seen Kaiden so relaxed since they had met.

On the opposite side of the room, he spotted the other soldiers, most notably Amam, sleeping with an empty wine bottle near, his chin glistening with drool.

Shaking his head and chuckling, Khalfani contemplated waking Tekem, eager to talk to his best friend and ask how the rest of the day had gone for him and the other soldiers. Before he could act on the thought, though, he froze, almost certain that he'd just heard someone call his name.

His thoughts immediately went to Isis, but he knew the voice he'd heard wasn't hers.

He also knew that somehow, he had *felt* the voice rather than heard it…

Slowly pulling the door back closed, Khalfani returned to the hallway. He listened carefully, but heard nothing. Still, something beckoned him…

He could not make sense of it, but it was like an invisible energy pulling him like a gravitational force to the hideout's entrance. His legs moved as if with minds of their own, soundlessly leading him to the entrance's landing. He pressed the button, elevating himself upwards. Before he knew it, he was outside, standing beneath the dark, cloudy sky, and gazing into the purple eyes of a large sable wolf.

The wolf was so beautiful he intuitively knew it was female. For the longest time, all he could do was stare at it in awe.

He'd seen that shade of purple in the wolf's eyes before…

Khalfani swallowed, watching the wolf turn away from him and sit with her back facing him. Astonished and unafraid, he inched closer to the wolf, wanting a closer look until a blindingly bright purple light stopped him dead in his tracks. Suppressing the instinct to cry out, Khalfani shielded his eyes, the light's warmth tingling against his eyelids and the back of his hands.

Slowly, the light began to dim, and Khalfani was able to lower his hands and reopen his eyes.

In place of the wolf now stood a woman, the long, intricate braid hanging down her back instantly familiar and recognizable. The hue of the purple glow that had previously blinded Khalfani suddenly triggered a memory; in his mind's eye, he recalled the purple light beam that had soared into the sky after Aurora's death.

His jaw nearly dropped to the floor.

Slowly, she glanced back at him from over her shoulder.

In that moment, Khalfani knew she was not quite the same Aurora Imamu that he'd known throughout the years. She was even more stunningly beautiful than she had been, and the decorative tattooing along her face glimmered as if made of diamond, rather than ink.

This was not warrior Aurora. This was Goddess Aurora.

She turned back around to face the east, as if awaiting the dawn of a new day. Khalfani continued to stare at her, speechless. A part of him wondered if he was dreaming—if he was really still lying in bed beside Isis, fast asleep. Before he could ponder it any further though, Aurora turned slowly around, locked eyes with him, and bowed her head, her magnificent braid falling elegantly over her shoulder. Clearly, she had wanted to give him a few moments to process what was happening before interacting with him. Now it seemed as if she was about to begin speaking.

Though Khalfani already felt frozen in place, the gesture halted him even further.

Aurora, bowing to him? Why would she do such a thing? He couldn't fathom a reason for his subconscious mind conjuring such an image, even in a dream.

When Aurora stood upright and looked him in the eyes again, her voice drifted to him like a bell. "You have no idea how powerful you are, Your Grace," she said. "I have a lot of things to tell you that you don't yet understand. But trust me, you will, in time."

Khalfani blinked, stupefied.

Aurora nudged her head, beckoning him closer.

"Come to me," she said.

Feeling he had no choice but to obey, he moved towards her, and they ended up perched upon a rock, a short distance away from the secret hideout's hidden entrance. As Khalfani took a seat next to Aurora, he realized that he suddenly felt a little too intimidated to look directly at her. Hence, he resorted to staring at the dusty ground before him.

"I understand that you and Isis are very close," Aurora said, and then smiled. "She is your bride now and her parents are very pleased. However, I have to request that you not share with her what I'm about to tell you."

Khalfani nodded, he was relieved that her parents were happy with their decision, but still he already felt slightly uncomfortable. He didn't like the thought of keeping secrets from Isis, especially now that they were married.

Likely sensing his distress, Aurora gave an understanding nod. "It is not that I wish you to lie to her. It's simply that she needs to discover her full power in her own time and in her own way—not through you."

Khalfani glanced at her, his worry subsiding and his curiosity piquing.

"Khalfani," Aurora continued, "I know you've been feeling different. That you've noticed changes within yourself. Correct?"

He swallowed and forced his head to nod. Again, he thought back to the battle, and the foreign yet innate power he'd abruptly felt inside himself. Not to mention the difference he'd observed in Isis.

"There's a reason for that. It's time that you know—you and Isis will be the last of the gods walking among men—after Maat Mahmoud leaves the realm of the living, that is." Aurora smiled. "Yes, I'm sure you've noticed changes in Isis as well, and you've no doubt always known Maat had powers that you could not explain."

"I'm sorry. *What?*" Khalfani said, so dumbfounded by what he'd just heard that his voice finally permitted him to speak. As far-fetched as it sounded, there was a part of him that could very well accept Maat as a god and Isis as a goddess.

But, himself? How could he be one of the last gods walking among men when it was the blood of Kek Abaza that ran through his veins?

Aurora met his gaze, her beautiful eyes so intense that Khalfani struggled again to maintain eye-contact despite wanting to tell her that she must be mistaken. "The battle with Kek and the Darkness is bigger than us, Khalfani. Even bigger than you and Isis." She lifted her gaze and proceeded to stare ahead. "We're dealing with a classic battle between good and evil. I know it's a lot to cope with, but at no cost can you let evil prevail. And I mean that—no matter what..."

Khalfani swallowed, his eyes wide as he thought about how the battle had already cost them so much. It had cost them Aurora herself. He also begrudgingly accepted that the time for him to question whether she was serious about his status as a god had passed; she clearly had more information she wished to relay, and it felt rude to interrupt now.

He glanced at her again, finding it a little easier to look at her when she wasn't making direct eye-contact.

"There's an ancient evil, The Darkness, that's existed since before even the creation of mankind, Your Grace," she resumed, staring off into the distance, yet still making Khalfani squirm. He wasn't accustomed to such a prestigious title. "And ever since the beginning, that evil has been trying and testing out ways to either dominate or destroy all that exists, all that is good, including humankind. It happened to find the Retrograde as the most effective means, realizing that it could demolish entire planets at a time—just like what it did to Ximxija. So, it trailed the Retrograde, feeding off of the fear and destruction that it brought. It strengthened it as much as it could until it found a source that it could use to give it an advantage."

Khalfani was immediately taken back to that day in the Mahmoud complex, watching the planet of Ximxija fall victim to the Retrograde's clutches. He remembered the fear he'd felt, knowing his own planet was soon to be on the Retrograde's agenda.

A deep frown involuntarily formed on his face, thinking about how his own *pa* was playing a role in aiding the destruction—aiding The Dark Order. It was something he wanted so desperately not to think about, for each time he did, his stomach clenched with fury.

"I know you sometimes wonder why you're in this position—the position of being the son of the man the Darkness has joined forces with," Aurora said, again speaking as if she could read Khalfani's thoughts. "The Darkness chose your *pa* because it was drawn to his essence. He's always had a tendency toward jealousy and hatred, and those are the kind of emotions the Darkness loves to feed on." She paused and returned her penetrating stare to Khalfani. "I'm not telling you this to make you feel bad about your *poje.* I'm telling you this because those are precisely the kind of emotions you're going to have to learn to avoid at all costs, and it won't be easy."

Khalfani's jaw clenched, and he halfway wondered if he should be offended. His whole life thus far had been spent trying to make sure he would never be the kind of man his *pa* was. Thus, he felt the warning was unwarranted.

"You have to understand, Khalfani, because of who you are, both the Light and the Darkness would love to claim you. They both want to win you over for their mission. I know you sometimes feel like this battle comes down to you versus your *pa.* But remember, it's much bigger than that. And it's also important to remember that you most certainly aren't alone in this battle. You have Isis, and you're going to need her. She's your partner in more than one way. And being a goddess in her own right, she's wrapped up in all of this, just as much as you are. And…" Aurora smirked, "she's the only living god who's more powerful than you are."

Khalfani chuckled. Even though he was still having a hard time believing himself to be a god, if he was, it didn't surprise him that Isis would be the one greater than he was.

"She's valuable. I hope you realize the full extent to what you have in her."

He nodded. "I do," he said, honestly meaning it. Even if he hadn't understood anything else in the world, he would have known that Isis was special.

Aurora smiled again. "You know, she's going to be the mother of your son someday. And your son is going to be extremely special too. He's going to finally bring peace into this chaotic world of yours."

Khalfani's ears rang with this latest tidbit of information. A lump formed in his throat, making him incapable of responding. And he was also pretty sure that he could literally feel his heart swelling.

His son?

He was going to have a son?

With Isis.

He'd never heard of anything that sounded more perfect. If he hadn't been so touched to hear the news, he would have been a little embarrassed by the tears that had sprung into his eyes upon hearing it.

His son wasn't there yet, but he already hoped he would be just half as good of a father as Maat Mahmoud was to Isis.

"I see that news pleases you," Aurora said with a serene smile. "Take the pride you feel in knowing that you will be the father of Isis's son, and use it to help you fight the Darkness, Khalfani. You're going to need all the strength you can get, and the love you feel toward Isis and your unborn son can be the sources of your greatest strength. Fighting the Darkness is going to be the most difficult battle you'll ever have to face…And while I hate to say this, it is necessary to remain a realist about this—there's no guarantee the outcome will be in your favor."

Khalfani's mood immediately sobered, thinking about his son being born into a world that was defeated by the Darkness. He suppressed a shudder.

"I will always be here fighting with you," Aurora added, "but of course, you know that already. That being said, however, I won't always be able to intervene. There's only so much I can do to help now, but trust that I most certainly will help whenever the gods allow it. So, please, take some solace in that. I and the Gods of Light are with you and Isis."

Khalfani nodded, and a silence passed between the two of them as he reflected on all that she'd just told him. It was definitely a lot to take in, and he already knew that it was going to feel overwhelming at times. Yet, he also already knew that just as Aurora had said, his love for Isis and their son-to-be was going to help him keep going, no matter what.

He supposed it was just like what Aurora had felt with Apple—a love that gave her the courage to do whatever she needed to, even if it meant sacrificing herself for the greater good.

"Aurora," he said, a new curiosity suddenly coming to him, "have you ever been in love?" He realized that in all the time he'd known Aurora, it was odd that this was something he didn't know.

She cast a sad smile at the ground and slowly nodded her head. "Yes," she whispered. "And he was one of the mightiest, bravest warriors I'd ever known. His name was Urion…"

There hadn't been a day that went by when Aurora didn't still envision his handsome face—his sharp blue/gray eyes, brown hair, and chiseled jawline…

There also wasn't a day that went by when she didn't recall the fateful day when she saw his face for the last time. Her mind suddenly clouded over with a vision of its own.

The rival nation they'd been battling had proven to be full of formidable opponents. Aurora, who had always been a skilled fighter, had been handling her own, though—or at least, so she thought.

With so many blasts and bullets surrounding her, she'd felt the one that nearly ended her before her mind could even distinguish where it had come from. Right in the middle of the battlefield, she turned instantly, her weapon aimed as she desperately tried to figure out who was targeting her. But the scene was so chaotic…

"A.I.!" Urion's voice yelled out. It didn't even matter that there was so much noise surrounding her—his voice, she would always hear. Her eyes instinctively found him and saw that he was running right in her direction, his light-colored eyes blazing with panic.

She stared back at him, startled and confused, wondering what he saw that she didn't.

His teeth were clenched in a snarl as he ran faster, desperate to get to her. "DUCK DOWN! IT'S UP ABOVE!" he yelled.

A confused Aurora looked upward, finally realizing that she was being targeted by a sniper drone. But she couldn't move quickly enough. She'd barely even had time to aim her weapon when Urion's body slammed into hers, knocking her to the hot ground beneath them.

She screamed, feeling his body on top of hers, jerking with the two shots that took his life…

Shots that all missed her, for he was acting as her shield. His dead weight pressed against her, and she could feel his blood pouring from his body onto hers...

She sobbed, her mind blank with grief that would consume her for the rest of her life.

"I've never loved another man the way I loved Urion," Aurora said, still looking off into the distance. Another sad smile animated her beautiful, now sorrowful face. "I lived the rest of my life, hoping that I would at least be reunited with him in my afterlife, but no such luck yet." She paused, her expression thoughtful. "After losing Urion, I gave up on love. I knew that I would never be able to experience anything again that came anywhere close to what I felt with him. But then, unexpectedly, as you know, Apple came into my life. A part of the reason why I was initially reluctant to take her in was because I didn't think my heart knew how to love again, in any capacity. But through her, I did find love again, albeit in a different way.

"Still, it wasn't hard to face death when I had the slightest hope that I would finally see Urion again." She lifted her head to the sky and took a deep breath. "I'm not ungrateful about it, though. I know the gods have found favor in him."

"You'll find him again," Khalfani said automatically without even doubting it.

Aurora smiled. "Thank you. But I'm okay, even if I don't. I'm at peace with how my life went because I know I served my purpose. Now, I'm grateful for the position I've been given in the afterlife. In a way, I feel this new role of mine," she gestured to her otherworldly being and the glow around her, "is even greater. I'm on to the next great adventure."

She stood, and Khalfani suddenly felt panicked, not wanting his time with her to end yet. He hurriedly climbed to his feet, his heart pounding. "Wait, how do I defeat Kek? And, I need to know please, if Apple is okay. Have you two at least been reunited?" he asked frantically.

Already retreating, Aurora looked at him one last time. *"Apollonia is stronger and more beautiful now than she was before. She is a goddess and a powerful one at that. The gods were pleased by her kindness, knowing that she will always lead first with love and fairness. They allowed her this privilege as a good deed toward me, which I am eternally thankful for. She also fights with you now, even in the afterlife. You will see her soon enough. As for defeating Kek, it won't be easy, but it is possible..."*

CHAPTER 17

For a moment, the only noise to fill the break room were the sounds of Rania's sniffles as she tried to stifle her crying. Her husband was now off on his way to face off against a dangerous archenemy. In the meantime, her daughter had married without her even being able to see her walk down the aisle. Rania was not angry that Isis had married. She loved Khalfani and could not be happier that they had formed a lifelong alliance both in life and in love. Rather, she was just so hurt that she could not share in the joy of the occasion with her daughter. It seemed as if the Retrograde was taking away everything and everyone that she held dear. It wasn't fair. Tiny white particles of dust floated through the air as she clutched a handkerchief in her hands, dabbling at her red, puffy eyes with it.

Sitting across from her, Mukhalas empathized with her pain. Yet, another part of him couldn't help marveling at how beautiful she was, even while distraught and sobbing. It shouldn't have surprised him though; he had always found Rania beautiful, right from the day he first laid eyes on her.

Never having been married or had children of his own, he sometimes thought back on those many, many years ago, when he had first met Rania. Although Mukhalas was a handsome man in his own right—some might even say more handsome than Maat Mahmoud—he had always suffered from almost debilitating shyness. The only time he ever felt brave was on a battlefield, where he could release his pent-up emotions and channel them in protecting those he cared about.

Upon encountering a girl as stunning as Rania, his confidence had been shaken, and he couldn't fathom having the courage to pursue her, even though they had cultivated a friendship. Night after night, a young Mukhalas thought and dreamed of Rania, trying in vain to work up the nerve to let his romantic interest be known.

But instead, he introduced her to his best friend, Maat Mahmoud. He and Maat had become close after Maat and Kek had fallen out of favor with each other—Maat no longer able to take Kek's jealous nature despite their friendship since boyhood. Mukhalas had been at Maat's side ever since, the loyal and dedicated friend he needed and hadn't been able to maintain in Kek.

Still, he could never prevent his mind from wandering off into 'what if' territory…

What if he'd had the confidence to ask Rania out on a date instead of Maat? What if when Maat had asked if he was all right with him taking out Rania, he had been honest and let his feelings for her be known, instead of pretending he had no interest in her and was perfectly fine with the two of them and their quickly budding romance? Would he be sitting with her right now, holding her hand as her husband instead, worrying about their child fighting a war?

The thought running away with him, Mukhalas sat back in his chair and averted his gaze, knowing that now was not the time for the 'what if' thinking. Besides, whenever he got too preoccupied with such thoughts, he reminded himself that things had likely turned out just as they were meant to. He convinced himself that, in reality, he probably had never had a real shot with Rania, in the first place. He was from a wealthy family, but nowhere near to the extent as the Mahmoud family.

Maat Mahmoud had won Rania, fair and square, and had the means to take care of her far better than Mukhalas could. Thus, Mukhalas had decided long ago that his purpose was to just be there for his best friend and contribute to their dynasty in other ways.

Such as right now—simply being there in a time of need, especially as Maat's righthand man. He knew he was the only person Maat trusted with his wife, which was an honor he took seriously and never wanted to damage.

Rania sighed. "I'm sorry," she said. "I've just been feeling like such a mess lately, with all that's going on…"

Mukhalas smiled sympathetically. "No need to explain or apologize to me, Rania. I know what you're going through. And I know how strong you are. But sometimes," he gestured to the handkerchief crumpled in her hand, "you've just got to let those emotions out. And there's nothing wrong with that."

She smiled appreciatively and wiped the last of her tears away. "You always know the right thing to say. Go figure Maat has worshipped the ground you walk on for all these years. He's so lucky to have you as a friend."

Mukhalas shook his head. "No, the luck is all mine, having you *both* as friends."

"Thanks." Rania paused for a second and then sighed again. "Well, my husband didn't exactly send you here to watch me cry." She chuckled, as did Mukhalas. She then tilted her head sideways. "You've been sitting here the whole time, though, looking pretty deep in thought. What's on your mind?"

Mukhalas swallowed, instantly feeling his skin warming and hoping he wasn't blushing too noticeably. He didn't need Rania knowing that he had simply been thinking about how much he'd been in love with her for all these years before she slipped through his fingertips and right into Maat's arms. He scratched the back of his head and cleared his throat, forcing his voice to remain nonchalant as he spoke. "Nothing. Just the earlier times. The simpler times…"

Rania smiled. "Like when you first introduced me to Maat?" she said, a happy glow of reminiscence piercing through her sorrow.

Mukhalas forced a laugh. "Yeah. I remember when Maat was about to go on his first date with you. The poor man was a nervous wreck!" *And so was I,* he thought while forcing another laugh up his throat.

Rania's eyes widened, and she laughed heartily. "No, no…Now, surely, you can't tell me that your buddy wasn't always as smooth and suave as he presents himself to be!"

Mukhalas leaned forward, a playful gleam in his eyes. "Did I ever tell you about the time my family invited him along for our family vacation, and he and I got lost because he was trying to meet up with this tourist girl who'd flirted with him? This was way before you were around though, mind you."

Rania shook her head and grinned. "No, but I'm all ears."

Mukhalas laughed and slapped his knee. "We were teenagers, of course. And he nearly gave me a heart attack because all I could think of was how upset his parents would be if something happened to him while under my family's watch – the son of the president of Cairo! My parents would have had a lot of explaining to do. It's a funny story anyway…"

And with that, he settled back in his chair and launched into an evening of funny stories and travels down memory lane to help Rania pass the time.

* * *

It took a little while, but Maat managed to convince Elias and the rest of the guards that he was fine. While they weren't used to seeing Maat right in the middle of having a vision, they knew better than to question him. Thus, despite their reservations, they swallowed back any questions they had and returned to their vehicles, ready to proceed with their mission.

As they rode along, on some level, they all kept hoping the grim scenery would lift. But on, it continued. Devastation from every direction, seemingly stretching on for eternity.

As Maat stared out the window from the backseat with a deep scowl planted on his forehead, his eyes roamed the destruction, imagining what it had been like for his soldiers while they fought.

During the drive, Elias kept glancing back at Maat through the rearview mirror.

Maat glanced up, noticing Elias's stare and sensing that his adviser had something to say. Expecting a serious matter to be on Elias's mind, Maat was taken aback to see the slow smile spread across Elias's face. Maat lifted a confused eyebrow, unable to comprehend what could produce a smile in the midst of their current surroundings.

When Elias glanced back at Maat again, only to find Maat also looking at him, he cleared his throat and spoke. "I was just wondering, sir," he said, and then broke into an even wider smile, "how you and Mrs. Mahmoud met." His question seemed so loud due to how quiet everything else was, the only noises being the soft hums of the vehicle engines driving along the blood-stained road.

Surprised by the question, Maat let out an off-guard laugh. "May I ask what brought that to mind?"

Even the guard beside Elias was curiously glancing at him sideways.

Elias shrugged his shoulders. "I guess, as I look at all this around us," he frowned and gestured to their surroundings, "I thought of your words from earlier. And I wonder how you can have such strong hope and conviction during a time like this. I realized it's because you have reasons to fight. You have a family that everyone can tell means the world to you. From there, I just started wondering how you and the missus met, and how you knew she was the one for you."

The guard in the passenger's seat remained quiet, but now, his silence felt different. Maat could tell he was listening in, likely wanting to hear the story to help take his mind off the grisly atmosphere around them.

Maat nodded. "I see," he said. "Well, I guess with Rania, as cliché as it sounds, it really was like love at first sight. She was just so beautiful, and I could automatically tell that the person she was on the inside was just as beautiful as who she was on the outside. Even though I came from a rather well-to-do family, I could care less about her background. I simply cared about her." Maat paused, thinking back to the past and preparing to launch into the story of the day he first met Rania. The memory was still just as sharp in his mind as if it had just happened.

"I met Rania—"

But that was as far into the story as Maat was able to get before the sound of metal-on-metal boomed through the air. The crash was quick, violent, and sudden—Maat's caravan slamming into the military vehicle beside it.

Maat felt the seatbelt around him tightened, his body jerking painfully at the collision. He could hear his name being yelled frantically, Elias and the guards more concerned for his safety than they were for their own. Elias twisted in the driver's seat, his teeth clenched and sweat beading down his forehead.

But before anyone could say anything else, they all saw the black mist forming outside. It covered the vehicle windows, blocking the already minimal lighting outside.

Maat stared out at it, his skin prickling. A cold chill went down his spine, and then everything went black altogether.

* * *

There was a gasp on Isis's lips as her eyes flung open, abruptly awakening from a deep sleep. Breathing heavily, she turned onto her side, instantly comforted by the sight of Khalfani beside her, the faint light beaming through the light panel along the wall, casting a soft glow on his smooth olive skin.

He turned toward her, concern filling his eyes. "What's wrong, *ti biyeh*?" he asked gently, crouching to put his face near hers and running a hand softly down the side of her face.

For a second, Isis's heart swelled at the phrase, *ti biyeh. My love.* Her parents used it so frequently with each other; it was a little unusual to hear it directed at her. She briefly wondered if Khalfani had subconsciously picked up the phrase from them.

But then she pushed the thought from her mind, remembering her current predicament. She took several deep breaths, trying to slow her racing heart. Then she shook her head. "I don't know," she finally said, still somewhat breathless as she answered Khalfani's question. She frowned. "I just feel like something's wrong, even though I don't know what. But whatever it is, though, I have a bad feeling about it..." She brought her hand to her forehead and sighed. "I know that sounds crazy."

"It's okay, Ninna," Khalfani said, rubbing gentle, massaging circles over her bare back before kissing her. "You're not crazy. It's inevitable that trouble lies ahead." He paused, kissed her again, wrapped his arms around her, and then sighed. "I wish more than anything that we could just continue our honeymoon. But we'll have to leave this sanctuary soon, I suppose. Back to the real world. Back to our mission..."

"Yeah," Isis murmured into the side of his neck before kissing it. "Well, we have a little longer...Let's just enjoy that."

"I'd like that," Khalfani said. He stared at her for a moment longer, relishing her beauty—her tousled bed-hair and her curves outlined beneath the thin sheet covering her. He then pulled her in for another kiss, the feel of her lips and skin temporarily easing his worries as thoughts of what Aurora said about their future came to mind.

Thinking of his future family—Isis and his unborn son—Khalfani felt peace before the upcoming chaos.

Meanwhile, someone very close to Khalfani was preoccupied, thinking about his past family—Tije and his now distant son.

The memories were like an assault; he couldn't get them out of his mind, no matter how hard he tried. He was plagued with thoughts of happier times as if battling the one shred of decency that perhaps still lived in his otherwise blackened heart. Thoughts of Tije's beauty…

The desperation he'd had to have her to himself. The need he'd felt to be able to call her his own. The dread he'd felt after learning she knew about his plans with The Sharir Device…

Before meeting her, he had never wanted someone so badly. The only thing that had rivaled his desire for her had been his desire for power. But she could never relate to it.

Now, it was like her ghost was right there, taunting him. He could smell the pleasantly light fragrance of her smooth skin in his nose. He could hear the way she laughed—so light and freely, her voice chiming like bells when she was happy. As the years went by, her laughter grew more and more scarce with Kek. Eventually, he only ever heard it when she had the young Khalfani in her arms. It had driven Kek half mad to stop seeing her beautiful smile directed at him…

He hated when she had fallen into the habit of only looking at him with fear in those big green eyes of hers…

His fingers clutched at air, his eyes closed for the second as he recalled the softness of her hair on his fingertips back when he used to stroke her luscious mane of hair when he held her. That had felt so much better than the later years, when he would clutch her hair to pull her back towards him when she would try to walk away rather than answer his questions…

Stress. The stress had made her soft hair grow dry and brittle towards the end, though it hadn't marred her beauty.

He remembered the pride in her eyes when Khalfani was born. Holding their son in her arms for the first time, Tije had smiled so widely that her jaw muscles grew tired and trembled. She'd looked up at Kek with tears of joy in her eyes. Things had temporarily grown rocky between them by that point, but once the boy was born, Kek had believed the infant was going to be the solution to making everything okay again.

He'd even been proud himself, envisioning having a strong, miniature version of himself to teach and mold. To help him take over the world…

He'd kissed Tije's soft lips, tasting the happy tears on her face as he did so.

Thinking back on all of this now, it was astounding to Kek how such joy could morph into such misery.

The slight smile that had been on his face upon reliving the memories of happier times faded, getting replaced with a deep glower when he was suddenly struck with the memory of Tije's dead body in his arms…

Tije, once so easy to hold and carry, had suddenly felt heavier than anything he'd ever felt. His arms had strained under her dead weight. It was like the beautiful butterfly he'd been holding in his palm had suddenly lost all of its color and turned into an ugly gray moth—dead, dry, and crumbling apart.

Kek grit his teeth and shook his head, a fury coming over him. Yes, he had loved Tije once, but that had been a mistake of a weak mind. And weak, he was no more. She had been weak. Their son was weak.

But Kek—he'd always known that he was special. And his beliefs had been confirmed by the Darkness choosing him to assist the Retrograde, this time around.

Being the chosen one was his reward for putting up with such weak individuals, he was sure of it. And that included his dear former friend, Maat Mahmoud.

In his laboratory, Kek settled before his Sharir device, thoughts of Maat filling his mind. With a few button presses, the Sharir device located his nemesis, showing the great Maat Mahmoud sitting in the backseat of a vehicle, staring out the window at the lovely destruction around him. His vehicle was surrounded by military cars, and Kek knew they all thought they were on a mission to put a stop to him.

He hissed at their audacity. He couldn't wait to show them that they had another thing coming if they thought they could stop him…

It wasn't long before he was laughing his head off, watching the aftermath of the crash.

Evil joy swelling in his blackened heart, Kek exited his laboratory, stepping outside onto the balcony. Looking out over the land beyond him, he fixed his gaze in the direction Maat and his entourage had been coming from.

A smile so wide that it nearly cracked his jaws formed on his face. He saw the dark mist in the distance, floating through the air, heading his way after completing the task he had given it.

Sensing Kek's presence summoning it, the black mist drifted more quickly through the air, eager to reunite with him after a job well done. And he stood there, welcoming it with open arms.

He outstretched his hand, and the mist condensed and landed in his palm. With doting eyes, Kek watched the mist swirling in his palm, the feel of it cold yet comforting. Bringing it to eye-level, Kek could sense the mist's loyalty, a distinct air of curiosity emanating from it as if asking him what it should do next.

Kek, with a snarl on his face, thought about what he wanted to achieve next. With his eyes closed and his face lifted to the sky, he clenched his teeth. The veins showing through his skin blackened, wiggled, and thickened until they appeared to seep out, joining the black mist in his palm.

Kek groaned, his skin burning from the effort of forcing the Darkness out and willing it to obey his commands. A layer of sweat broke out over his entire body, and he felt close to collapsing at any second. But he pressed on, his plans too delicious to relent.

The black mist in his hand began to warm, eagerly waiting for his instruction.

Returning his attention to the swirl of Darkness in his hand, Kek hissed, "Kill them all." As if pleased with the instruction, the mist lifted itself out of Kek's hand, swirling a mile-a-minute. It stretched and elongated, and not before long, became a tornado.

Responding to Kek's vehemence, the Dark tornado began to whirl more violently. Trees were uprooted, shaking the ground as they toppled over and destroyed the landscape around them. The tornado moved on, ripping apart any dwellings in its path as it went on its mission and hurdled toward Maat and his entourage.

Meanwhile, more Darkness continued to burst through Kek's skin. With one last final burst, the last of it exploded out of him, creating a thick mass of deep black fog. Swirling slowly, the fog thickened, taking on a solid appearance, albeit an indistinct one. It loomed before Kek, gradually growing more defined as the seconds ticked by. Not before long, a black beast stood before him, its immense body resembling a powerful bull.

Kek stared at the beast fondly, and it stared right back at him, two deep ruby-red pupils forming as its eyes. In the silence, the beast's body heaved, as if literally breathing. And right below its shining red eyes, the creature's nostrils widened, smoke billowing out with each breath it took.

The beast appeared to deepen its breathing until huffing out a large breath that sent a more solid form of smoke drifting into the air. Immediately, this cloud of smoke occupied a space beside the beast, where it began to swirl into its own shape. Not before long, the black bull sent two more puffs of smoke billowing out of its nostrils, until three distinct swirls surrounded it, all of them taking on a life of their own.

The three shapes swirled and thickened in the air until they formed strong animal torsos that stood upon long, elegant, sturdy legs. The torsos sprouted heads, and on top of those heads grew antlers with ends as pointed and sharp as knives. Not before long, three solid, pitch-black deer of Darkness stood around the original beast, all of them facing Kek, their ears alert. Waiting.

Standing proudly as the wind whipped around him, Kek laughed and looked towards the black beasts before him. "Go, find them!" he said, the tone of his voice just as dark and void of light as the monstrosities he had created.

The Dark deer pawed the ground with their black hooves and raised their heads to the sky. And then they gracefully leapt off the immensely large balcony, Darkness swirling around their hooves and legs as they ran.

Kek watched them drift away, already relishing in the chaos he knew they would soon be causing. *At least I have reliable messengers whenever I can't get the job done myself,* he thought smugly.

Kek's grin widening once again, he looked toward the direction he knew Maat and his entourage were stranded. His laughter rang into the night, anticipating the moment when the great Maat Mahmoud met his end…

He wanted to see the look in Maat's eyes when he realized he had no way to escape the Darkness.

He'd been waiting what felt like forever to finally get the upper hand over Maat, and now, his time of waiting was over.

Lastly, he turned to the Dark bull, who continued standing by obediently. Kek's eyes locked with the creature's bright red ones, and his lips curled into a furious snarl.

He knew there was one fool-proof method of getting things to go exactly as he wanted them. And that was to get ahold of Isis Mahmoud. Getting Isis meant getting not only Maat, but also his wretched son, Khalfani Abaza, as well.

It was killing two birds with one stone. Victory would never taste sweeter.

"BRING HER TO ME!" Kek roared. "I have plans for her." he continued.

With a huff and a nod of its enormous head, the bull slowly turned around and walked away, its red eyes blazing as it set off to carry out the command.

Whistling to himself, Kek moved to a higher point on his balcony, giving himself a better viewpoint of the landscape before him. He looked down at his property—not quite as big and lavish as the Mahmoud palace, but it was sizable nonetheless and still a source of pride for him, for he had worked hard to obtain it.

Sensing the dedication of the Dark messengers, his mouth dropped open into a victorious laugh, his sharp, elongated teeth glistening under the crackles of lightning in the sky.

CHAPTER 18

"This stuff is awesome," Mirko said, gawking at the weapons around him.

"Yeah," Aiari agreed, carefully studying a gun he'd pulled off the shelf before him. "These are so excellently put together. The craftsmanship. What I wouldn't give to talk to whoever designed these..."

"You're such a nerd, Aiari," Easton teased.

Khalfani glanced around at his fellow soldiers. Noticeably different was Kaiden, who stood next to Aiari, examining a weapon. He looked like a changed man. His stance showed confidence, and he no longer appeared to be as shy around the others. A few minutes earlier he overheard him speaking jovially with Tekem. The rest of the group also stood wide eyed and enlivened. If he didn't feel so stressed, he probably would have laughed, for they all looked like excited children in a toy store.

The wedding and honeymoon phase had officially come to an end. Early that morning, he and Isis had finally spoken to

Maat to discuss their next moves. Maat had formally congratulated them on their wedding. Then they'd gone over tactics to fight the Darkness, as well as the safest route to take towards Kek's lair—although it had been stressed that no route was completely safe. Nevertheless, Khalfani and Isis had been informed that he and a team of guards were setting off to make their way to Kek first. Hence, the plan was for Cairo's army to catch up to provide reinforcement.

Now, it was time to relay the information to the others.

Additionally, they'd gratefully been told to help themselves to whatever they wanted from the weapons room the other soldiers had discovered after the wedding.

"That stuff is there for you guys anyway," one of the hideout's guards had told them.

There had even been several tailors present at the hideout to fit and design new fighting attire for them all, under Rania Mahmoud's orders.

As they all stood around now, more thoroughly examining their new weapons and trying on their new attire, Khalfani paced the floor, concentrating on the sounds of his footsteps as he tried to relax his racing mind. Yet, his skin prickled apprehensively. While he assumed it was just nerves about the upcoming battles, deep down, he sensed something else wrong.

Glancing around the room again, he spotted Isis standing off to herself in a corner, her mouth pouted in a troubled frown.

Immediately, he headed her way. "What's wrong, Ninna?"

She chewed her bottom lip for a moment. "I can't reach my *poje*."

Khalfani's tingles of apprehension suddenly intensified. Even though they had both spoken with Maat not long ago, something felt off for him to not answer a call now, especially since they had vowed to keep in touch during their journeys.

Plus, Isis was his daughter; he would always answer, for her, if he could.

"I just…I don't know," Isis resumed. "I felt the need to check in with him again. Something just doesn't feel right…Do you think—"

"He's fine," Khalfani interjected, not wanting her to even finish her question.

She bit her lower lip again. As nervous as she looked, she managed to keep her voice steady when she spoke. "Okay. Well, I was going to try calling my *eva* to see if she's heard from him over the past few hours, but I think I'll wait…"

Khalfani nodded. "Right. Let's just wait to hear back from him first. C'mon, Ninna. We got this." Then, taking her hand in his, he led her back toward the rest of the group, both of them silently refusing to give voice to the worry going through their minds. Neither of them wanted to be in denial, but they both knew that now wasn't the time to send everyone else into a panic.

Khalfani, however, kept hearing Aurora's words running through his head—particularly what she'd said about he and Isis being the last of the gods walking among men after Maat left the living realm.

He clenched his teeth, hoping that wouldn't come true for many, many years…

From the corner of his eye, he saw Isis's concern. It wasn't until then that he noticed how tightly he'd been squeezing her hand in reaction to the thoughts he'd been mulling over. He loosened his grip and tried to give her a reassuring smile. Her expression remained, though; she was too smart and too skilled at reading Khalfani's moods. Nevertheless, she stayed quiet in attempts to keep her own composure. When they released hands, Isis wrapped her arms around herself to keep from wincing due to her disturbing thoughts.

Khalfani turned to the other soldiers. They all gathered around, their eyes glued to him as he contemplated what he wanted to say and how he was going to say it.

"Well, everyone—first and foremost, Isis and I want to thank you all for participating in our wedding celebration." He glanced back at her, and she nodded her head, smiling appreciatively at the others as they all clapped and gave their 'congratulations' again.

Khalfani cleared his throat and resumed. "However, like we all knew, the celebration couldn't last forever. Now, it's time to get back to business. I hope everyone is well-rested, refreshed, and ready to restart the fight."

"Woo! Yeah!" Mirko cheered, showcasing his trademark enthusiasm for fighting.

"What's the plan, Khal?" Amam asked, his huge, hulking figure stepping forward.

"The plan," Khalfani said, "is simply to win. To win at all costs because losing is too much of a cost to pay." He swallowed, once again remembering Aurora's visit to him; it was so hard to keep it a secret, especially from Isis. "Now, in order to do that, we have to accept that we haven't even encountered the worst yet. If you think what we already went through was bad," he shook his head, "you had better start mentally preparing yourself right now for worse."

Lia closed her eyes for a second and clutched Tekem's arm.

"You been speaking to someone about this?" Tekem asked.

Khalfani nodded and swallowed again, trying to force away quickly the dread that sprang into his chest. "Yes. My wife and I have been in regular contact with President Mahmoud." Saying his name sent a swoop through his stomach, and he felt a wave of anxiety from Isis, who stood behind him, off to this right. "He informed us that we are fighting the Dark Order." As expected, he saw the confused glances pop onto the soldiers' faces.

"The what?" Easton asked.

"The Dark Order," he repeated. "It's essentially what is now strengthening the Retrograde to unconscionable levels. The Darkness is the power that the order summons to destroy. It is an evil entity. And its sole purpose is to fight against the Light—or all that is good in our world."

"*Leum*," Kaiden said under his breath.

"So, we're literally fighting evil?" Orsel said in nearly a whisper.

"Yes," Khalfani said softly. "But we do have an advantage, and that advantage is knowing that we are backed right now by The Light. The Light is what preserves what is good. In fact, it's been brought to our awareness that direct light is the trick to getting the Darkness to back off. It's almost like it's allergic to it. That being said, it won't destroy the Darkness, but it will help give us a fighting chance against it. It will give us precious seconds to either defend or attack. Our best weapons are those large particle ray guns." He gestured to the shelf behind Aiari, who wasted no time pulling one of them down and tossing it to Khalfani.

"I knew those guns looked badass," Aiari commented.

"Yeah." Khalfani held the gun gingerly in his hand. "They have lights attached to them—light bright enough to destroy proton molecules in living organisms."

"Speak English, man," Amam said.

Khalfani briefly chuckled. "The light from these guns can do damage to the living, and can temporarily be enough to throw the Darkness off-balance during a battle. So, we'll definitely be using them."

"Sounds good to me," Kaiden said. "Let's get this over with."

Isis stepped forward. "Just be aware that the best time to strike the Darkness is the very second you see it start to materialize."

"Right," Khalfani agreed. "Thanks, Ninna. Remember that, you guys. As soon as you see the Darkness materializing, aim and fire. That will help buy us some time. Now..." His voice trailed off as he set the gun down and began fumbling with his communication device. A light suddenly beamed out of it, and he aimed it at a nearby wall, turning on its 4-D projection feature. Images filled the wall, displaying a pathway. "This is the route we'll be taking," he said, his mind thinking back to the last conversation he and Isis had with Maat.

"That's not too far from here, is it?" Kaiden asked.

"No, it isn't," Khalfani said. "It's only about four miles north from here, but the journey won't be easy. Remember what's out there and what could be lurking around any corner, waiting for us. It's going to be a challenge. Mark my words, the path won't be clear..."

* * *

Maat's eyelids felt heavy as he slowly opened them to the sound of Elias's distressed voice and a hand shaking his shoulder.

"Sir? Mr. Mahmoud?"

Maat blinked, feeling wetness dripping down his forehead. Struggling to move his arm, he managed to touch the spot just above his brow and flinched. The skin stung, and when he drew back his hand, blood covered his fingertips.

"Are you all right, sir?" Elias asked.

Maat mentally scanned his body, noticing the only discomfort he felt seemed to be from the abrasion on his brow. "Yes, I think so." He squirmed, trying to return to an upright position in the smashed vehicle. Peering out of the cracked window, his mind started racing.

"Easy, sir," the guard in the front seat warned. "Before you move too much, let one of us check you out for further injury. We might need to call for medical assistance."

Maat shook his head, a deadly chill suddenly coming over his body. "No, we have to get out. Now!"

"Okay, sir. Let's just make sure everyone is all right first," Elias said calmly.

"WE NEED TO GET OUT OF HERE RIGHT NOW!" Maat yelled, struggling out of his seatbelt and gritting his teeth as he tried to force the door open. "UNLOCK THESE DOORS! GET OUT OF THE VEHICLE! SIGNAL THE OTHERS!"

Rattled by Maat's sudden harshness and urgency, Elias and the guard sprung out the car, making it out just after Maat did.

"OUT! EVERYONE OUT!" Maat yelled to the other guards.

They all jumped out of the other vehicles, visibly nervous.

"Sir! I'm sorry, sir! I don't know how I lost control of the car!" one of them said, panicked as he approached Maat. "The crash, it just seemed to happen out of nowhere!"

"Hush!" Maat hissed. "Follow me!" And without further ado, he set off running as fast as his legs would carry him, his sights on a brick building he'd spotted.

As he ran, he could hear the others whispering and muttering, trying to understand the reason for his sudden haste. But fortunately, he also heard them obediently following him.

The building he saw was one of few still standing. And as if on cue, the moment he started running towards it, the Darkness reappeared, descending on the area in the shape of a massive tornado.

Several of the guards swore.

"RUN!" Maat urged them, pressing his own legs to move faster.

Yet, his voice could hardly be heard over the clang of metal flying through the air, the vehicles some of the guards had just exited getting blasted into the air by the tornado.

Metal and glass shards flew dangerously in the wind.

A blood-curdling scream sounded through the air. Glancing backwards, Maat's stomach lurched at the blood he saw soaring through the air—a piece of metal from a vehicle having collided with one of the men.

No longer needing instruction from Maat, fear and adrenaline sent the guards racing forward.

As the tornado whipped around them, another scream pierced the air.

Looking upwards, Elias saw a guard hovering above him, swept up into the black whirlwind. Gritting his teeth, he jumped up, attempting to reach the soldier's daggling, outstretched hand as the tornado flipped him upside down.

"ELIAS!" Maat screamed, knowing his advisor was fighting a lost cause.

Noticing the situation, another guard charged at Elias, pushing him forward, resigned to the fact there was nothing they could do for the guard suspended in air. Not before long, the tornado swallowed him entirely, leaving no traces of him behind.

Maat glanced over his shoulder again, his eyes widening at the sight of the pitch-black tornado that appeared to be targeting them specifically. He had never seen anything like it. His legs aching, he reached the building, quickly ducking inside and realizing that it was the town theater. The formally plush carpeting felt thin under his feet, the walls were smeared with dirt, the air was stale, and everything was covered in a layer of dust.

Wheezing with a stitch in his side, he waited at the entrance for the rest to catch up. One-by-one, the remaining soldiers ducked into the theater after him, one of them dragging along a shell-shocked Elias.

"KEEP MOVING!" Maat screamed and then proceeded to run farther into the building.

The others following him without question, they raced to a stairwell and made their way to the basement of the building.

Suddenly, a deafening crash drowned out the sound of their hurried footsteps. Maat looked upwards as he ran, absurdly thinking a commuter train had somehow torn through the building.

The walls shook, making the whole group momentarily pause, terrified the building itself was about to come crumbling down with them inside of it.

But then, as abruptly as it all started, it stopped.

Maat, Elias, and the rest of the group stood, the only sounds now around them being their own labored breathing.

"Come on," Maat said, breaking the silence and continuing downward until reaching the basement floor landing.

The group simply stood for a while, too many thoughts and too much fear running through their minds—not to mention the grief of having just lost two of their members. No one had seen those casualties coming.

Some of Elias's senses coming back to him, he stared at Maat. "H-How did you kn-know?" he stammered.

Maat stood with his hands resting on his knees, crouched over and attempting to catch his breath in the basement's dank air. "I need you all to listen to me carefully," he said, looking around at what remained of his group. Too many times on this journey thus far, his orders had been questioned.

He shuddered, thinking about how much worse things could have been, had they waited too long to run just now…

"When I tell you all to move, run, duck—just do it. Do not question me. Don't even pause to wonder why. Just follow my orders. They may not always make sense at the time, but they will later. I just need you all to trust me. I didn't get this far in life not knowing what I'm talking about."

The guards looked at him and muttered agreement and apologies, though some of them still appeared too shocked to really take in what he was saying.

"Okay," Maat resumed, "right now, we need to get to Illyian…" His voice trailed off, his inner-eye abruptly assaulted with the previous vision he'd had of Isis getting swallowed into the Darkness. The mere thought causing his hands to tremble.

"We need to find that bastard Kek and bring him and his device down, no matter what it takes," Maat continued. Balling his fists at his sides, he took a deep breath, vowing that he would not permit the vision come to fruition.

All of the soldiers looked around. Maat rarely swore, especially when describing others. Clearly, his intention was not bringing Kek in as a prisoner. He wanted Kek out of the way, permanently.

"Sir," Elias said, speaking gently, "since it seems that... whatever that was has stopped now...perhaps we should go see if any of our vehicles were spared?"

"All right," Maat agreed. "But please, stay alert at all times."

The group gingerly made it back to the upper level of the abandoned theater, where they instantly saw one of their vehicles.

"Guess that explains the noise," one of the guards mumbled.

Maat recalled the moment when he thought it sounded like a freight train had suddenly gone by. It made sense now; the tornado had tossed one of the vehicles straight through the theater. It lay in the middle of the floor with scattered bricks around it.

"Found one," Elias said.

A few of the guards chuckled, and even Maat was able to allow himself a small smile. "Check to see if that one works," Maat told Elias. "The rest of us will see if there are more outside."

Elias carefully approached the vehicle sitting haphazardly on the theater floor, while the rest of the group cautiously walked around it to follow Maat outside. It was dark, but not in the same unrelenting way it had been when the tornado was chasing them.

Unfathomably, the destruction around them had grown even worse in the aftermath of the tornado. Though no one wanted to say it, they all had their eyes on the lookout for any traces of the guards who hadn't managed to escape the tornado. But as they suspected, there was nothing.

A couple of their vehicles lay in pieces along the road, shattered. One was still whole, but flipped over. Meanwhile, some had merely been pushed farther down the road and still appeared to be intact.

Maat nodded his head appreciatively. "This is pretty good, considering—"

"We can probably flip this one back over," a guard commented, gesturing to the truck that was flipped upside down. Several of them proceeded to approach it, and after a lot of pushing and exertion, they managed to flip it back upright and erupted in a small round of cheers for the victory.

They all turned when they heard the roar of an engine, further pleased to see Elias driving the vehicle that had been blown inside the theater. He rolled down the window and poked his head out. "I was just thinking—I know a way to get to Illyian. We can go around the back of the mountains. Granted, it'll take a little longer than normal, but it'll be safer."

Maat curtly nodded his head. "That's exactly what we need. I don't care if it takes longer. We need an alternate route because the direct route will garner too much attention—and that's the last thing we need." He glanced around at the other guards, hearing the blissful sounds of the spared vehicles' engines cranking to life. "Hop in, everyone, and follow Elias!"

* * *

Kek Abaza, who had been standing on his balcony and breathing in the beautiful chaos, closed his eyes and tapped into the psyche of the Dark beasts he'd sent out to attack Khalfani and Isis. Seeing as they were made from the Darkness and the Darkness continued to run through his veins, it didn't take long for him to sense where they were.

They were still on the way towards the area where he knew Isis and Khalfani to be hiding. Meanwhile, he could see a small black swirling mist returning from the wreckage of Maat's attack.

Kek smiled, knowing this could only mean one thing…

Reopening his eyes, he headed back into his laboratory, eagerly making his way towards his Sharir device. Although the feed was not as clear as usual and scrambled, not providing him with a clear picture, he could still see the remaining vehicles that had escaped the tornado…

The remaining vehicles of Maat's entourage—they were heading for the mountains, clearly in retreat mode.

Kek cackled. If his beasts were heading for Isis and Khalfani, and Maat's entourage was retreating, it had to be because finally, *finally*, Maat Mahmoud was dead. Things had worked out better, and far easier than even he had planned.

"He's dead," Kek roared joyously, springing up from his seat in elation. "The great Maat Mahmoud, President of Cairo, is dead alas! Sleep well, you would-be visionary. I will see you in the deepest pits of hell!"

Smiling widely, his elongated teeth protruding over his cracked lips, Kek lulled, "Now, Isis Mahmoud, it's your turn. You will become my greatest weapon of all." His vision reddened with fury at the thought of the girl—and at the thought of his treacherous disappointment of a son.

* * *

Isis, Khalfani, and the remaining soldiers slowly began their trek into the woods to face The Darkness. Khalfani could only imagine what it would be like to see his father again. He knew what had to be done. He could only hope that the gods would give him the strength to fully carry out his mission.

Isis noticing the distress on Khalfani's face, touched his hand. "Khal, it's going to be okay," she said as she walked slowly through the woods with her head on a swivel, scanning their surroundings for danger.

She didn't have to wait long.

It was in that very moment that the group began to hear it. It was the thunderous sound of hooves galloping furiously in their direction. The hairs on the back of Khalfani's neck stood up, his heart began to palpitate.

Meanwhile, Isis's eyes widened. She could feel the evil approaching. It was something that she had never felt before. Deep inside, she knew that she was the prime target of whatever was headed their way. She wondered if she was truly ready. And just like that fateful day when she was surrounded by changelings in the ballroom, her heart began to pound, a small fire inside of her had been ignited.

"Khal?" Isis questioned, unsure if she was having a panic attack or if something else was happening to her at that moment.

"He's here," Khalfani replied.

The woods around them darkened suddenly. The galloping grew louder and louder, and panic began to arise throughout the group until all at once, the galloping stopped.

"What the hell was that?!" Mirko screamed, his voice devoid of his usual confidence.

Suddenly Orsel let out a blood-curdling scream as she turned to her left, only to look into the soulless eyes of The Darkness itself.

The entire group unable to move, stood frozen in fear.

"This can't be real," Tekem said as he quickly pushed Orsel back, his face twisted in disgust.

But it was real. Evil itself was upon them and ready for a fight.

"May the gods help us all," Khalfani prayed, as he took in a deep breath, bracing for the worst.

ACKNOWLEDGEMENTS

Thank you, Mommy, for always being my champion. You always tell me that I can do anything. And growing up, you showed me what it was like to face mountainous obstacles and overcome them, one by one. Whenever I face challenges today, I reflect on your story, dust myself off, and move forward. I love you so much. #bestmamaever

Thank you, Andreas, for being my husband, lover and friend for over a decade. You're still the only one for me after all of these years.

Thank you, Katharina, my stepdaughter and personal ray of sunshine. You will probably never know how grateful I am to have you in my world. Love you, Munchkin.

Thank you to my army of enormously sized and handsome brothers: Rob, Ron, Craig, Romont, and Cornell. Thank you all for scaring away every boyfriend that I ever tried to date until I met my husband. You guys pissed me off then, but I'm finally grateful for it now. Each of you is so brilliant in your own unique way. Love you all.

Thank you, Uncle Herb K. Ames, for being so supportive of my husband and I during our transition back to life in the United States and beyond, and also for your incredible example of what it means to be an entrepreneur.

Thank you to my beautiful cousin Maggie who also served as my first official book reviewer and to my Aunt Ann who always sends me words of encouragement and lovely greeting cards. Love you!

Vielen Dank an meine Deutsche Familie das ich sehr stark liebe. Ich vermisse euch sehr und drücke euch fest (Mama Alma, Papa Alex, Schwesterchen Lydia, Tanta Olga, Tanta Lily, Unkle Waldemir, Unkle Paul, Unkle Edward, Unkle Rudolph, Unkle Helmut, Meine Schöne Cousine Irene Kammerer, Natalie und Regina)

Thank you, Teri Edwards, my writing partner in crime. I could not have done this without you. Your support means everything. I appreciate you, your expertise and professionalism beyond words.

Thank you to my editor, Lisa Whrite and your team at editingbuddies.com, for your hard work on this project with me. I am already looking forward to our next collaboration.

Thank you to Dr. Sam Verniero and Lenora for being incredible leaders and beacons light in a darkened world.

Thank you to Dane, Adrian and John from E-Book Launch, my interior and jacket design team. You guys are absolutely incredible. Thank you for making the process so easy.

Thank you, Joe Howell, my business partner at Maswell Films. You have always been encouraging to me, and I appreciate it so much.

Thank you, Marlon Mizrahi, for being an outstanding creative that is not only genius in ideas but also a witty and sincere individual that cares about others.

Thank you, Rob Brodie, my manager from North End Entertainment. Rob, it is great to know that you have my back. Thank you for your transparency and for making great things happen for me every day.

Thank you, Timothy E. Burke, my mastermind friend, colleague, CEO of The Bigger Picture Films, RUON AI, and about a thousand other successful companies. I am so grateful to work with you every day. You are a tremendous force and a gentleman. I will always have your back now and forever.

Thank you, Melora Walters. Wolf Women travel best in packs. I'm so glad to have you in mine. You are a true artist, and I do not say that lightly. Everything about you is so graceful; it's like watching a ballet. And yet you are a powerful woman who inspires me to do better. Never change.

Thank you, Lisa Ferrell. I will never forget the first day we met at the Atlanta Film Festival. I knew then that I had a friend for life. We must have spent close to a thousand dollars between True Food Kitchen and Upbeet that year on lunch dates, but it was worth every penny. You are amazing. Your love for the industry is infectious.

Thank you, Chris Butcher, for being the best sounding board for ideas, a creative genius and just an overall wonderful person. I am very much looking forward to your upcoming film.

Thank you to my bestie, Y.B., we are two peas in a pod. It would be impossible to dream up a better best friend. You are a queen. Love you.

Thank you to anyone else that I may have missed because I could really go on and on forever. Please, know that I am grateful to all of the positive forces in my world.

And thank you, wonderful reader, for your support. I cannot express how grateful I am for you taking the time to join me on this adventure.

Be sure to read the second part of the *Retrograde* duology. We are just getting started! You can follow me on Instagram at @aliciagodmasch or visit www.aliciagodmasch.com, where I will drop release dates for upcoming books and perhaps a contest or two.

Love & Light.

ABOUT THE AUTHOR

RETROGRADE: THE DARKNESS

Alicia Godmasch grew up in Rockaway Township, New Jersey. Her upbringing and the influence by esteemed loved ones gave her a profound respect and affinity for business and the entertainment industry.

Her love of both industries paved the way for a career that encompassed both of her passions. She graduated Magna Cum Laude from Fairleigh Dickinson University in Madison, New Jersey, where she spent many a night, weekend, and her free time on sets, learning the trade from the ground floor up, while she earned a degree in Business Management.

Today, she is the Co-Owner of Maswell Films, an Atlanta based film production company. She's also the Executive Producer of The Bigger Picture Films, based out of Los Angeles and the CEO of Sunlight Casting, an Atlanta based talent casting agency.

When she's not hard at work on her film projects, Alicia enjoys traveling the globe, reading, writing, stargazing, the great outdoors, and spending as much time as possible with her loving husband of eleven years and her stepdaughter near their Metro Atlanta area home.

For more information about her and her books, visit her website here:

www.aliciagodmasch.com

CPSIA information can be obtained
at www.ICGtesting.com
Printed in the USA
LVHW030149250321
682393LV00003B/85/J